DEAD@17

AFTERBIRTH

DEAD@17

AFTERBIRTH

BY

JOSH HOWARD

PRODUCTION - **PATRICK BUSSEY**

SPECIAL THANKS - **LAURA HOWARD**

THIS VOLUME COLLECTS:

DEAD@17:

AFTERBIRTH #1-#4

WWW.JOSHHOWARD.NET

image

IMAGE COMICS, INC. - WWW.IMAGECOMICS.COM

ROBERT KIRKMAN - CHIEF OPERATING OFFICER
ERIK LARSEN - CHIEF FINANCIAL OFFICER
TODD McFARLANE - PRESIDENT
MARC SILVESTRI - CHIEF EXECUTIVE OFFICER
JIM VALENTINO - VICE-PRESIDENT

ericstephenson - PUBLISHER
JOE KEATINGE - PR & MARKETING COORDINATOR
BRANWYN BIGGLESTONE - ACCOUNTS MANAGER
SARAH deLAINE - ADMINISTRATIVE ASSISTANT
TYLER SHAINLINE - PRODUCTION MANAGER

DREW GILL - ART DIRECTOR
JONATHAN CHAN - PRODUCTION ARTIST
MONICA HOWARD - PRODUCTION ARTIST
VINCENT KUKUA - PRODUCTION ARTIST

INTERNATIONAL RIGHTS REPRESENTATIVE: **CHRISTINE JENSEN** (CHRISTINE@GFLOYSTUDIO.COM)

DEAD@17: AFTERBIRTH
ISBN: 978-1-60706-176-2
First Printing

PRINTED IN SOUTH KOREA

CHAPTER ONE

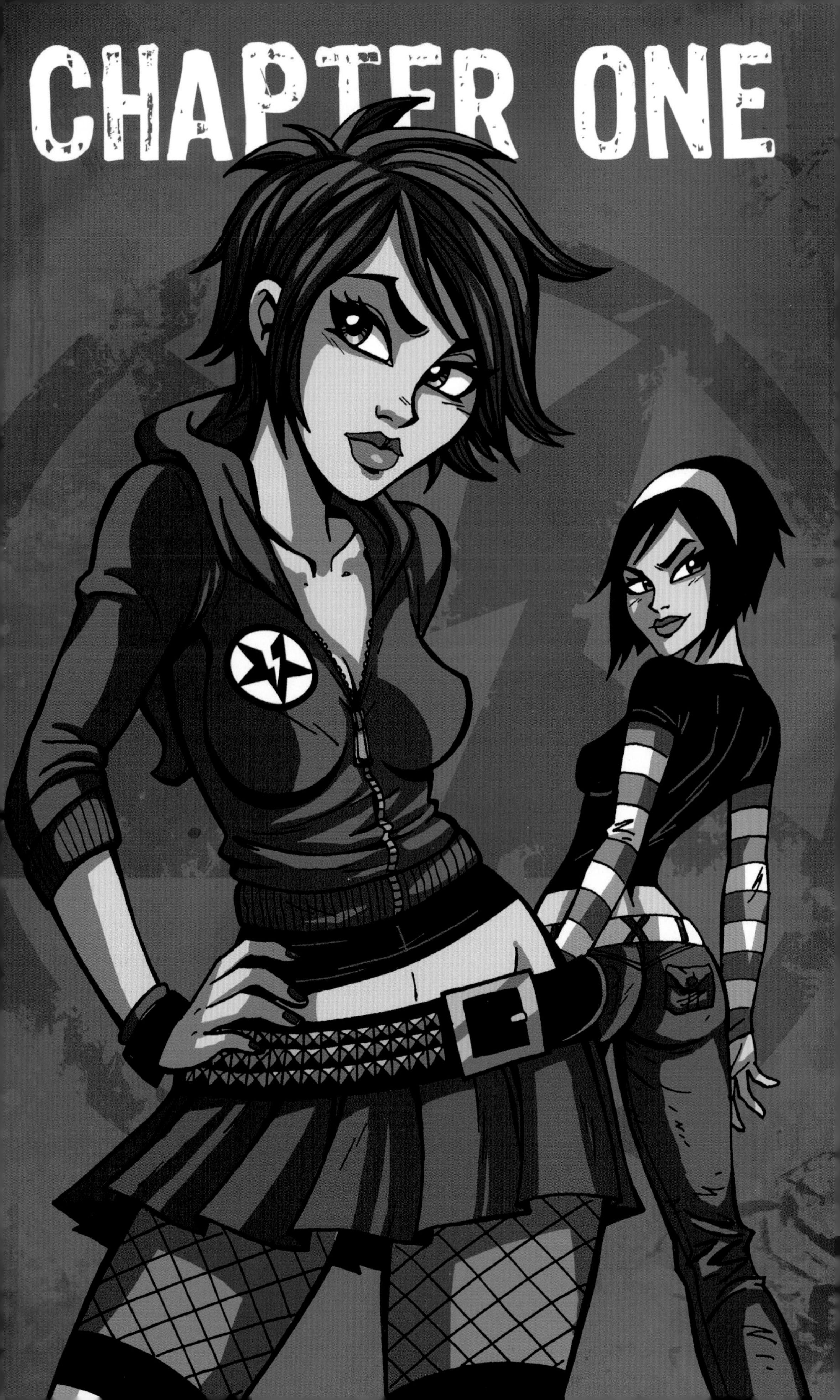

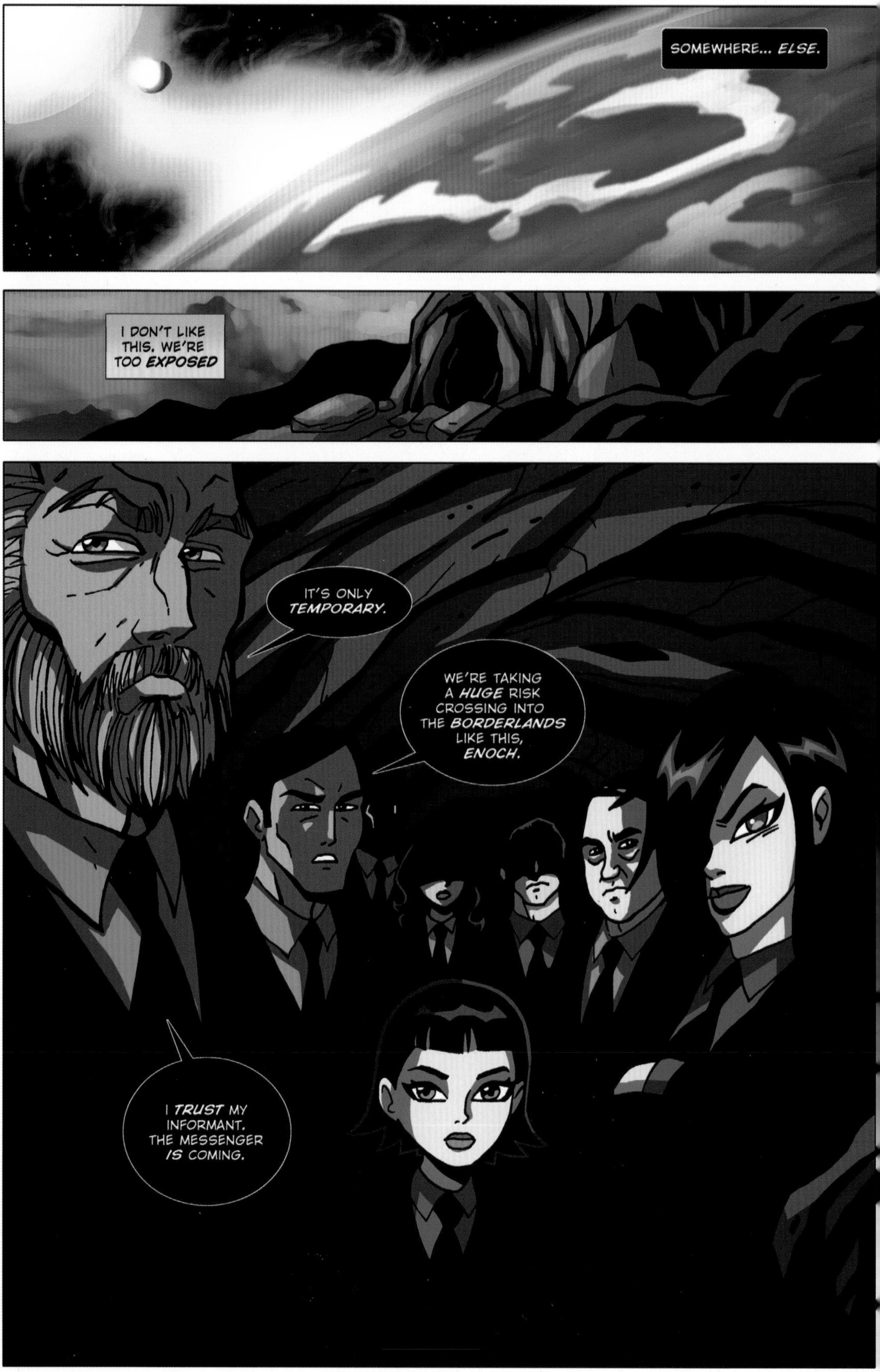
SOMEWHERE... ELSE.
I DON'T LIKE THIS. WE'RE TOO EXPOSED
IT'S ONLY TEMPORARY.
WE'RE TAKING A HUGE RISK CROSSING INTO THE BORDERLANDS LIKE THIS, ENOCH.
I TRUST MY INFORMANT. THE MESSENGER IS COMING.

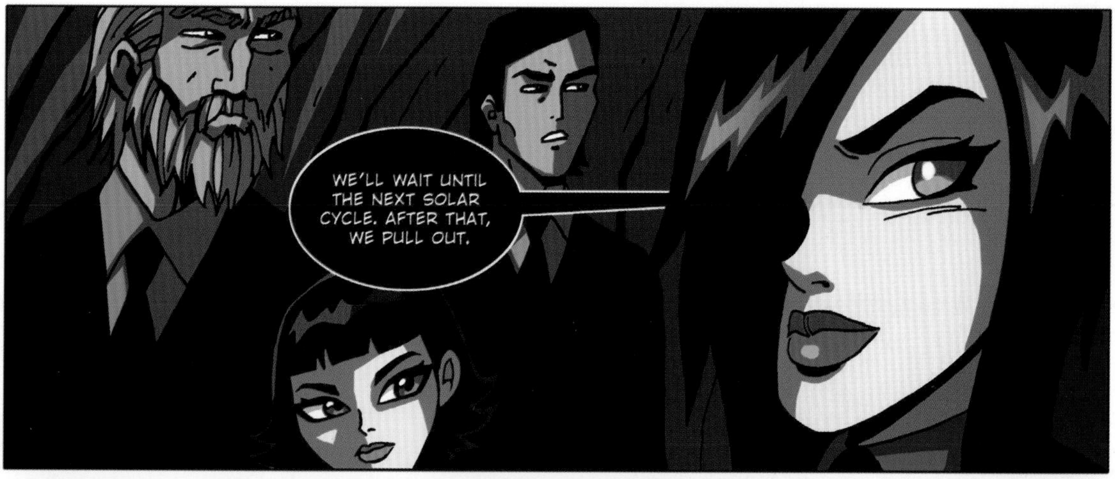
WE'LL WAIT UNTIL THE NEXT SOLAR CYCLE. AFTER THAT, WE PULL OUT.
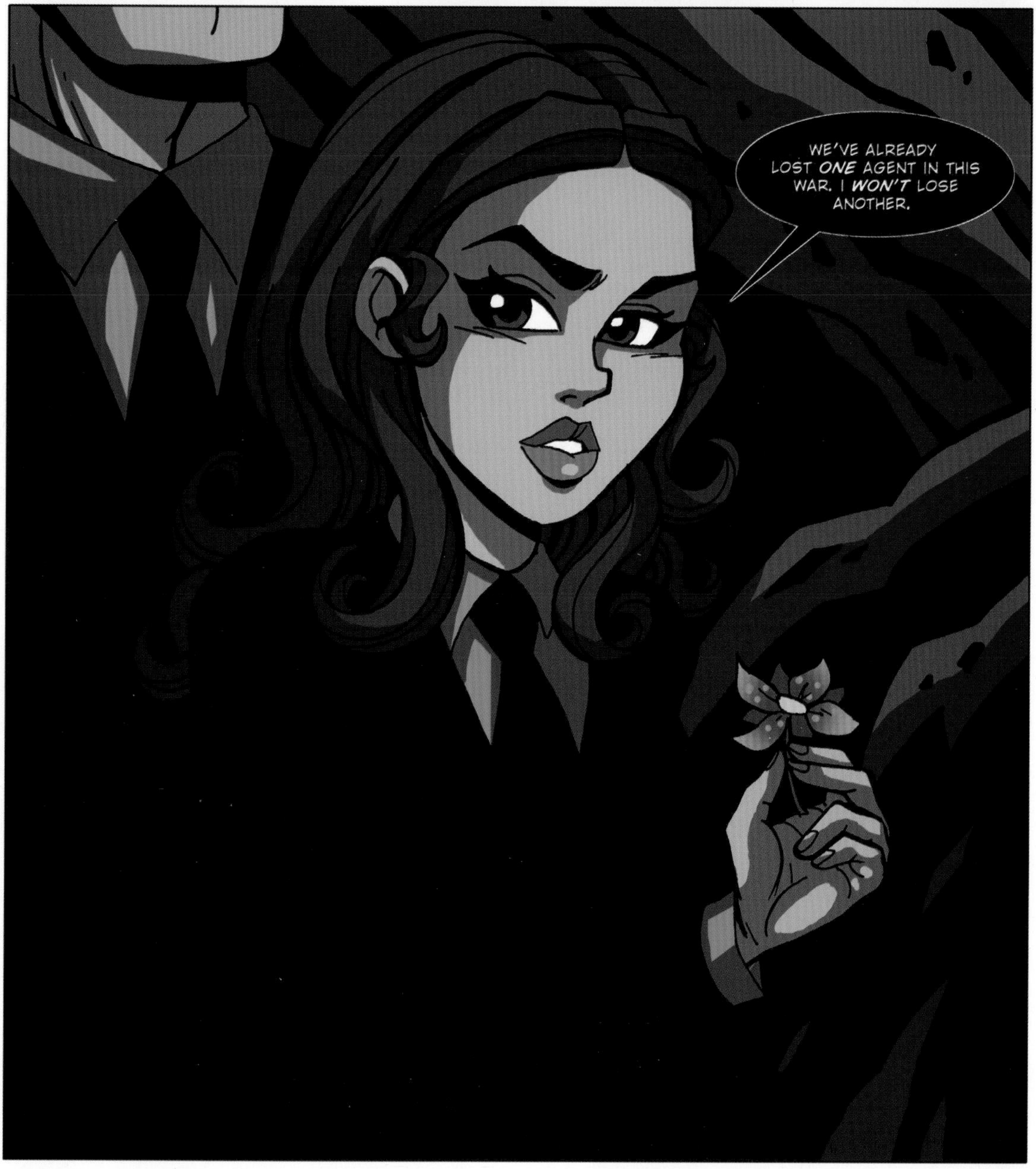
WE'VE ALREADY LOST ONE AGENT IN THIS WAR. I WON'T LOSE ANOTHER.

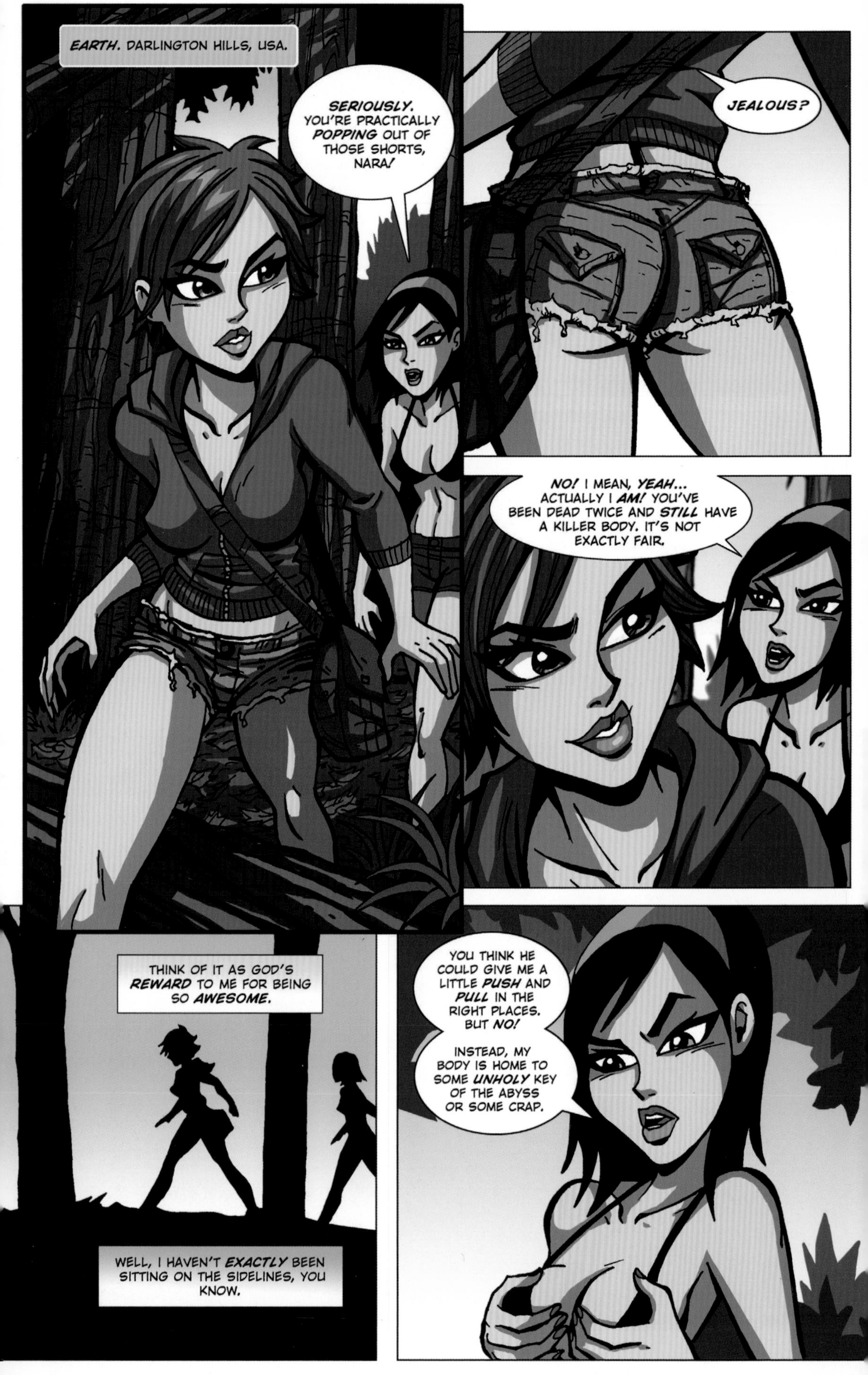

EARTH. DARLINGTON HILLS, USA.
SERIOUSLY. YOU'RE PRACTICALLY POPPING OUT OF THOSE SHORTS, NARA!
JEALOUS?
NO! I MEAN, YEAH... ACTUALLY I AM! YOU'VE BEEN DEAD TWICE AND STILL HAVE A KILLER BODY. IT'S NOT EXACTLY FAIR.
THINK OF IT AS GOD'S REWARD TO ME FOR BEING SO AWESOME.
WELL, I HAVEN'T EXACTLY BEEN SITTING ON THE SIDELINES, YOU KNOW.
YOU THINK HE COULD GIVE ME A LITTLE PUSH AND PULL IN THE RIGHT PLACES. BUT NO!
INSTEAD, MY BODY IS HOME TO SOME UNHOLY KEY OF THE ABYSS OR SOME CRAP.

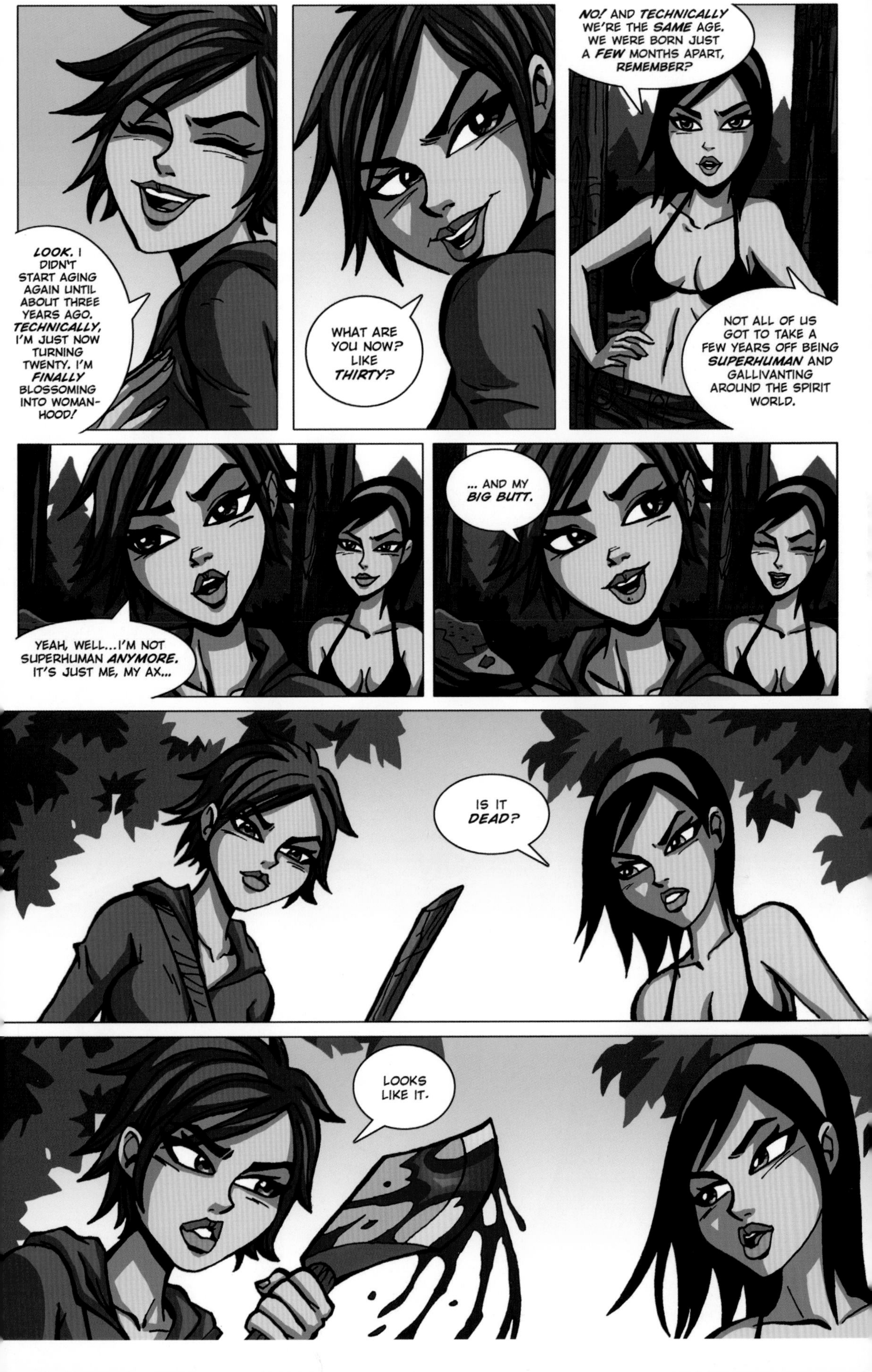
LOOK. I DIDN'T START AGING AGAIN UNTIL ABOUT THREE YEARS AGO. TECHNICALLY, I'M JUST NOW TURNING TWENTY. I'M FINALLY BLOSSOMING INTO WOMAN-HOOD!
WHAT ARE YOU NOW? LIKE THIRTY?
NO! AND TECHNICALLY WE'RE THE SAME AGE. WE WERE BORN JUST A FEW MONTHS APART, REMEMBER?
NOT ALL OF US GOT TO TAKE A FEW YEARS OFF BEING SUPERHUMAN AND GALLIVANTING AROUND THE SPIRIT WORLD.
YEAH, WELL...I'M NOT SUPERHUMAN ANYMORE. IT'S JUST ME, MY AX...
... AND MY BIG BUTT.
IS IT DEAD?
LOOKS LIKE IT.

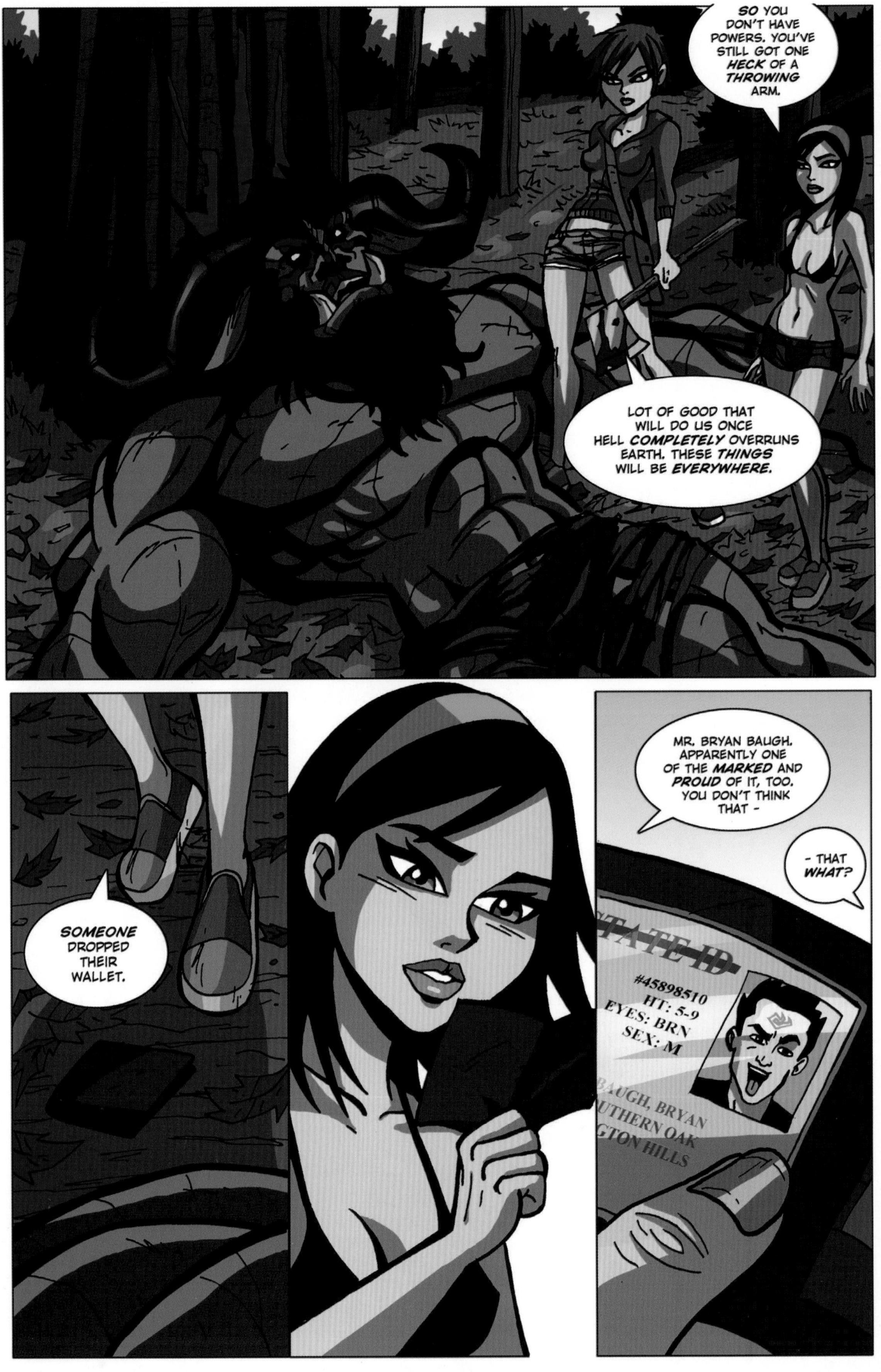
SO YOU DON'T HAVE POWERS. YOU'VE STILL GOT ONE HECK OF A THROWING ARM.
LOT OF GOOD THAT WILL DO US ONCE HELL COMPLETELY OVERRUNS EARTH. THESE THINGS WILL BE EVERYWHERE.
SOMEONE DROPPED THEIR WALLET.
MR. BRYAN BAUGH. APPARENTLY ONE OF THE MARKED AND PROUD OF IT, TOO. YOU DON'T THINK THAT -
- THAT WHAT?
#45898510
HT: 5-9
EYES: BRN
SEX: M
BAUGH, BRYAN

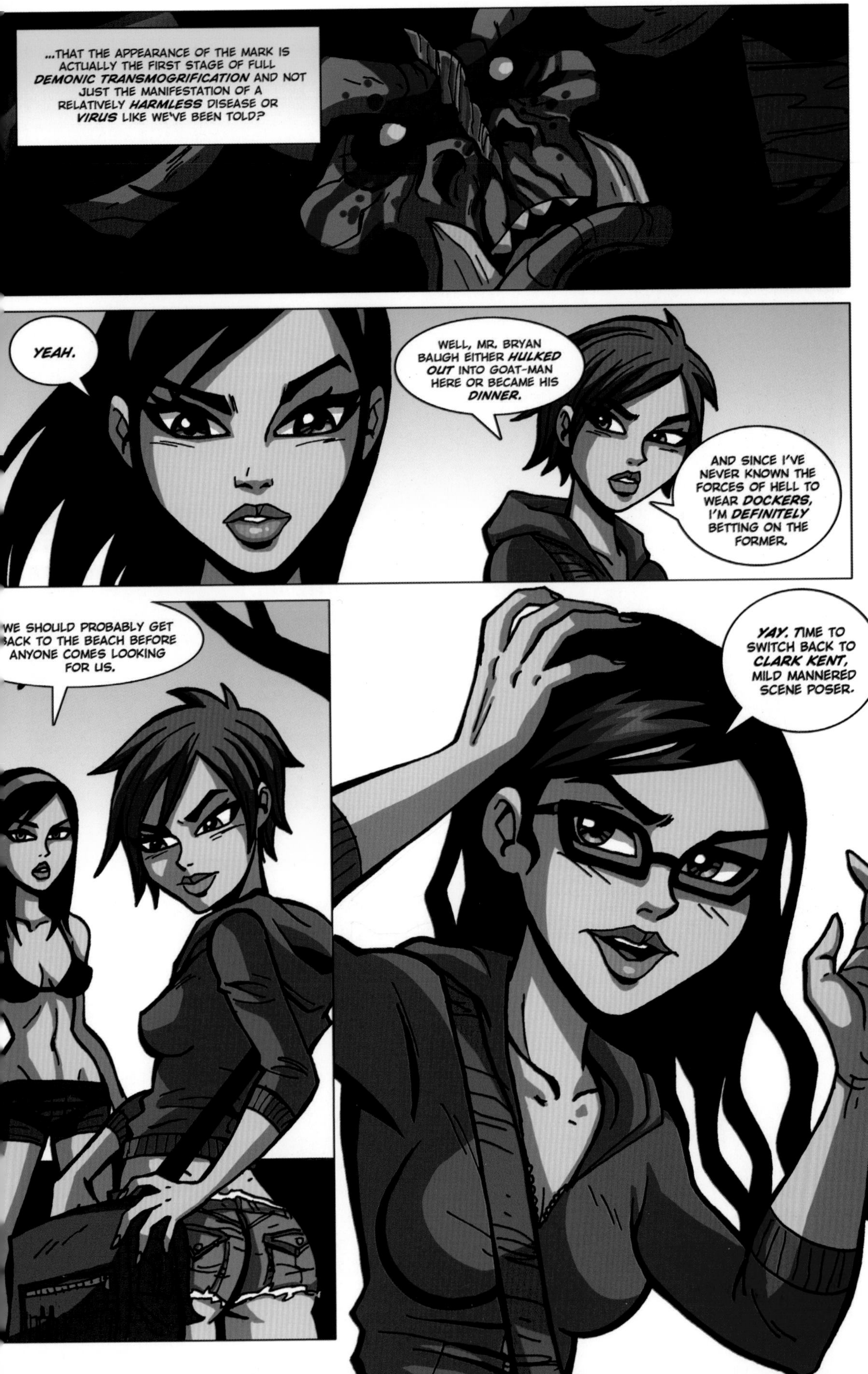
...THAT THE APPEARANCE OF THE MARK IS ACTUALLY THE FIRST STAGE OF FULL DEMONIC TRANSMOGRIFICATION AND NOT JUST THE MANIFESTATION OF A RELATIVELY HARMLESS DISEASE OR VIRUS LIKE WE'VE BEEN TOLD?
YEAH.
WELL, MR. BRYAN BAUGH EITHER HULKED OUT INTO GOAT-MAN HERE OR BECAME HIS DINNER.
AND SINCE I'VE NEVER KNOWN THE FORCES OF HELL TO WEAR DOCKERS, I'M DEFINITELY BETTING ON THE FORMER.
WE SHOULD PROBABLY GET BACK TO THE BEACH BEFORE ANYONE COMES LOOKING FOR US.
YAY. TIME TO SWITCH BACK TO CLARK KENT, MILD MANNERED SCENE POSER.

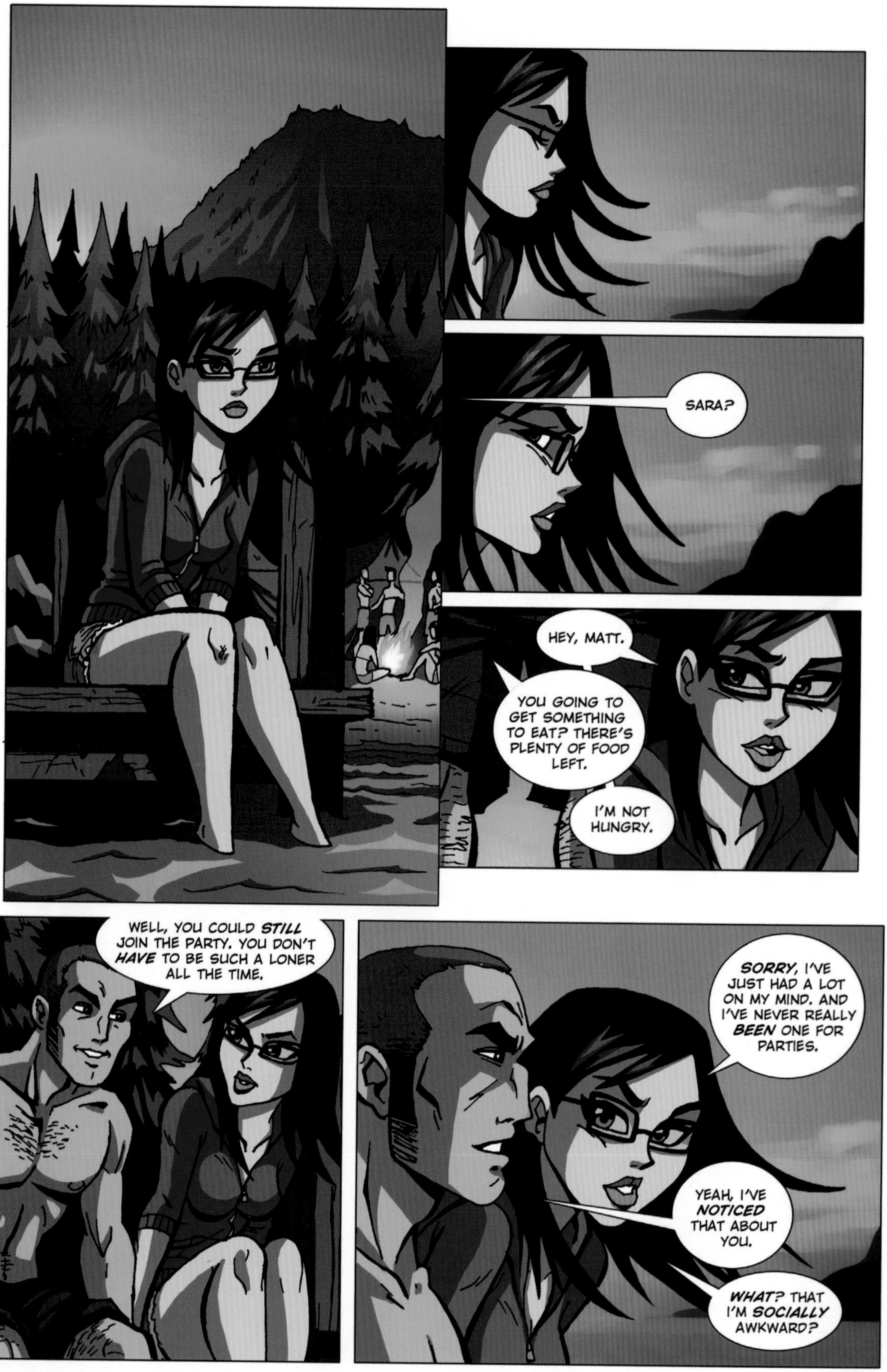
SARA?
HEY, MATT.
YOU GOING TO GET SOMETHING TO EAT? THERE'S PLENTY OF FOOD LEFT.
I'M NOT HUNGRY.
WELL, YOU COULD *STILL* JOIN THE PARTY. YOU DON'T *HAVE* TO BE SUCH A LONER ALL THE TIME.
SORRY, I'VE JUST HAD A LOT ON MY MIND. AND I'VE NEVER REALLY *BEEN* ONE FOR PARTIES.
YEAH, I'VE *NOTICED* THAT ABOUT YOU.
WHAT? THAT I'M *SOCIALLY* AWKWARD?

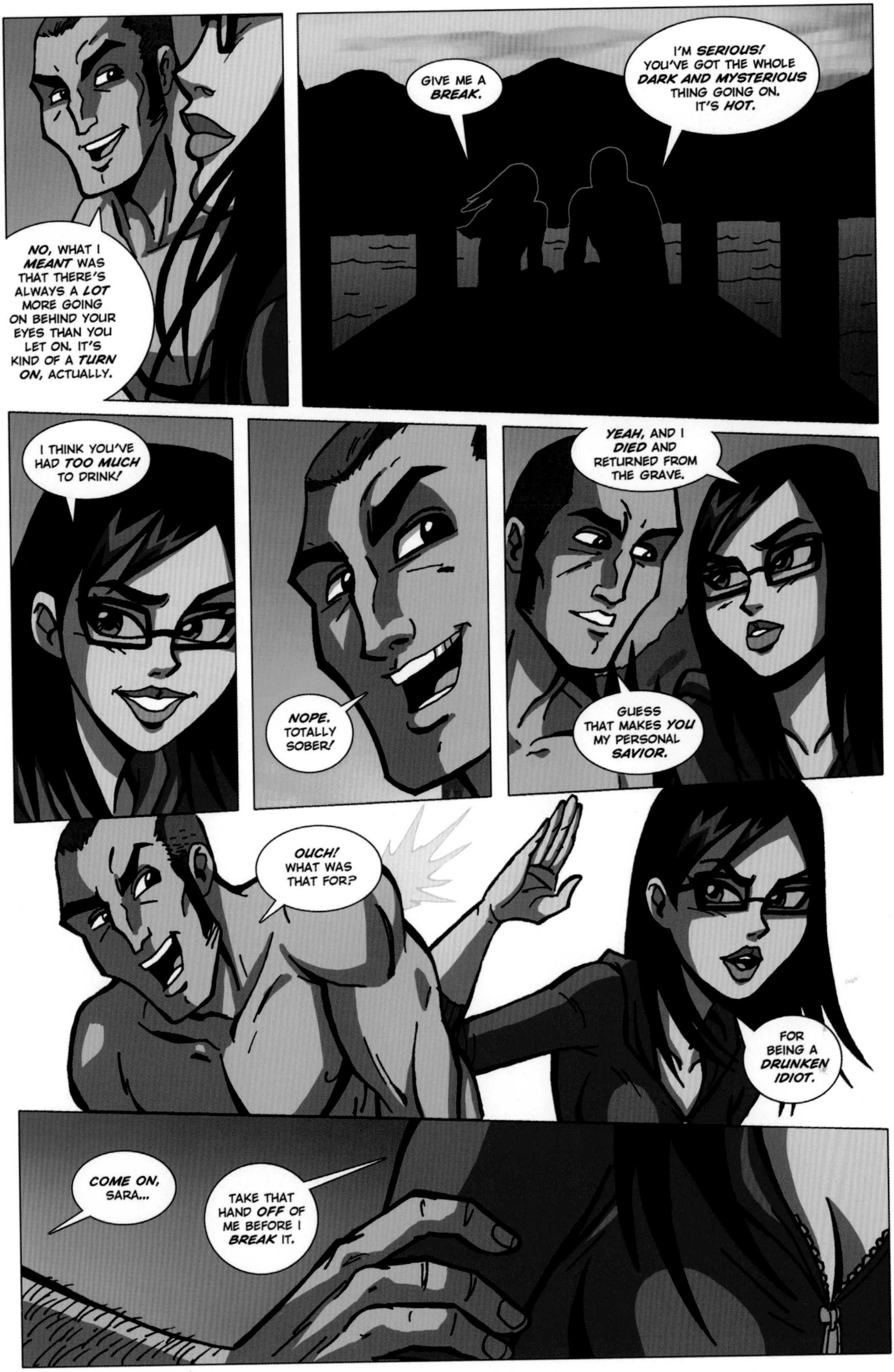
NO, WHAT I MEANT WAS THAT THERE'S ALWAYS A LOT MORE GOING ON BEHIND YOUR EYES THAN YOU LET ON. IT'S KIND OF A TURN ON, ACTUALLY.
GIVE ME A BREAK.
I'M SERIOUS! YOU'VE GOT THE WHOLE DARK AND MYSTERIOUS THING GOING ON. IT'S HOT.
I THINK YOU'VE HAD TOO MUCH TO DRINK!
NOPE. TOTALLY SOBER!
YEAH, AND I DIED AND RETURNED FROM THE GRAVE.
GUESS THAT MAKES YOU MY PERSONAL SAVIOR.
OUCH! WHAT WAS THAT FOR?
FOR BEING A DRUNKEN IDIOT.
COME ON, SARA...
TAKE THAT HAND OFF OF ME BEFORE I BREAK IT.

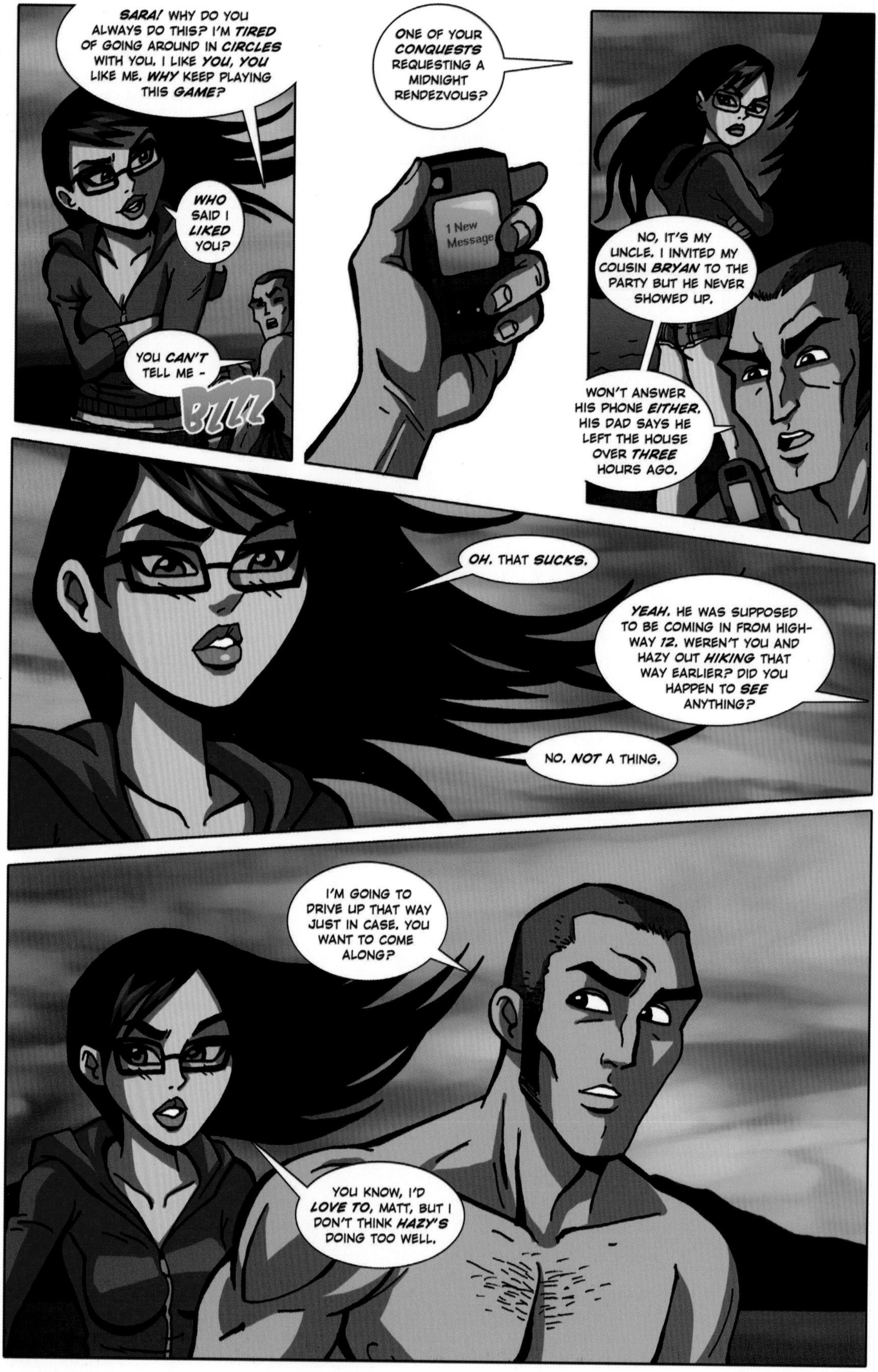

SARA! WHY DO YOU ALWAYS DO THIS? I'M TIRED OF GOING AROUND IN CIRCLES WITH YOU. I LIKE YOU, YOU LIKE ME. WHY KEEP PLAYING THIS GAME?
WHO SAID I LIKED YOU?
YOU CAN'T TELL ME -
BZZZ
ONE OF YOUR CONQUESTS REQUESTING A MIDNIGHT RENDEZVOUS?
1 New Message
NO, IT'S MY UNCLE. I INVITED MY COUSIN BRYAN TO THE PARTY BUT HE NEVER SHOWED UP.
WON'T ANSWER HIS PHONE EITHER. HIS DAD SAYS HE LEFT THE HOUSE OVER THREE HOURS AGO.
OH. THAT SUCKS.
YEAH. HE WAS SUPPOSED TO BE COMING IN FROM HIGH-WAY 12. WEREN'T YOU AND HAZY OUT HIKING THAT WAY EARLIER? DID YOU HAPPEN TO SEE ANYTHING?
NO. NOT A THING.
I'M GOING TO DRIVE UP THAT WAY JUST IN CASE. YOU WANT TO COME ALONG?
YOU KNOW, I'D LOVE TO, MATT, BUT I DON'T THINK HAZY'S DOING TOO WELL.

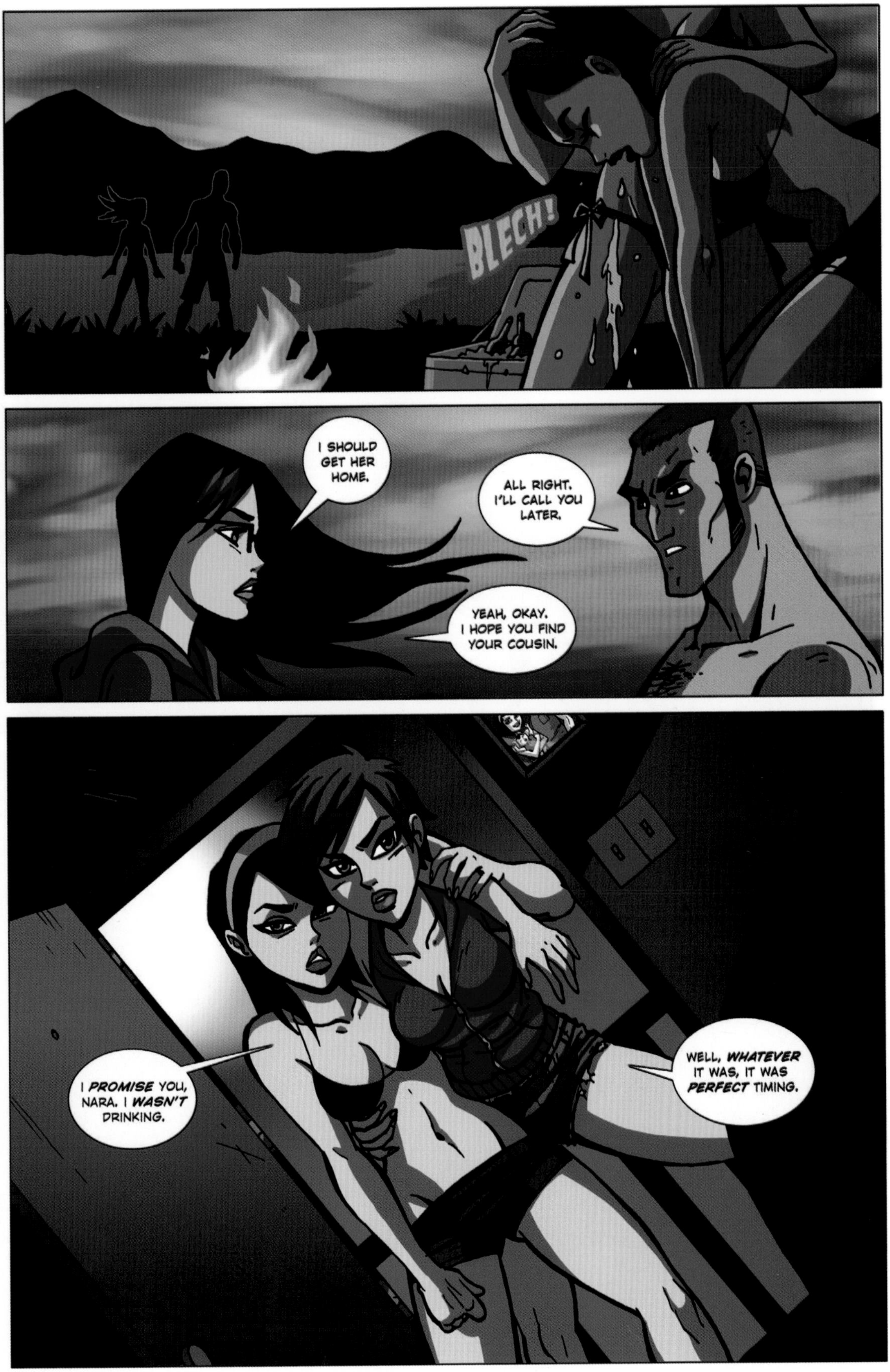
BLECH!
I SHOULD GET HER HOME.
ALL RIGHT. I'LL CALL YOU LATER.
YEAH, OKAY. I HOPE YOU FIND YOUR COUSIN.
I *PROMISE* YOU, NARA. I *WASN'T* DRINKING.
WELL, *WHATEVER* IT WAS, IT WAS *PERFECT* TIMING.

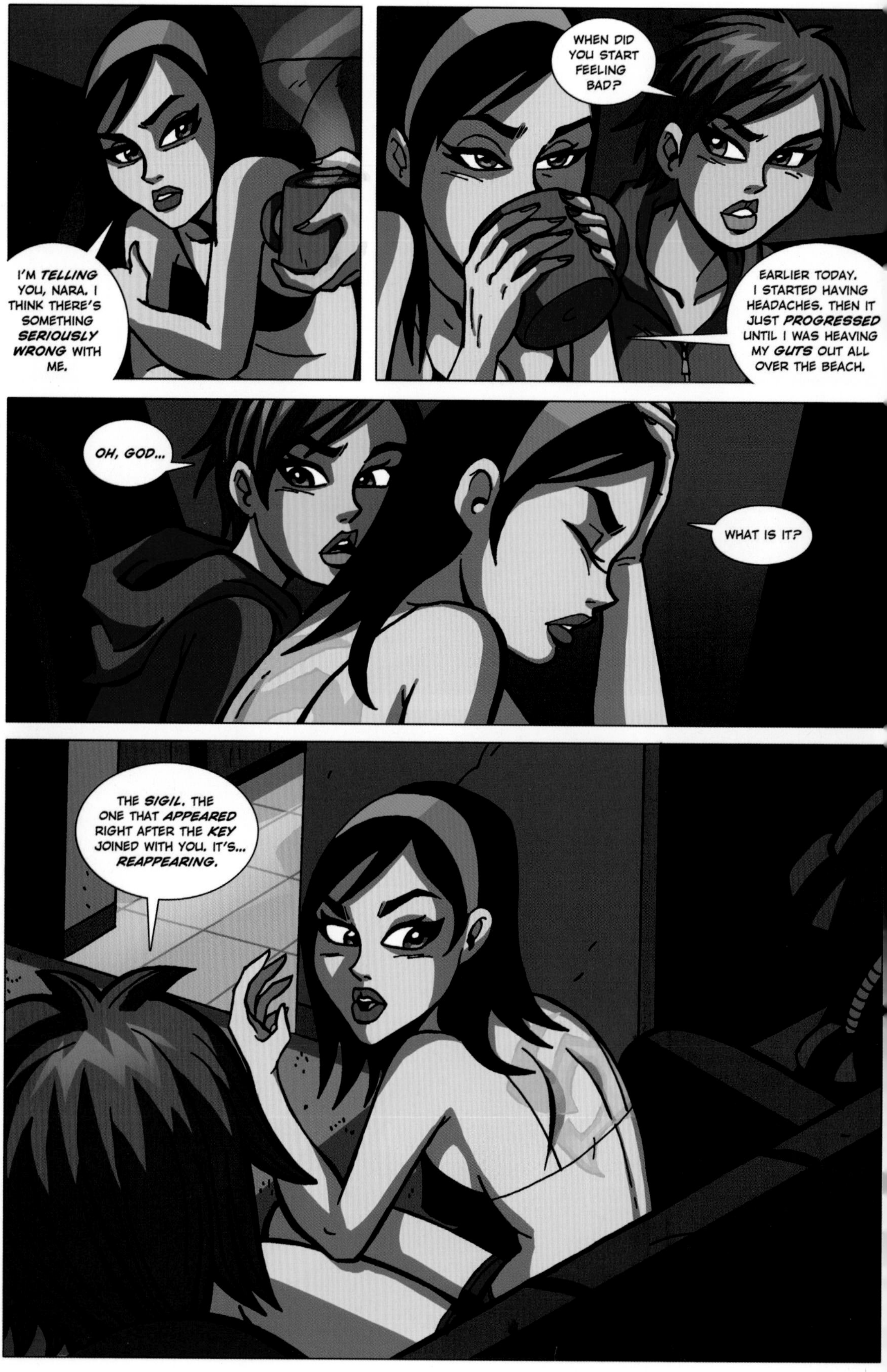
I'M *TELLING* YOU, NARA. I THINK THERE'S SOMETHING *SERIOUSLY WRONG* WITH ME.
WHEN DID YOU START FEELING BAD?
EARLIER TODAY. I STARTED HAVING HEADACHES. THEN IT JUST *PROGRESSED* UNTIL I WAS HEAVING MY *GUTS* OUT ALL OVER THE BEACH.
OH, GOD...
WHAT IS IT?
THE *SIGIL*. THE ONE THAT *APPEARED* RIGHT AFTER THE *KEY* JOINED WITH YOU. IT'S... *REAPPEARING*.

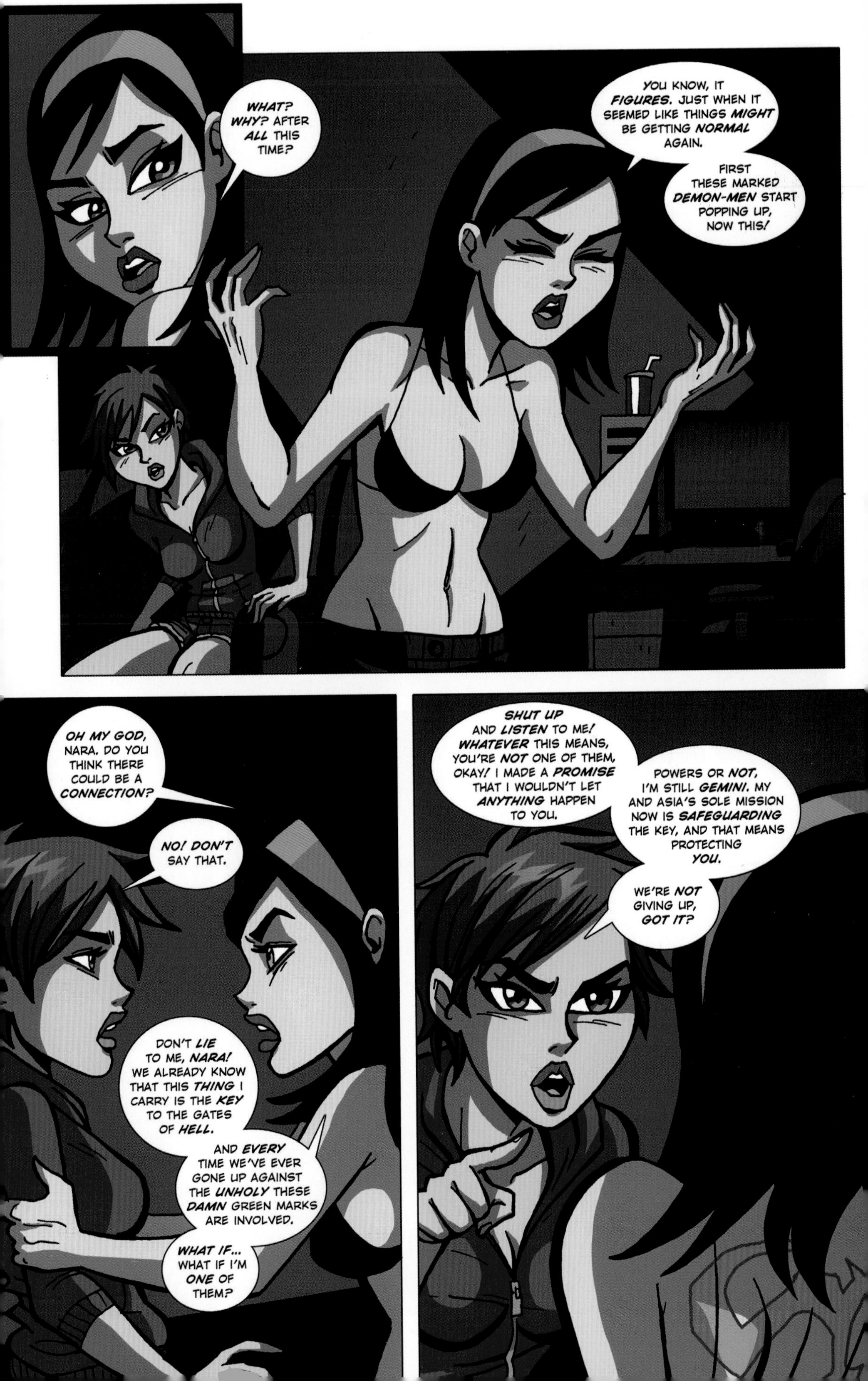
WHAT? WHY? AFTER ALL THIS TIME?
YOU KNOW, IT FIGURES. JUST WHEN IT SEEMED LIKE THINGS MIGHT BE GETTING NORMAL AGAIN.
FIRST THESE MARKED DEMON-MEN START POPPING UP, NOW THIS!
OH MY GOD, NARA. DO YOU THINK THERE COULD BE A CONNECTION?
NO! DON'T SAY THAT.
DON'T LIE TO ME, NARA! WE ALREADY KNOW THAT THIS THING I CARRY IS THE KEY TO THE GATES OF HELL.
AND EVERY TIME WE'VE EVER GONE UP AGAINST THE UNHOLY THESE DAMN GREEN MARKS ARE INVOLVED.
WHAT IF... WHAT IF I'M ONE OF THEM?
SHUT UP AND LISTEN TO ME! WHATEVER THIS MEANS, YOU'RE NOT ONE OF THEM, OKAY! I MADE A PROMISE THAT I WOULDN'T LET ANYTHING HAPPEN TO YOU.
POWERS OR NOT, I'M STILL GEMINI. MY AND ASIA'S SOLE MISSION NOW IS SAFEGUARDING THE KEY, AND THAT MEANS PROTECTING YOU.
WE'RE NOT GIVING UP, GOT IT?

WHAT *ABOUT* ASIA? IS SHE *STILL*...

I DON'T KNOW...

WE'RE *STILL* CONNECTED, BUT EVER SINCE WE TRIED TESTING THE *LIMITS* OF THE CONNECTION, TO SEE HOW *FAR* SHE COULD GET TO THE OTHER SIDE, I HAVEN'T HEARD FROM HER.

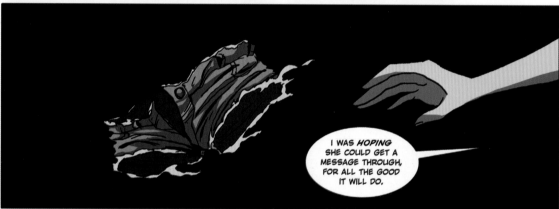

I WAS *HOPING* SHE COULD GET A MESSAGE THROUGH, FOR ALL THE GOOD IT WILL DO.

IF THESE OTHER *ZODIAC* ARE *REALLY* OUT THERE, WE COULD USE THEIR HELP.

LISTEN, I DON'T WANT YOU *WORRYING* ABOUT THIS. WE'LL GET THROUGH IT *TOGETHER*, LIKE WE ALWAYS DO.

IT'S MATT.

BRRR

HEY...YEAH, SHE'S FINE. I JUST GOT HER TO BED... YOU FIND YOUR COUSIN?...OH... *REALLY?*

I'M *SO* SORRY, MATT. IF THERE'S *ANYTHING* I CAN DO... YEAH...WELL, I'M *HERE* FOR YOU, OKAY?... ALL RIGHT, I'LL SEE YOU TOMORROW.

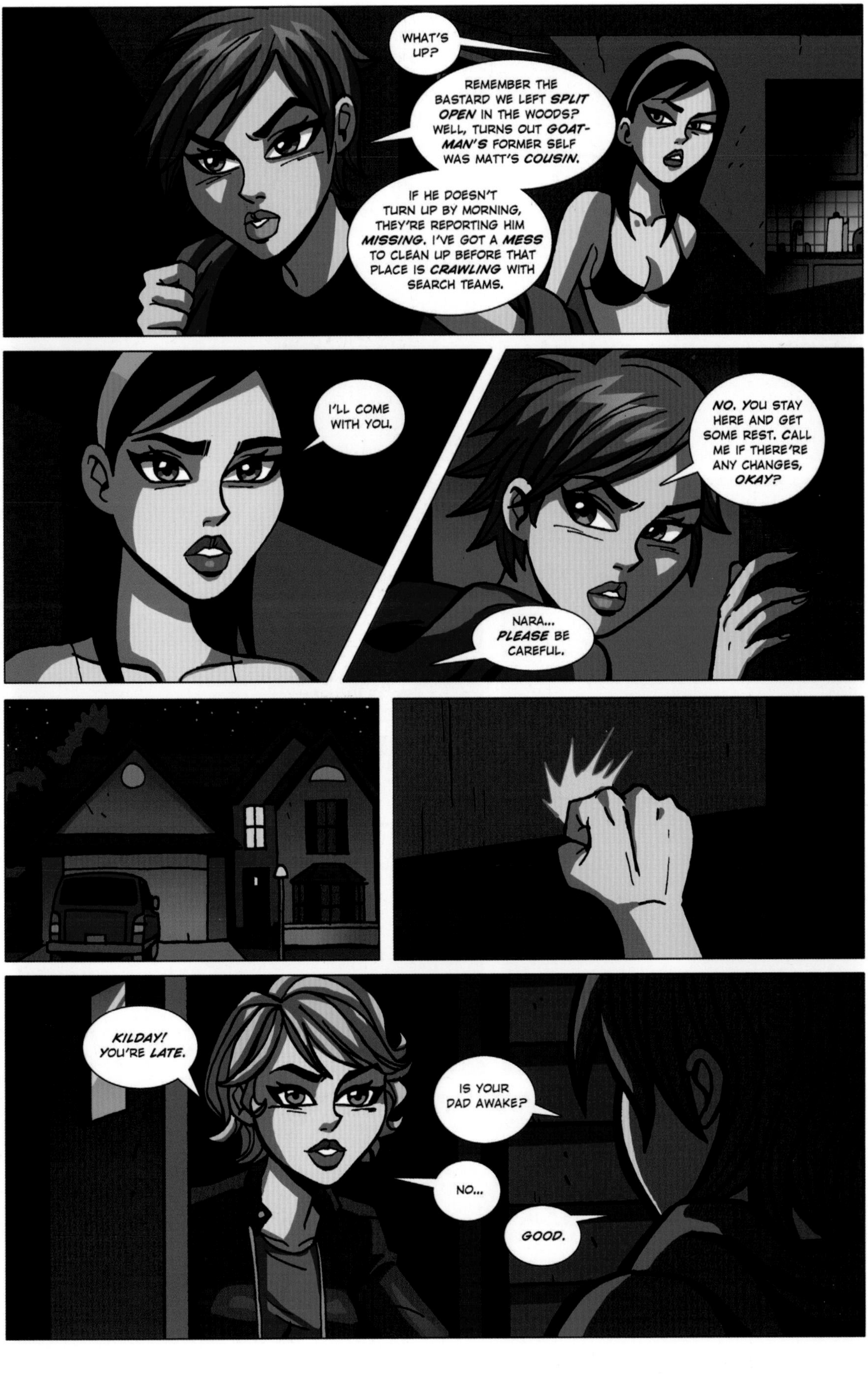
WHAT'S UP?
REMEMBER THE BASTARD WE LEFT SPLIT OPEN IN THE WOODS? WELL, TURNS OUT GOAT-MAN'S FORMER SELF WAS MATT'S COUSIN.
IF HE DOESN'T TURN UP BY MORNING, THEY'RE REPORTING HIM MISSING. I'VE GOT A MESS TO CLEAN UP BEFORE THAT PLACE IS CRAWLING WITH SEARCH TEAMS.
I'LL COME WITH YOU.
NO. YOU STAY HERE AND GET SOME REST. CALL ME IF THERE'RE ANY CHANGES, OKAY?
NARA... PLEASE BE CAREFUL.
KILDAY! YOU'RE LATE.
IS YOUR DAD AWAKE?
NO...
GOOD.

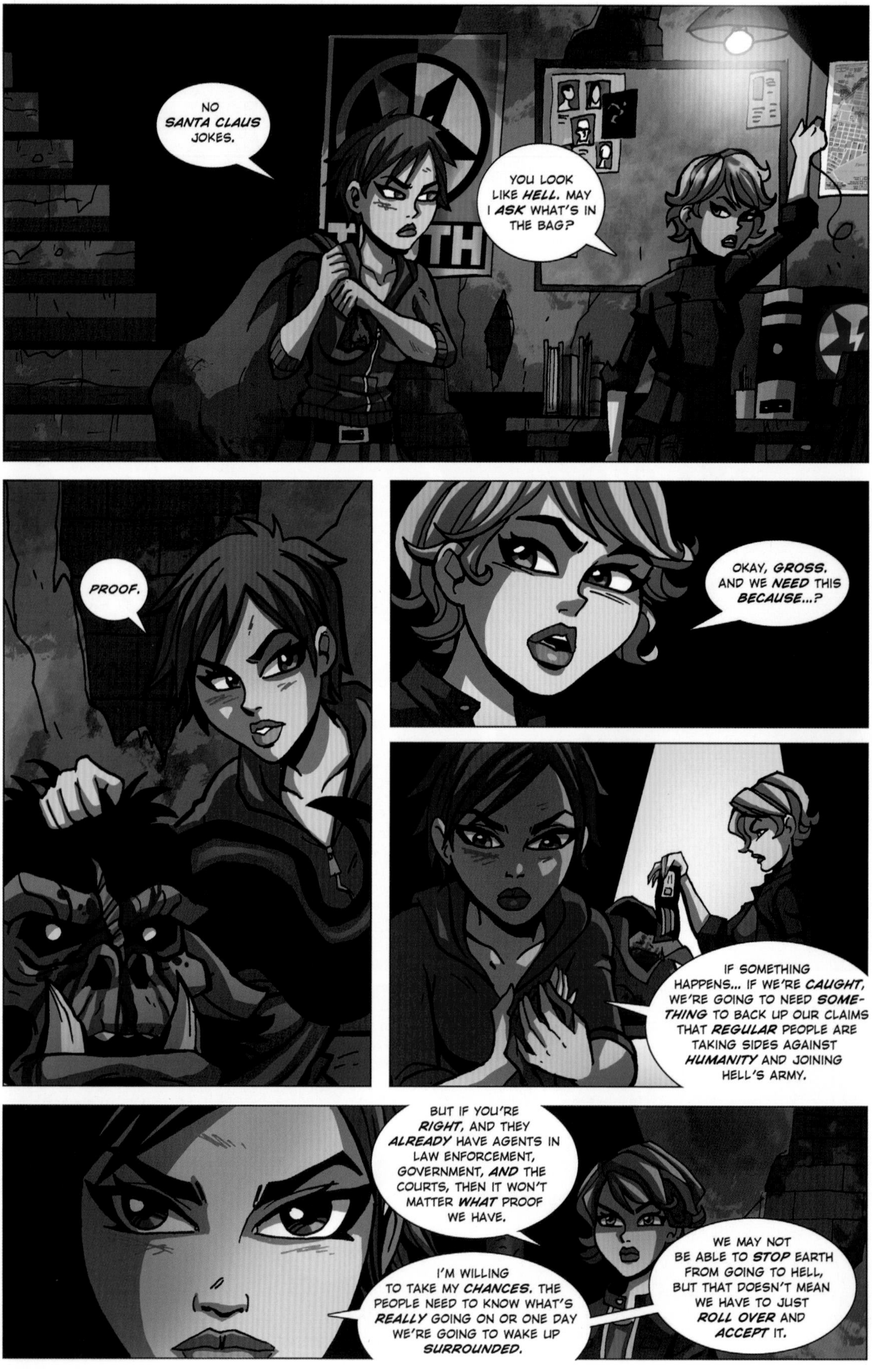
NO SANTA CLAUS JOKES.
YOU LOOK LIKE HELL. MAY I ASK WHAT'S IN THE BAG?
PROOF.
OKAY, GROSS. AND WE NEED THIS BECAUSE...?
IF SOMETHING HAPPENS... IF WE'RE CAUGHT, WE'RE GOING TO NEED SOME-THING TO BACK UP OUR CLAIMS THAT REGULAR PEOPLE ARE TAKING SIDES AGAINST HUMANITY AND JOINING HELL'S ARMY.
BUT IF YOU'RE RIGHT, AND THEY ALREADY HAVE AGENTS IN LAW ENFORCEMENT, GOVERNMENT, AND THE COURTS, THEN IT WON'T MATTER WHAT PROOF WE HAVE.
I'M WILLING TO TAKE MY CHANCES. THE PEOPLE NEED TO KNOW WHAT'S REALLY GOING ON OR ONE DAY WE'RE GOING TO WAKE UP SURROUNDED.
WE MAY NOT BE ABLE TO STOP EARTH FROM GOING TO HELL, BUT THAT DOESN'T MEAN WE HAVE TO JUST ROLL OVER AND ACCEPT IT.

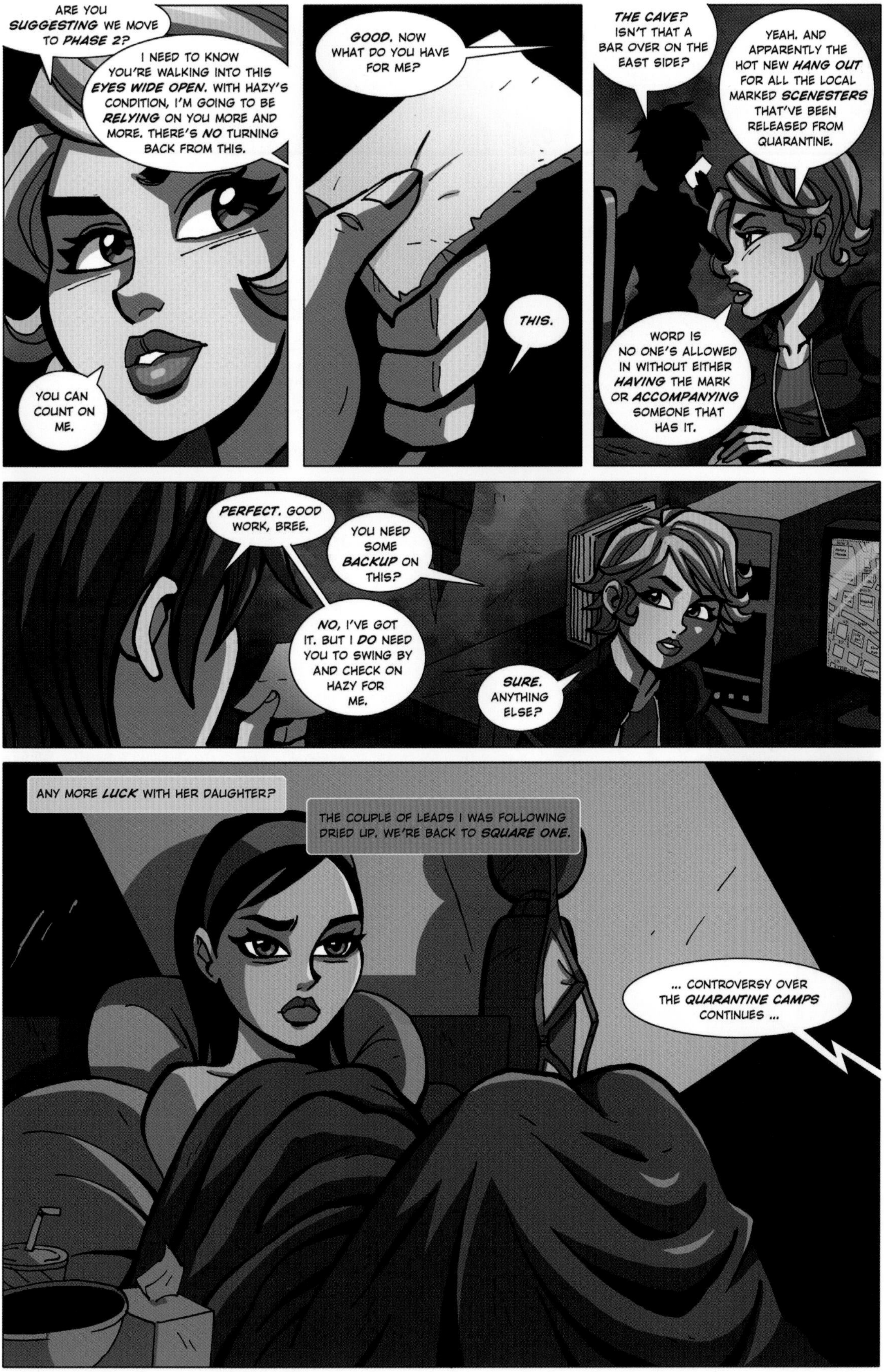
ARE YOU SUGGESTING WE MOVE TO PHASE 2?
I NEED TO KNOW YOU'RE WALKING INTO THIS EYES WIDE OPEN. WITH HAZY'S CONDITION, I'M GOING TO BE RELYING ON YOU MORE AND MORE. THERE'S NO TURNING BACK FROM THIS.
YOU CAN COUNT ON ME.
GOOD. NOW WHAT DO YOU HAVE FOR ME?
THIS.
THE CAVE? ISN'T THAT A BAR OVER ON THE EAST SIDE?
YEAH. AND APPARENTLY THE HOT NEW HANG OUT FOR ALL THE LOCAL MARKED SCENESTERS THAT'VE BEEN RELEASED FROM QUARANTINE.
WORD IS NO ONE'S ALLOWED IN WITHOUT EITHER HAVING THE MARK OR ACCOMPANYING SOMEONE THAT HAS IT.
PERFECT. GOOD WORK, BREE.
YOU NEED SOME BACKUP ON THIS?
NO, I'VE GOT IT. BUT I DO NEED YOU TO SWING BY AND CHECK ON HAZY FOR ME.
SURE. ANYTHING ELSE?
ANY MORE LUCK WITH HER DAUGHTER?
THE COUPLE OF LEADS I WAS FOLLOWING DRIED UP. WE'RE BACK TO SQUARE ONE.
... CONTROVERSY OVER THE QUARANTINE CAMPS CONTINUES ...

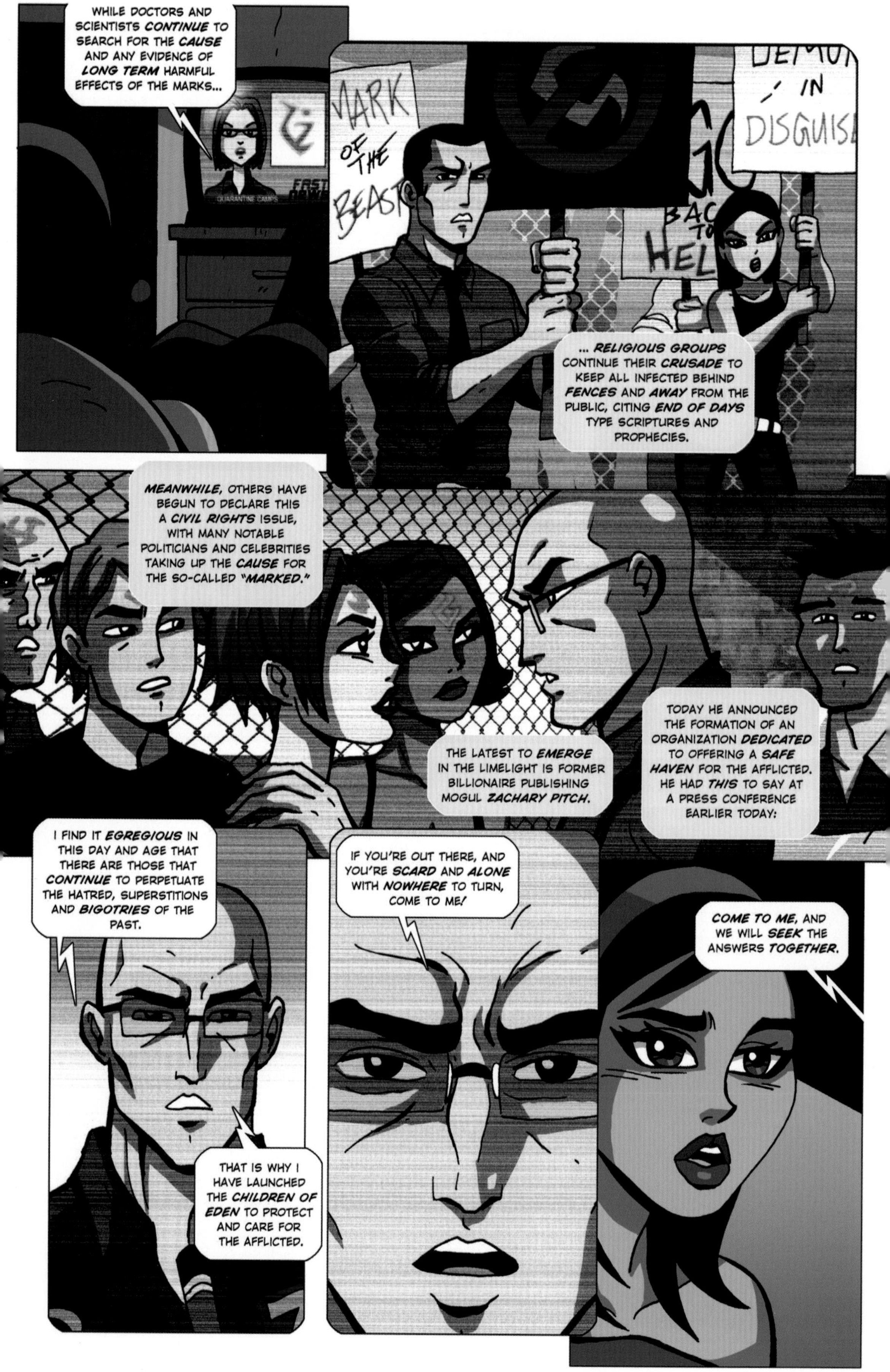
WHILE DOCTORS AND SCIENTISTS CONTINUE TO SEARCH FOR THE CAUSE AND ANY EVIDENCE OF LONG TERM HARMFUL EFFECTS OF THE MARKS...
QUARANTINE CAMPS
MARK OF THE BEAST
DEMON IN DISGUISE
BACK TO HELL
... RELIGIOUS GROUPS CONTINUE THEIR CRUSADE TO KEEP ALL INFECTED BEHIND FENCES AND AWAY FROM THE PUBLIC, CITING END OF DAYS TYPE SCRIPTURES AND PROPHECIES.
MEANWHILE, OTHERS HAVE BEGUN TO DECLARE THIS A CIVIL RIGHTS ISSUE, WITH MANY NOTABLE POLITICIANS AND CELEBRITIES TAKING UP THE CAUSE FOR THE SO-CALLED "MARKED."
THE LATEST TO EMERGE IN THE LIMELIGHT IS FORMER BILLIONAIRE PUBLISHING MOGUL ZACHARY PITCH.
TODAY HE ANNOUNCED THE FORMATION OF AN ORGANIZATION DEDICATED TO OFFERING A SAFE HAVEN FOR THE AFFLICTED. HE HAD THIS TO SAY AT A PRESS CONFERENCE EARLIER TODAY:
I FIND IT EGREGIOUS IN THIS DAY AND AGE THAT THERE ARE THOSE THAT CONTINUE TO PERPETUATE THE HATRED, SUPERSTITIONS AND BIGOTRIES OF THE PAST.
THAT IS WHY I HAVE LAUNCHED THE CHILDREN OF EDEN TO PROTECT AND CARE FOR THE AFFLICTED.
IF YOU'RE OUT THERE, AND YOU'RE SCARD AND ALONE WITH NOWHERE TO TURN, COME TO ME!
COME TO ME, AND WE WILL SEEK THE ANSWERS TOGETHER.

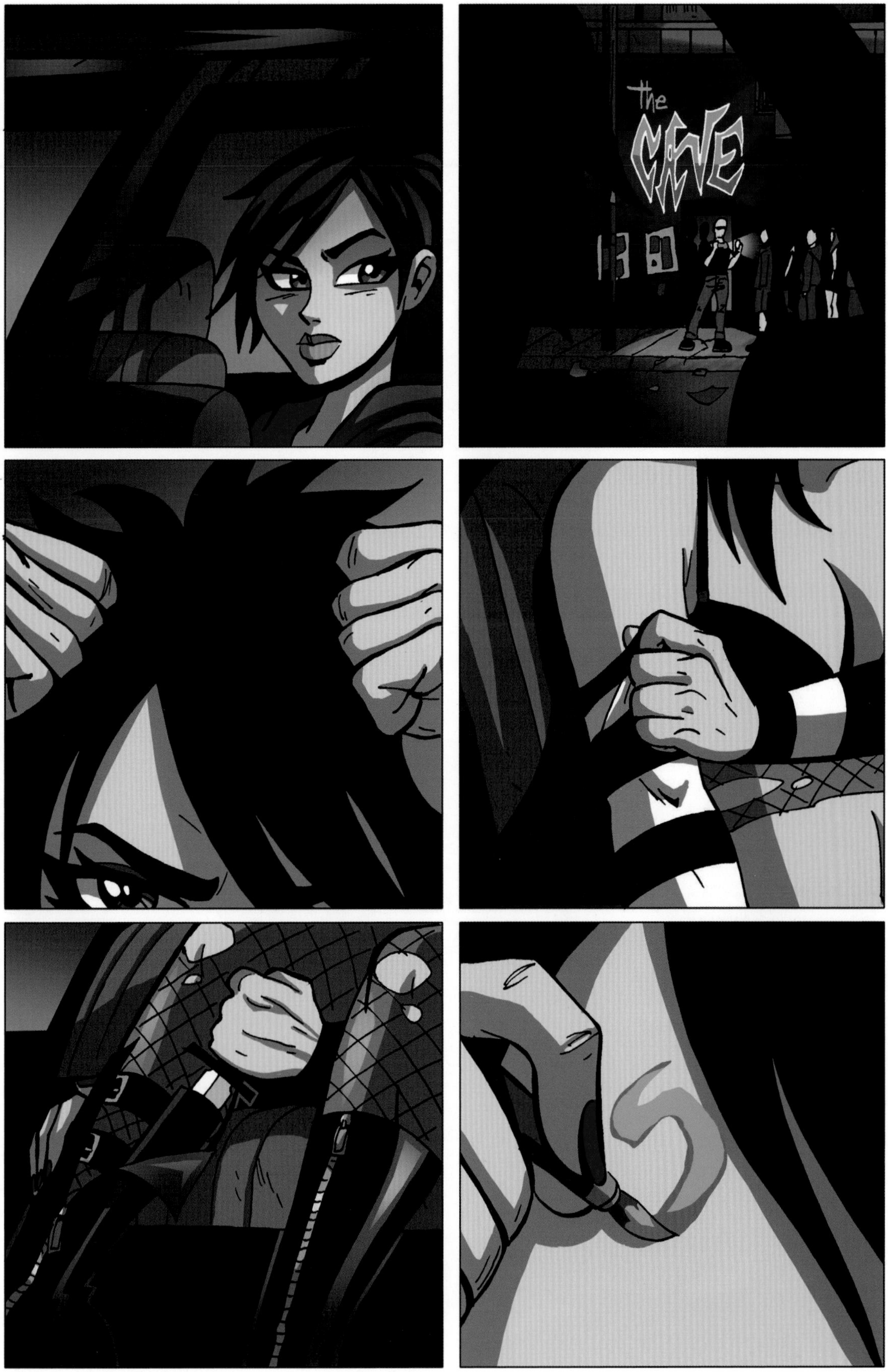
the CAVE

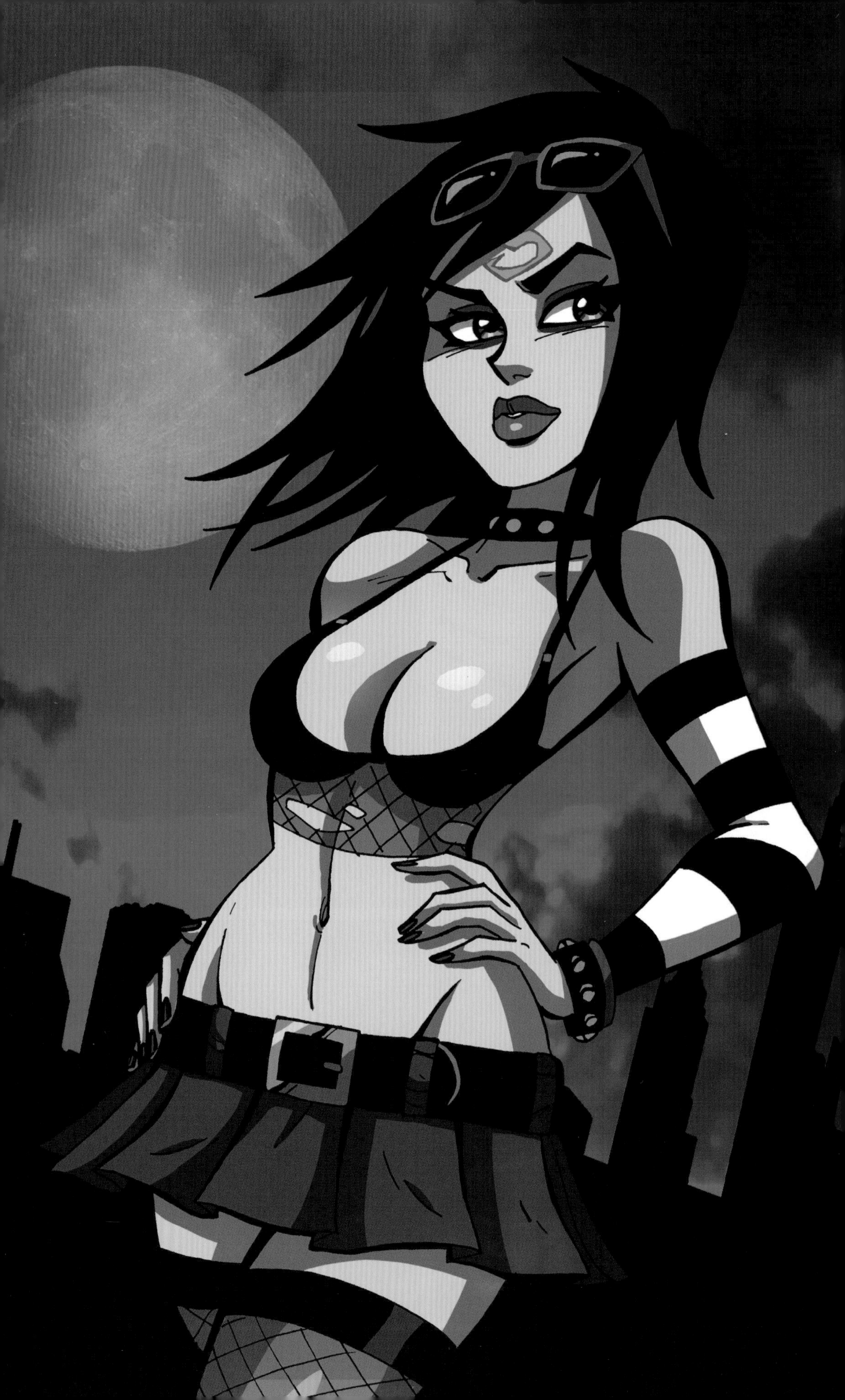

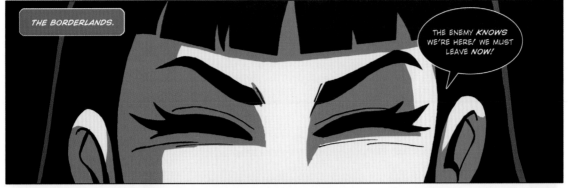

THE BORDERLANDS.

THE ENEMY *KNOWS* WE'RE HERE! WE MUST LEAVE *NOW!*

WHAT ABOUT THE *MESSENGER?*

THEY *FOLLOWED* HER HERE.

THERE! SOMEONE *APPROACHES!*

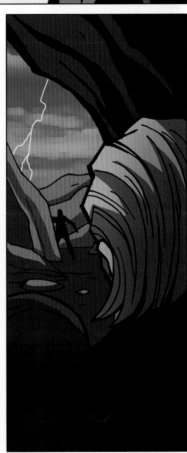

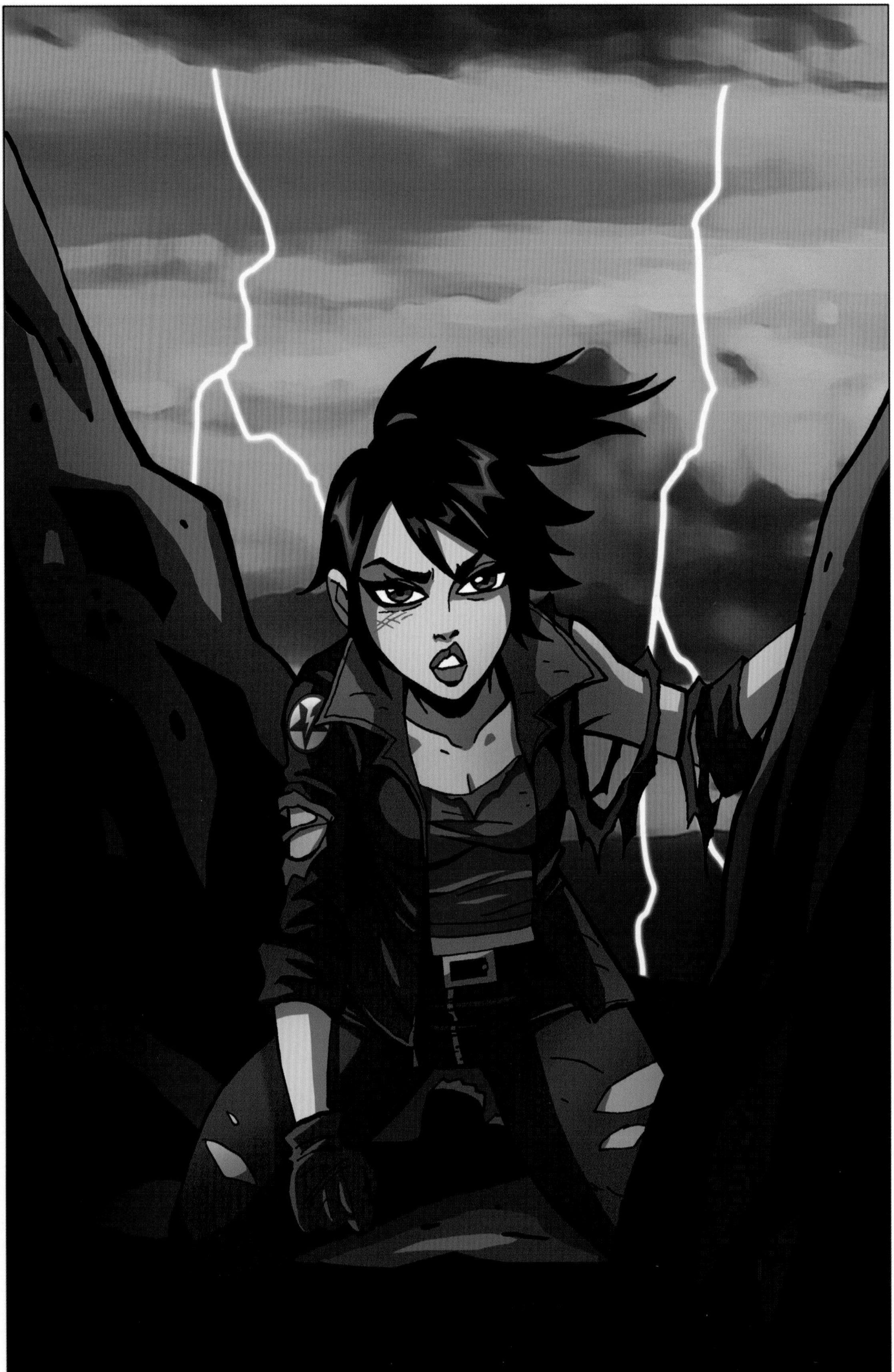

CHAPTER TWO

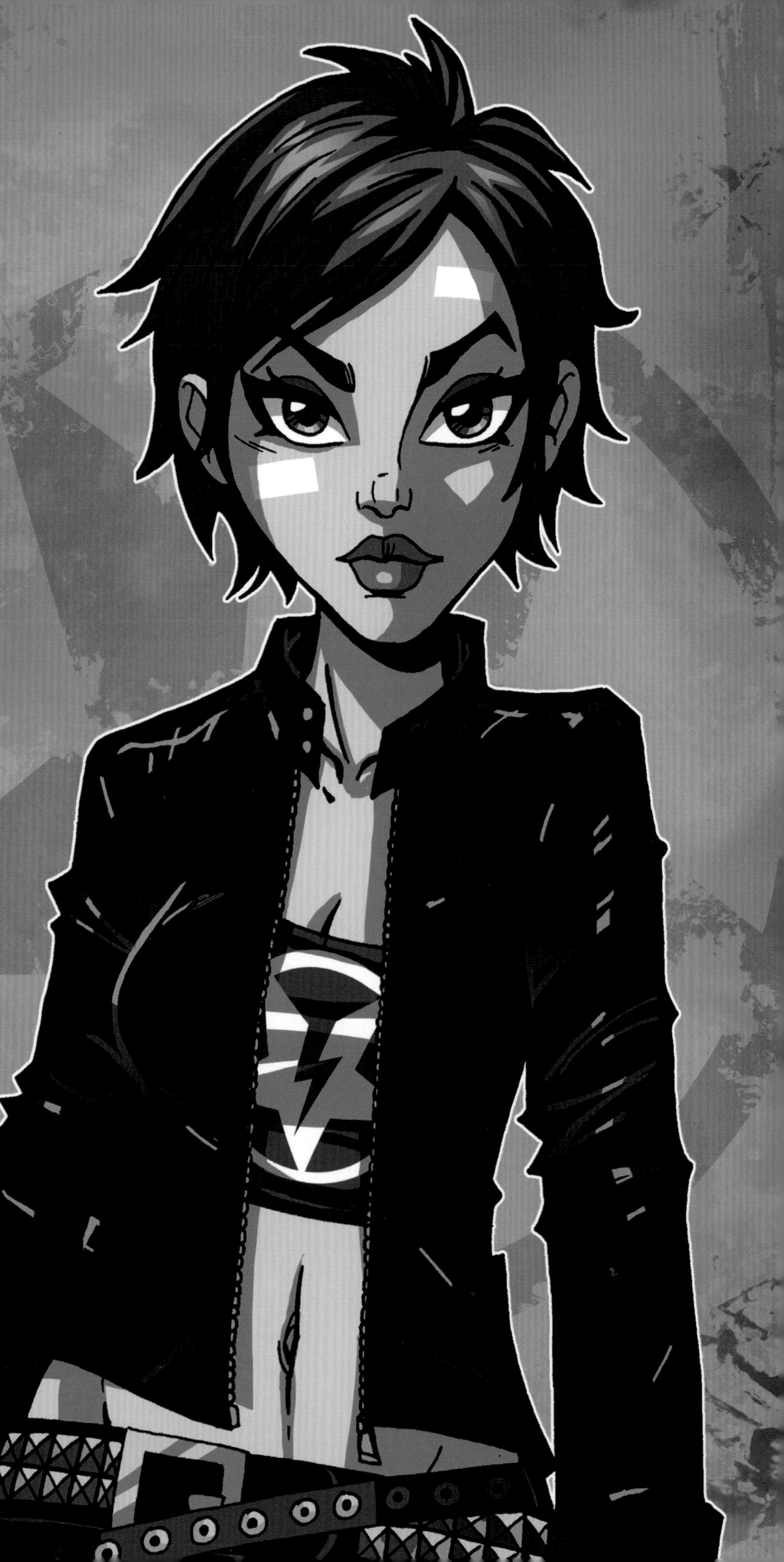

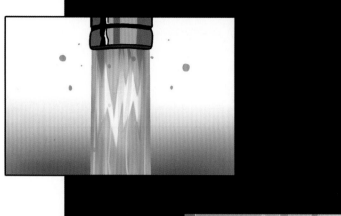

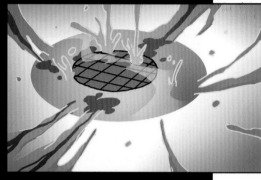

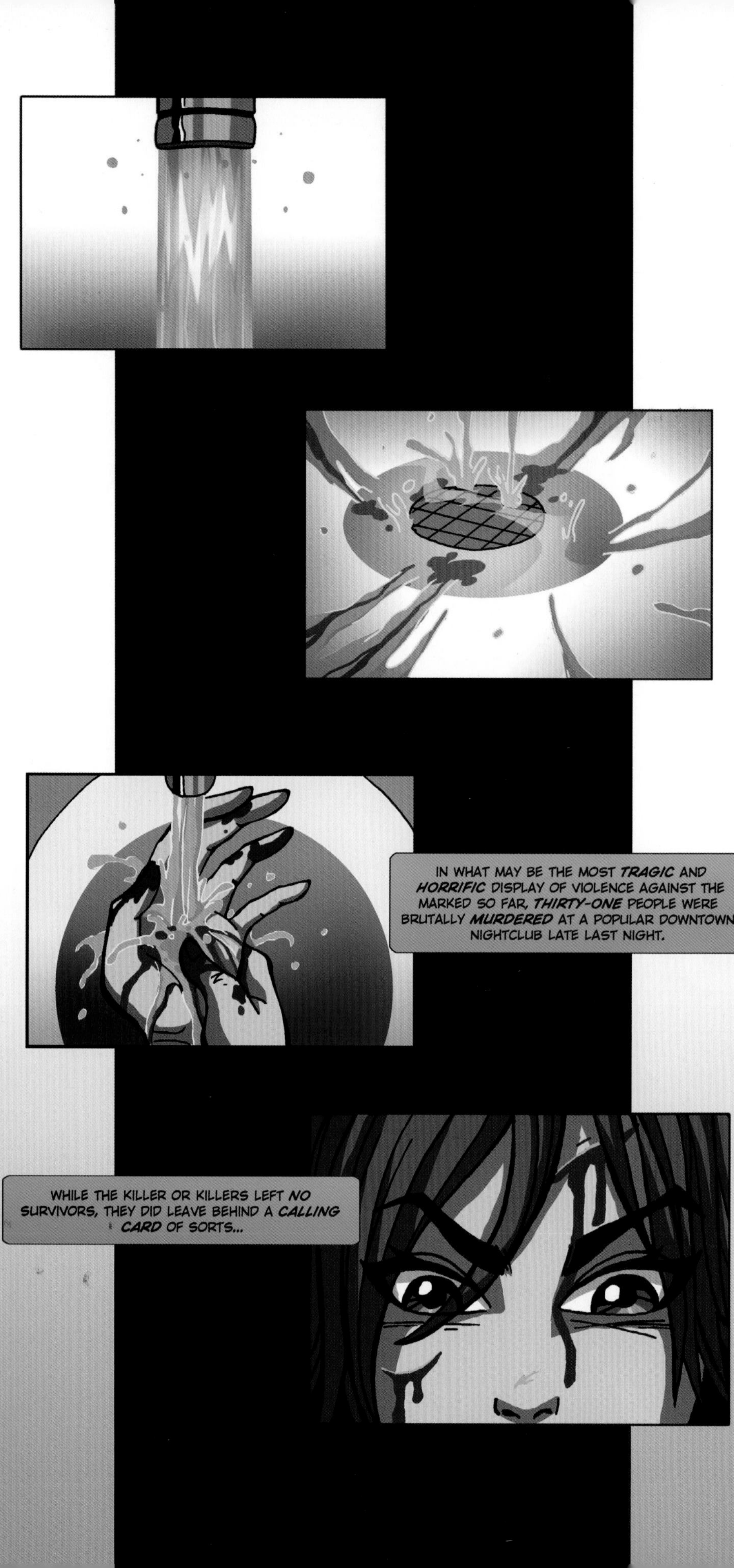

IN WHAT MAY BE THE MOST *TRAGIC* AND *HORRIFIC* DISPLAY OF VIOLENCE AGAINST THE MARKED SO FAR, *THIRTY-ONE* PEOPLE WERE BRUTALLY *MURDERED* AT A POPULAR DOWNTOWN NIGHTCLUB LATE LAST NIGHT.

WHILE THE KILLER OR KILLERS LEFT *NO* SURVIVORS, THEY DID LEAVE BEHIND A *CALLING CARD* OF SORTS...

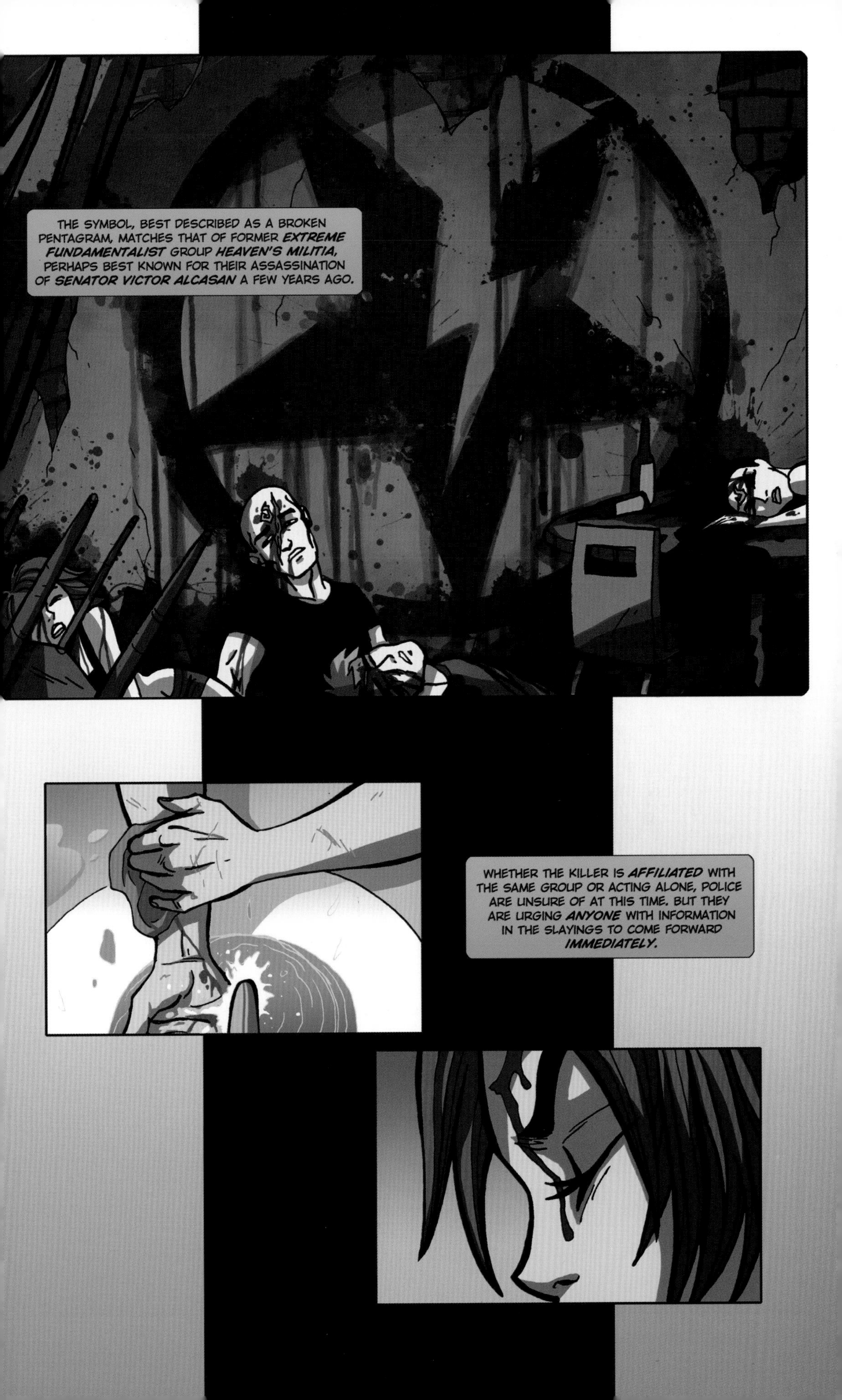
THE SYMBOL, BEST DESCRIBED AS A BROKEN PENTAGRAM, MATCHES THAT OF FORMER EXTREME FUNDAMENTALIST GROUP HEAVEN'S MILITIA, PERHAPS BEST KNOWN FOR THEIR ASSASSINATION OF SENATOR VICTOR ALCASAN A FEW YEARS AGO.
WHETHER THE KILLER IS AFFILIATED WITH THE SAME GROUP OR ACTING ALONE, POLICE ARE UNSURE OF AT THIS TIME. BUT THEY ARE URGING ANYONE WITH INFORMATION IN THE SLAYINGS TO COME FORWARD IMMEDIATELY.

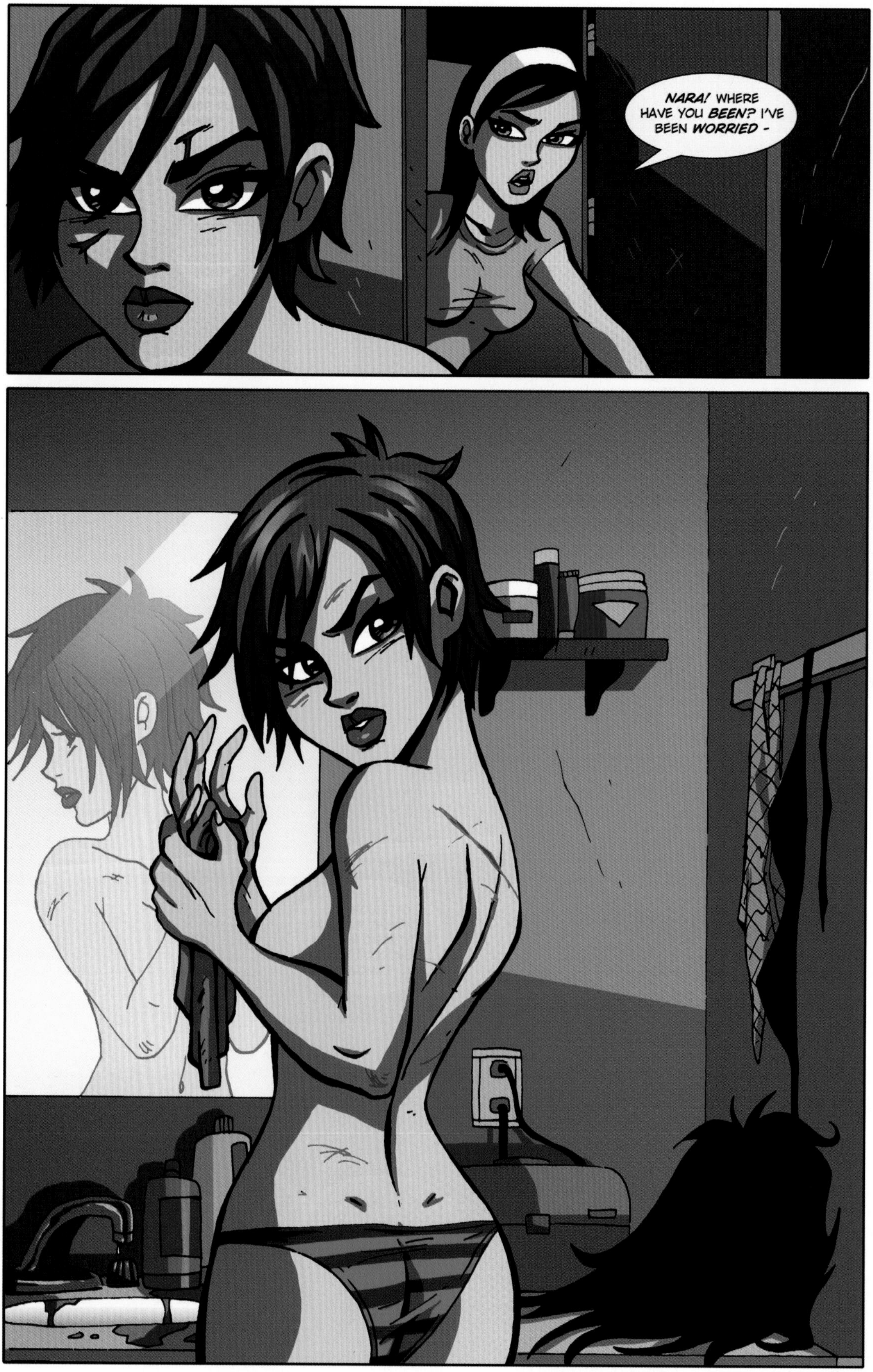
NARA! WHERE HAVE YOU BEEN? I'VE BEEN WORRIED -

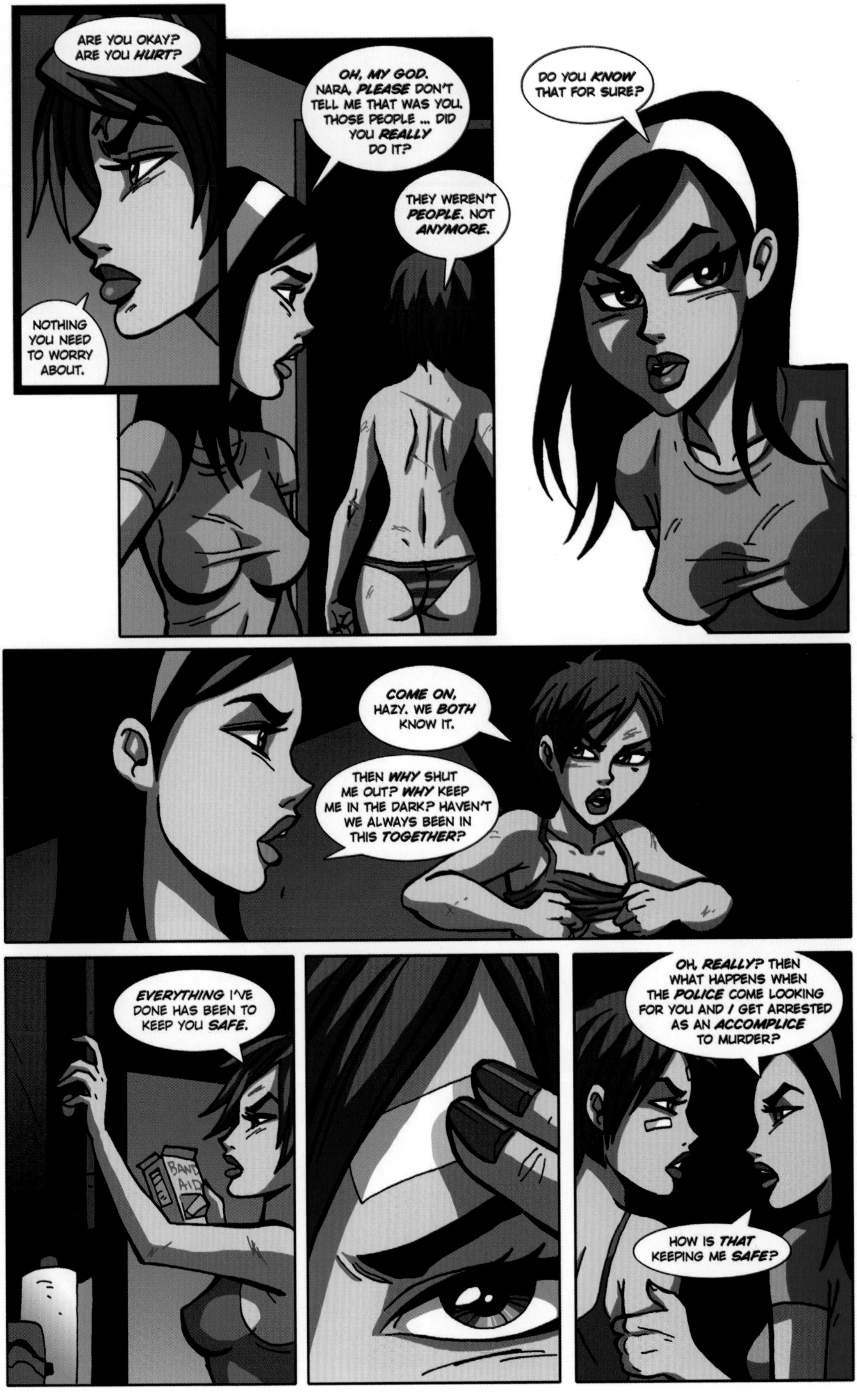
ARE YOU OKAY? ARE YOU HURT?
NOTHING YOU NEED TO WORRY ABOUT.
OH, MY GOD. NARA, PLEASE DON'T TELL ME THAT WAS YOU. THOSE PEOPLE ... DID YOU REALLY DO IT?
THEY WEREN'T PEOPLE. NOT ANYMORE.
DO YOU KNOW THAT FOR SURE?
COME ON, HAZY. WE BOTH KNOW IT.
THEN WHY SHUT ME OUT? WHY KEEP ME IN THE DARK? HAVEN'T WE ALWAYS BEEN IN THIS TOGETHER?
EVERYTHING I'VE DONE HAS BEEN TO KEEP YOU SAFE.
BAND AID
OH, REALLY? THEN WHAT HAPPENS WHEN THE POLICE COME LOOKING FOR YOU AND I GET ARRESTED AS AN ACCOMPLICE TO MURDER?
HOW IS THAT KEEPING ME SAFE?

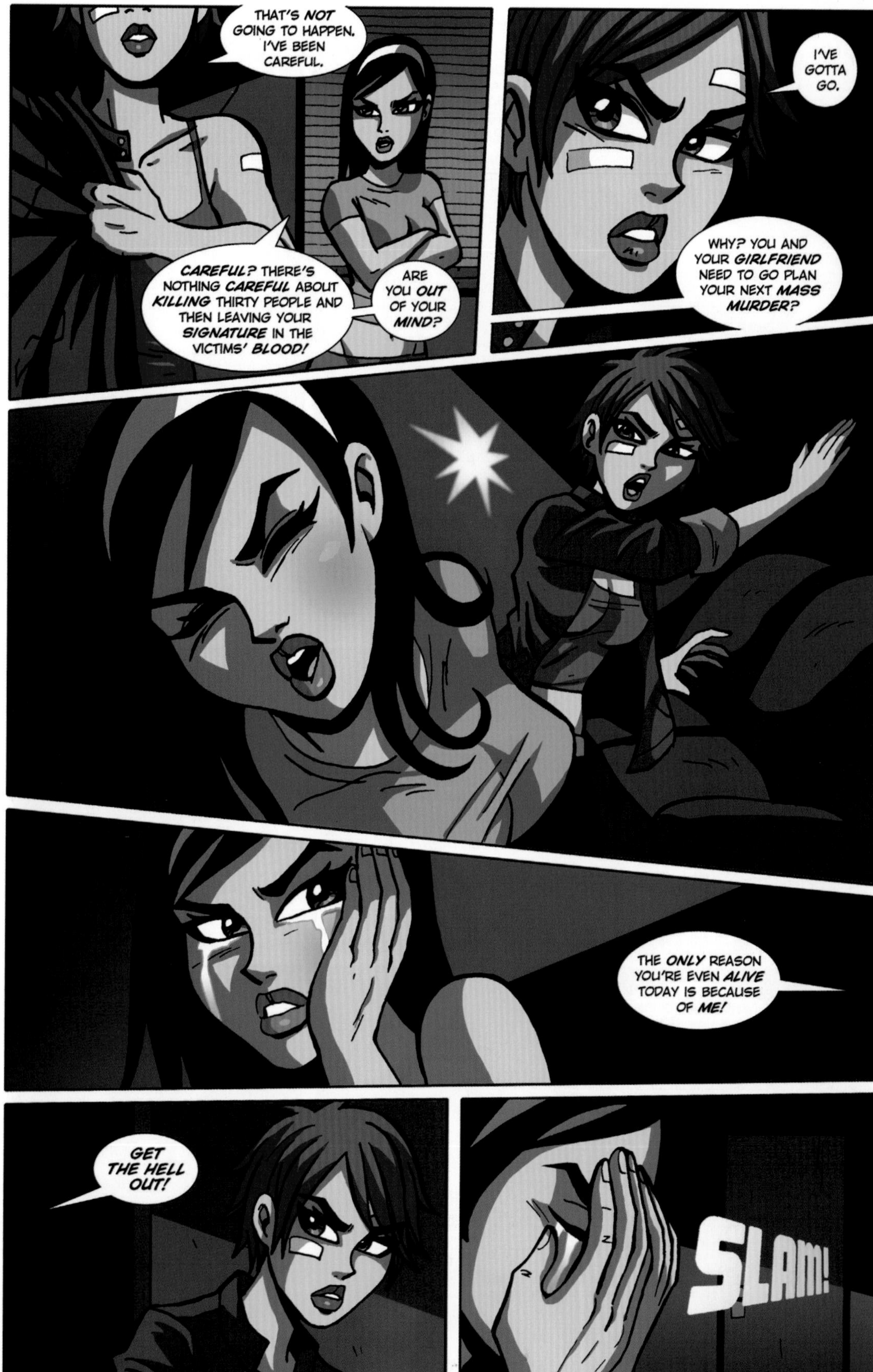
THAT'S NOT GOING TO HAPPEN. I'VE BEEN CAREFUL.
CAREFUL? THERE'S NOTHING CAREFUL ABOUT KILLING THIRTY PEOPLE AND THEN LEAVING YOUR SIGNATURE IN THE VICTIMS' BLOOD!
ARE YOU OUT OF YOUR MIND?
I'VE GOTTA GO.
WHY? YOU AND YOUR GIRLFRIEND NEED TO GO PLAN YOUR NEXT MASS MURDER?
THE ONLY REASON YOU'RE EVEN ALIVE TODAY IS BECAUSE OF ME!
GET THE HELL OUT!
SLAM!

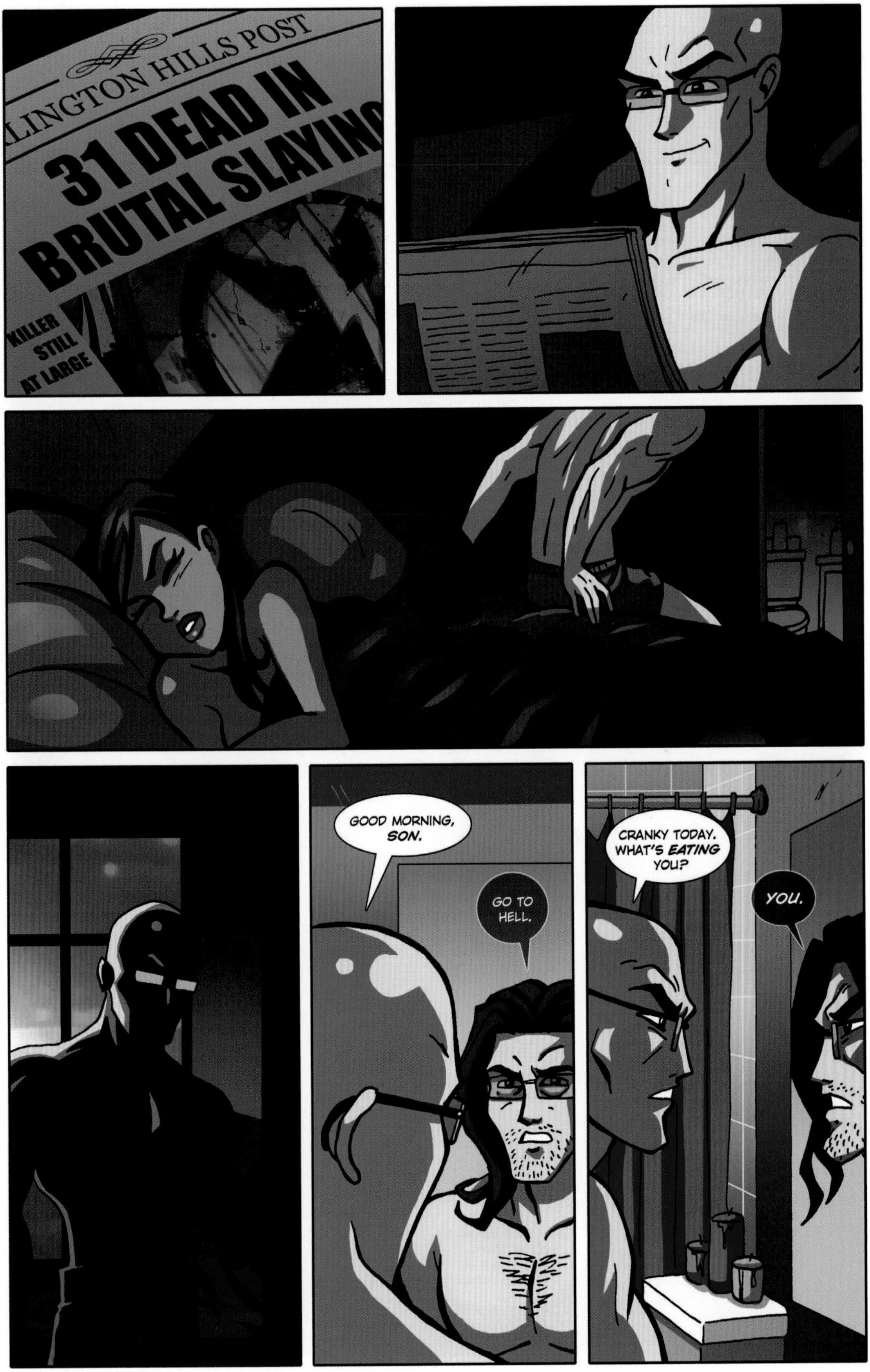

LLINGTON HILLS POST
31 DEAD IN BRUTAL SLAYING
KILLER STILL AT LARGE
GOOD MORNING, SON.
GO TO HELL.
CRANKY TODAY. WHAT'S EATING YOU?
YOU.

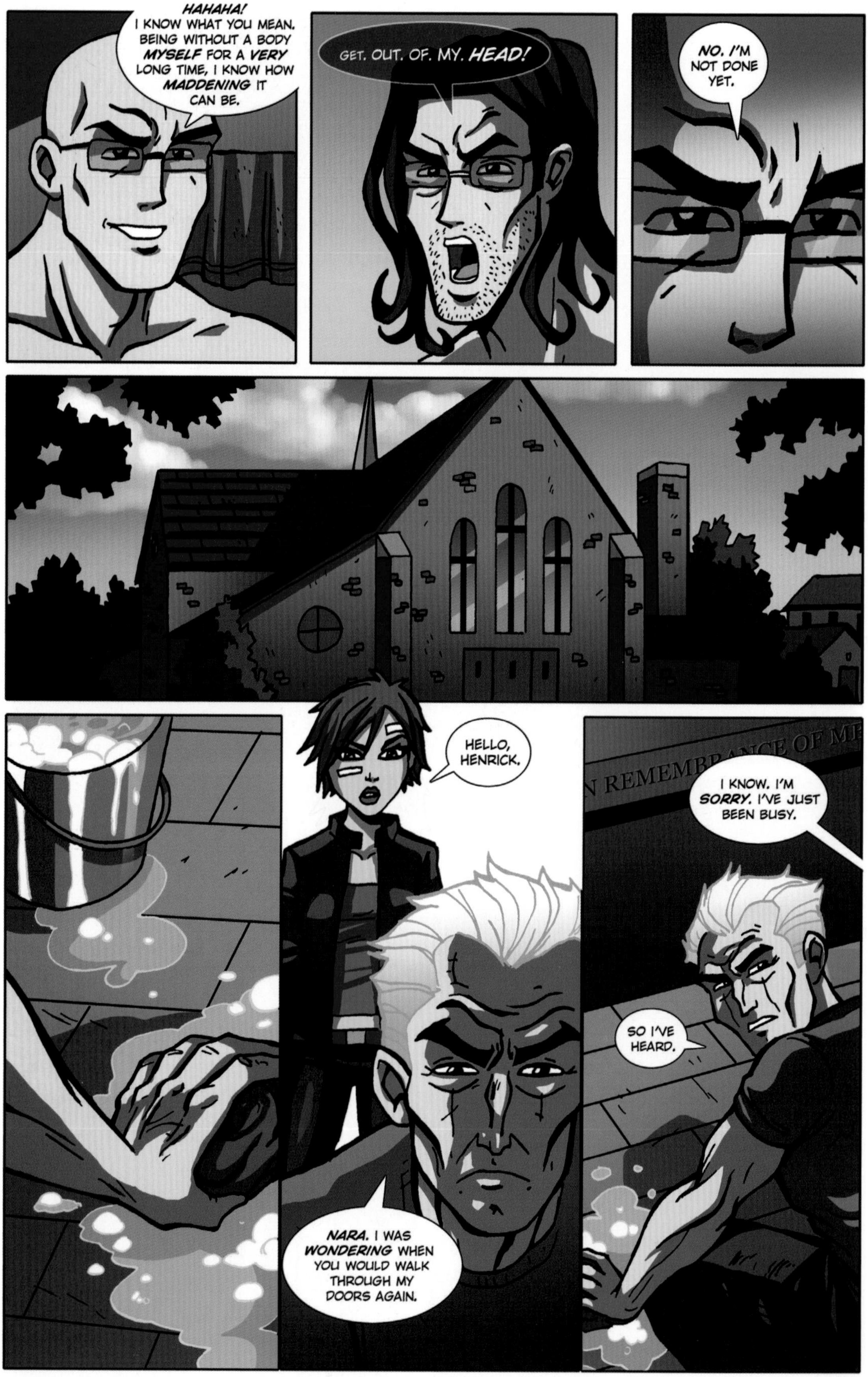
HAHAHA! I KNOW WHAT YOU MEAN. BEING WITHOUT A BODY MYSELF FOR A VERY LONG TIME, I KNOW HOW MADDENING IT CAN BE.
GET. OUT. OF. MY. HEAD!
NO. I'M NOT DONE YET.
HELLO, HENRICK.
NARA. I WAS WONDERING WHEN YOU WOULD WALK THROUGH MY DOORS AGAIN.
I KNOW. I'M SORRY. I'VE JUST BEEN BUSY.
SO I'VE HEARD.
N REMEMBRANCE OF ME

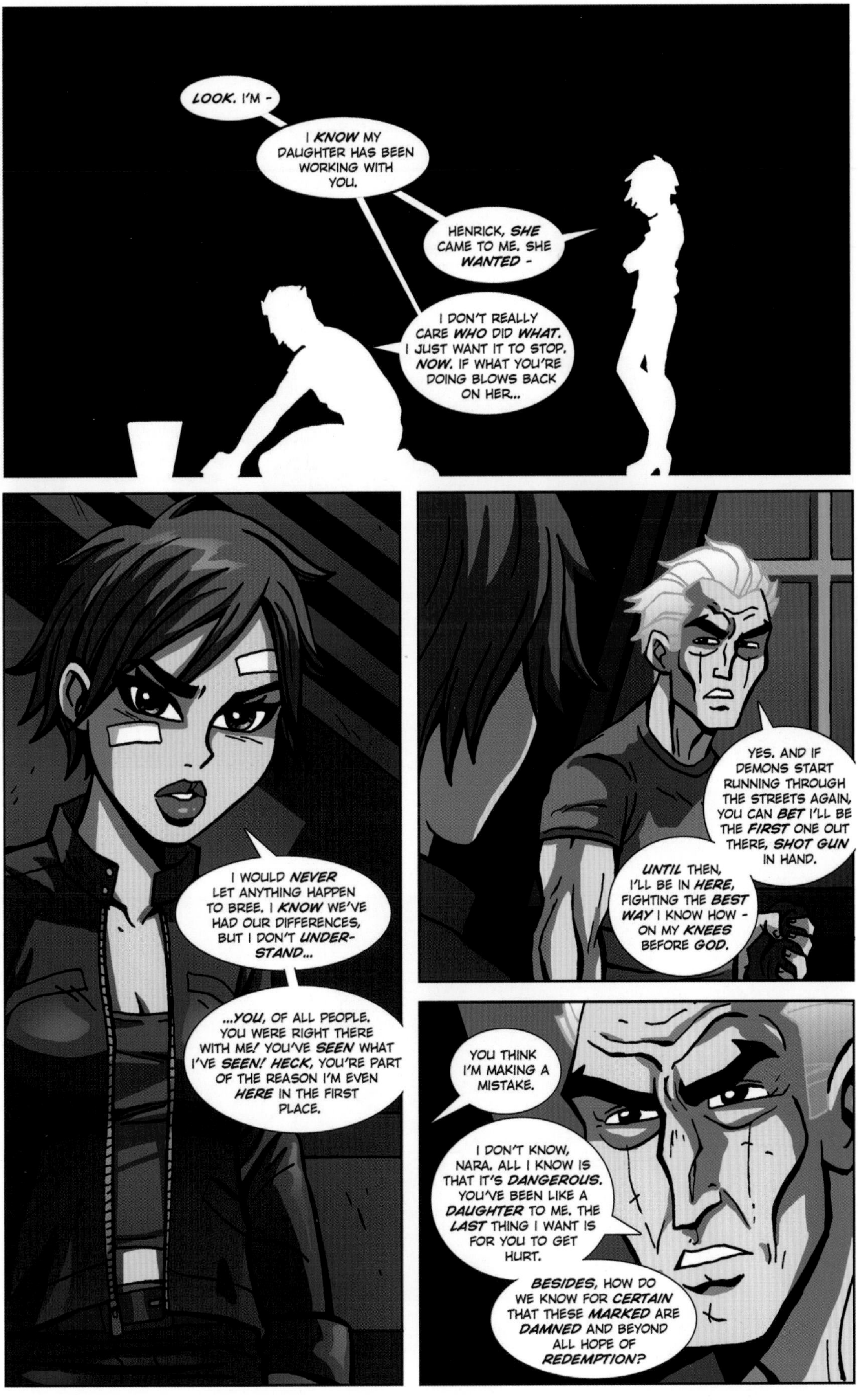
LOOK. I'M -
I KNOW MY DAUGHTER HAS BEEN WORKING WITH YOU.
HENRICK, SHE CAME TO ME. SHE WANTED -
I DON'T REALLY CARE WHO DID WHAT. I JUST WANT IT TO STOP. NOW. IF WHAT YOU'RE DOING BLOWS BACK ON HER...
I WOULD NEVER LET ANYTHING HAPPEN TO BREE. I KNOW WE'VE HAD OUR DIFFERENCES, BUT I DON'T UNDER-STAND...
...YOU, OF ALL PEOPLE. YOU WERE RIGHT THERE WITH ME! YOU'VE SEEN WHAT I'VE SEEN! HECK, YOU'RE PART OF THE REASON I'M EVEN HERE IN THE FIRST PLACE.
YES. AND IF DEMONS START RUNNING THROUGH THE STREETS AGAIN, YOU CAN BET I'LL BE THE FIRST ONE OUT THERE, SHOT GUN IN HAND.
UNTIL THEN, I'LL BE IN HERE, FIGHTING THE BEST WAY I KNOW HOW - ON MY KNEES BEFORE GOD.
YOU THINK I'M MAKING A MISTAKE.
I DON'T KNOW, NARA. ALL I KNOW IS THAT IT'S DANGEROUS. YOU'VE BEEN LIKE A DAUGHTER TO ME. THE LAST THING I WANT IS FOR YOU TO GET HURT.
BESIDES, HOW DO WE KNOW FOR CERTAIN THAT THESE MARKED ARE DAMNED AND BEYOND ALL HOPE OF REDEMPTION?

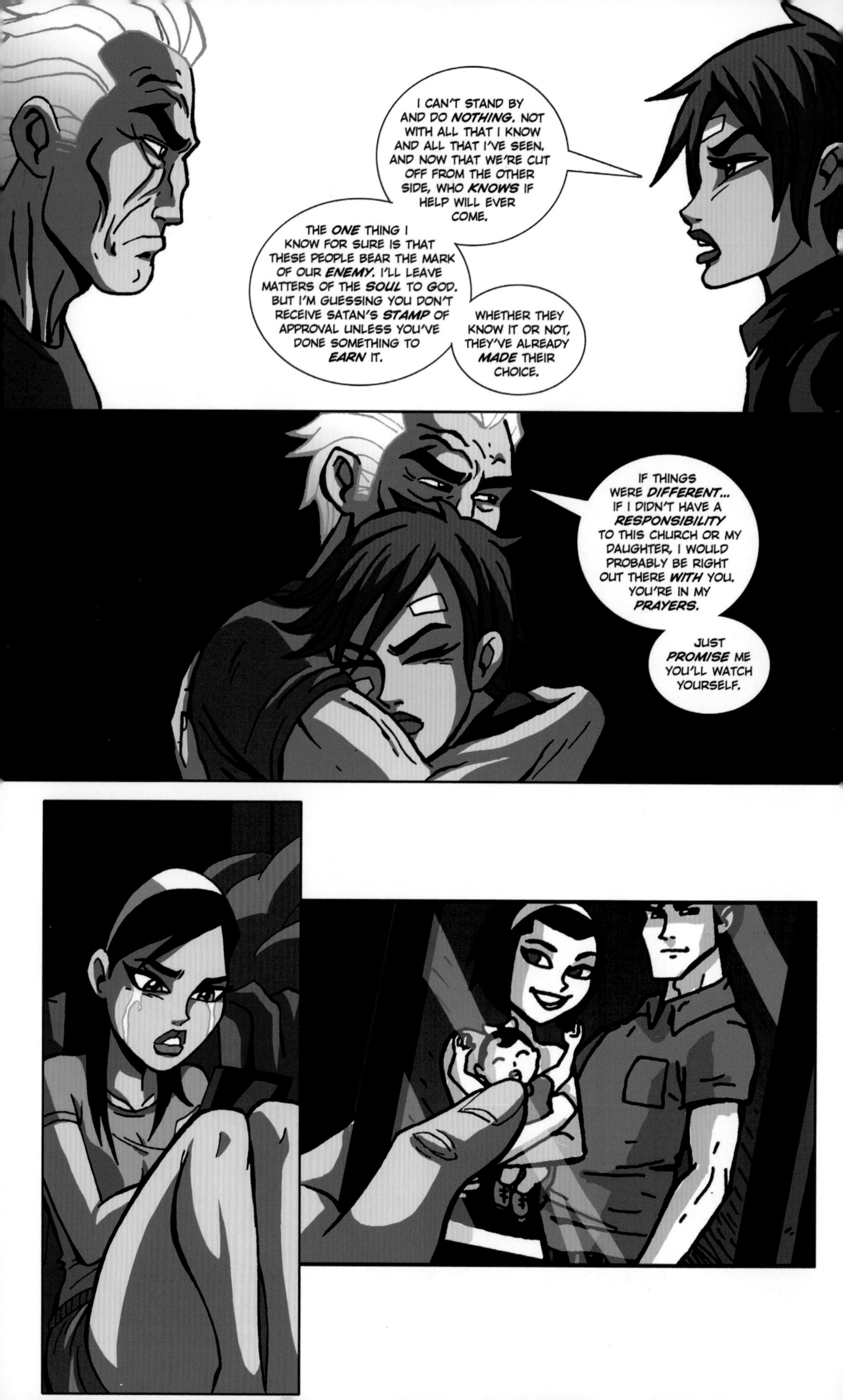
I CAN'T STAND BY AND DO NOTHING. NOT WITH ALL THAT I KNOW AND ALL THAT I'VE SEEN. AND NOW THAT WE'RE CUT OFF FROM THE OTHER SIDE, WHO KNOWS IF HELP WILL EVER COME.
THE ONE THING I KNOW FOR SURE IS THAT THESE PEOPLE BEAR THE MARK OF OUR ENEMY. I'LL LEAVE MATTERS OF THE SOUL TO GOD. BUT I'M GUESSING YOU DON'T RECEIVE SATAN'S STAMP OF APPROVAL UNLESS YOU'VE DONE SOMETHING TO EARN IT.
WHETHER THEY KNOW IT OR NOT, THEY'VE ALREADY MADE THEIR CHOICE.
IF THINGS WERE DIFFERENT... IF I DIDN'T HAVE A RESPONSIBILITY TO THIS CHURCH OR MY DAUGHTER, I WOULD PROBABLY BE RIGHT OUT THERE WITH YOU. YOU'RE IN MY PRAYERS.
JUST PROMISE ME YOU'LL WATCH YOURSELF.

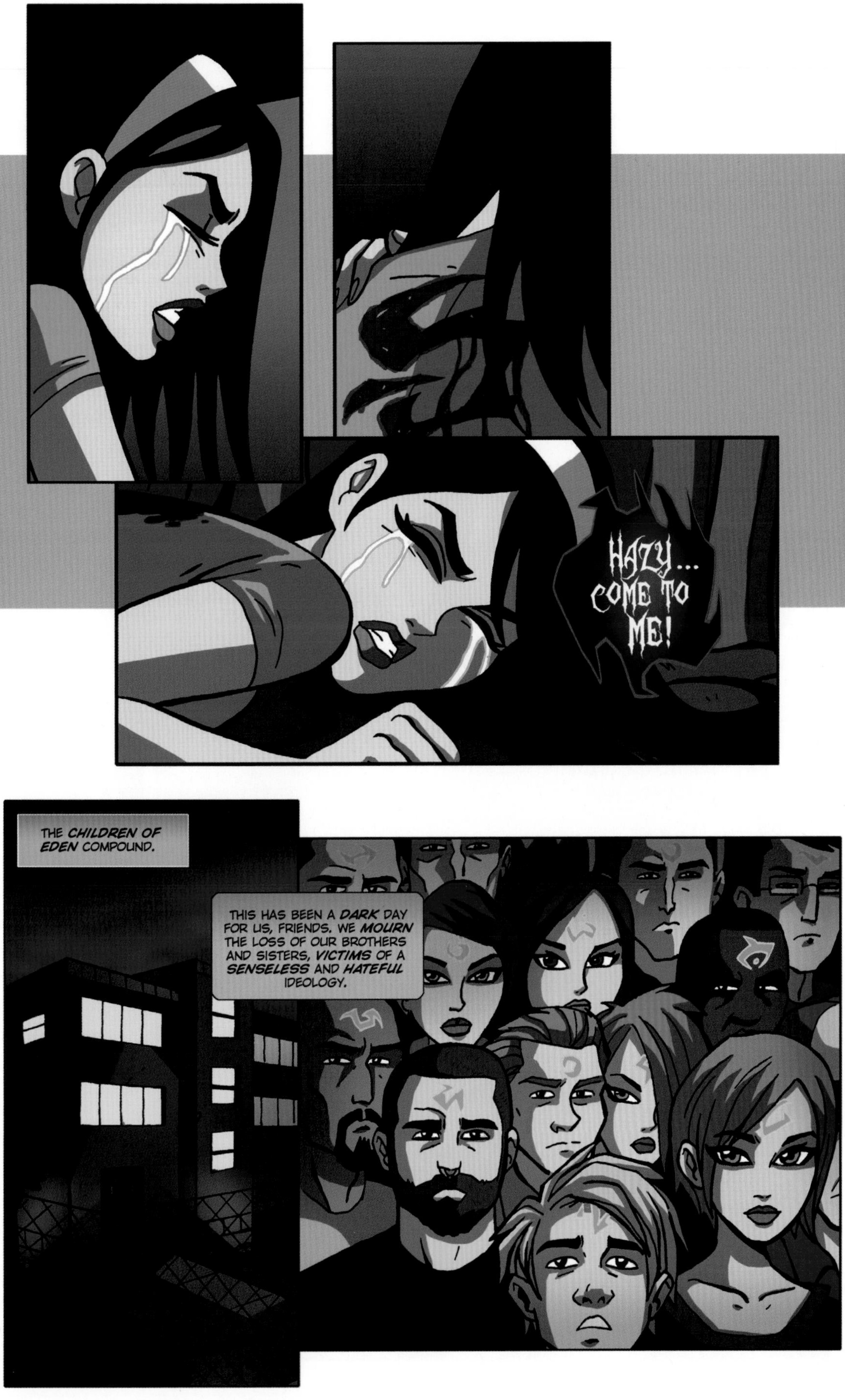
HAZY... COME TO ME!
THE CHILDREN OF EDEN COMPOUND.
THIS HAS BEEN A DARK DAY FOR US, FRIENDS. WE MOURN THE LOSS OF OUR BROTHERS AND SISTERS, VICTIMS OF A SENSELESS AND HATEFUL IDEOLOGY.

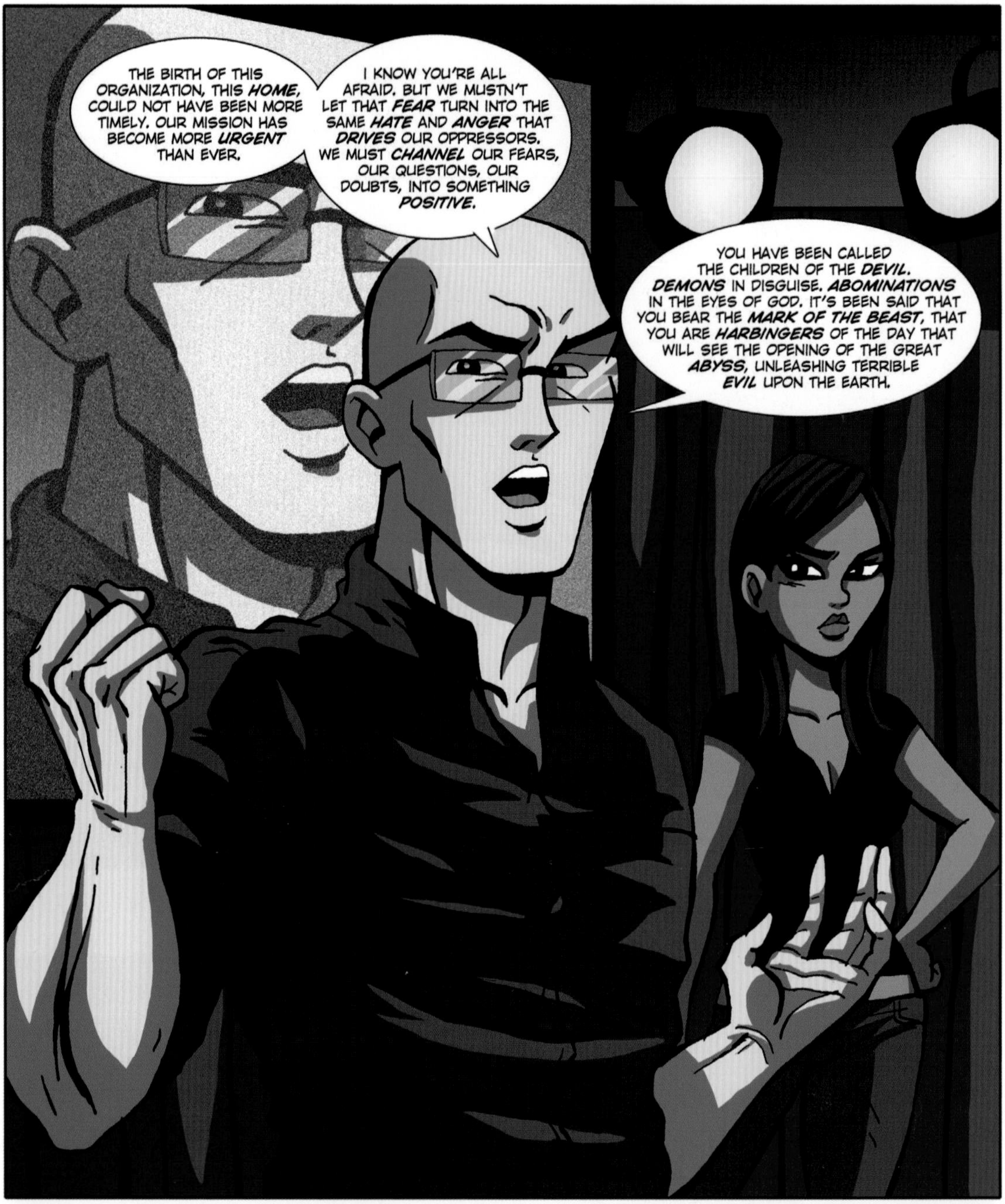
THE BIRTH OF THIS ORGANIZATION, THIS HOME, COULD NOT HAVE BEEN MORE TIMELY. OUR MISSION HAS BECOME MORE URGENT THAN EVER.
I KNOW YOU'RE ALL AFRAID. BUT WE MUSTN'T LET THAT FEAR TURN INTO THE SAME HATE AND ANGER THAT DRIVES OUR OPPRESSORS. WE MUST CHANNEL OUR FEARS, OUR QUESTIONS, OUR DOUBTS, INTO SOMETHING POSITIVE.
YOU HAVE BEEN CALLED THE CHILDREN OF THE DEVIL. DEMONS IN DISGUISE. ABOMINATIONS IN THE EYES OF GOD. IT'S BEEN SAID THAT YOU BEAR THE MARK OF THE BEAST, THAT YOU ARE HARBINGERS OF THE DAY THAT WILL SEE THE OPENING OF THE GREAT ABYSS, UNLEASHING TERRIBLE EVIL UPON THE EARTH.

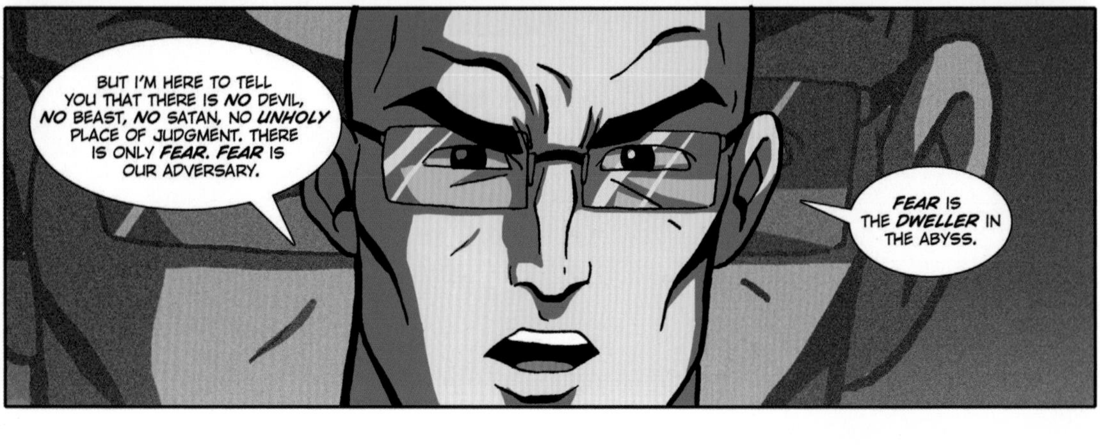
BUT I'M HERE TO TELL YOU THAT THERE IS NO DEVIL, NO BEAST, NO SATAN, NO UNHOLY PLACE OF JUDGMENT. THERE IS ONLY FEAR. FEAR IS OUR ADVERSARY.
FEAR IS THE DWELLER IN THE ABYSS.

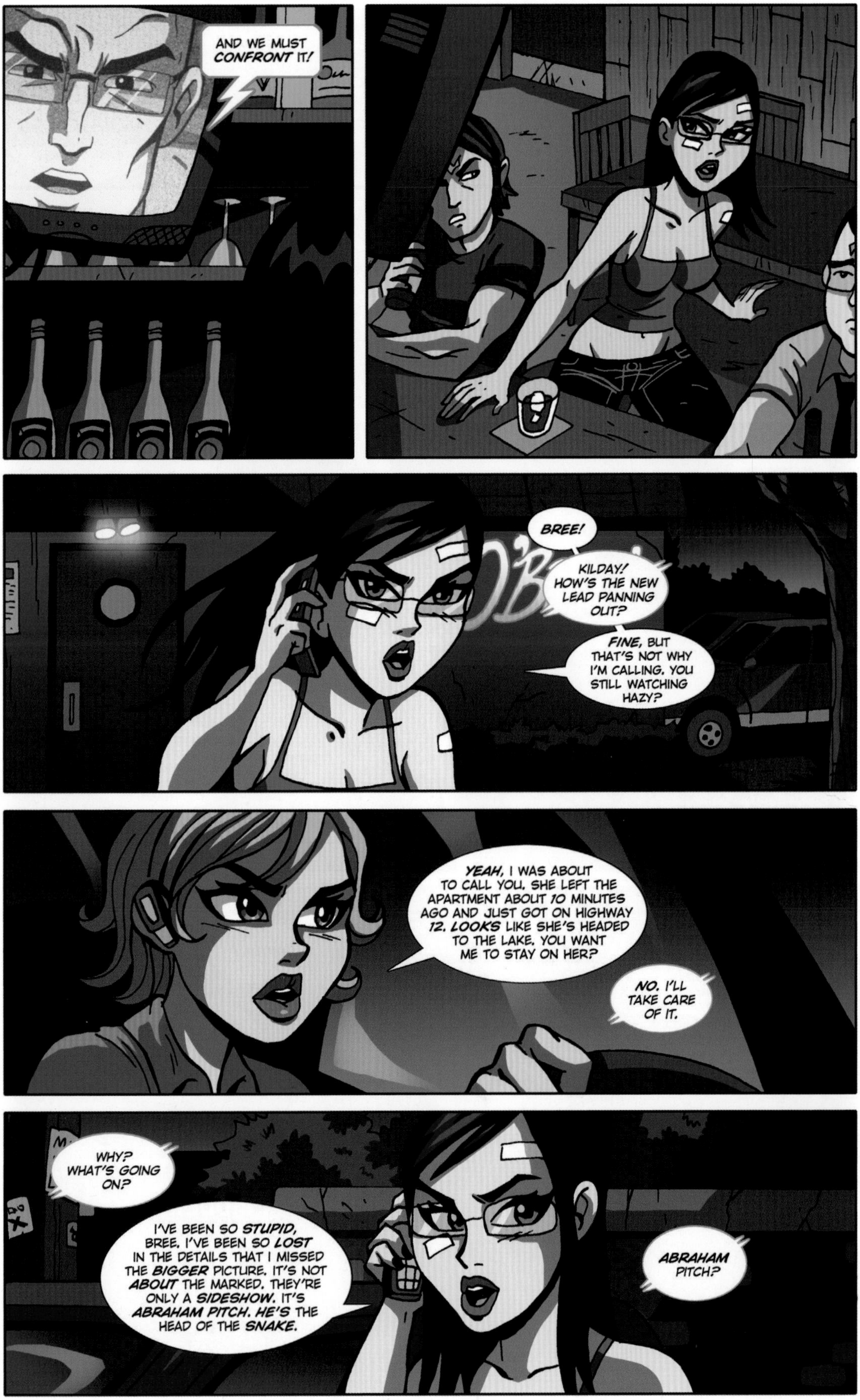
AND WE MUST CONFRONT IT!
BREE!
KILDAY! HOW'S THE NEW LEAD PANNING OUT?
FINE, BUT THAT'S NOT WHY I'M CALLING. YOU STILL WATCHING HAZY?
YEAH, I WAS ABOUT TO CALL YOU. SHE LEFT THE APARTMENT ABOUT 10 MINUTES AGO AND JUST GOT ON HIGHWAY 12. LOOKS LIKE SHE'S HEADED TO THE LAKE. YOU WANT ME TO STAY ON HER?
NO. I'LL TAKE CARE OF IT.
WHY? WHAT'S GOING ON?
I'VE BEEN SO STUPID, BREE. I'VE BEEN SO LOST IN THE DETAILS THAT I MISSED THE BIGGER PICTURE. IT'S NOT ABOUT THE MARKED. THEY'RE ONLY A SIDESHOW. IT'S ABRAHAM PITCH. HE'S THE HEAD OF THE SNAKE.
ABRAHAM PITCH?

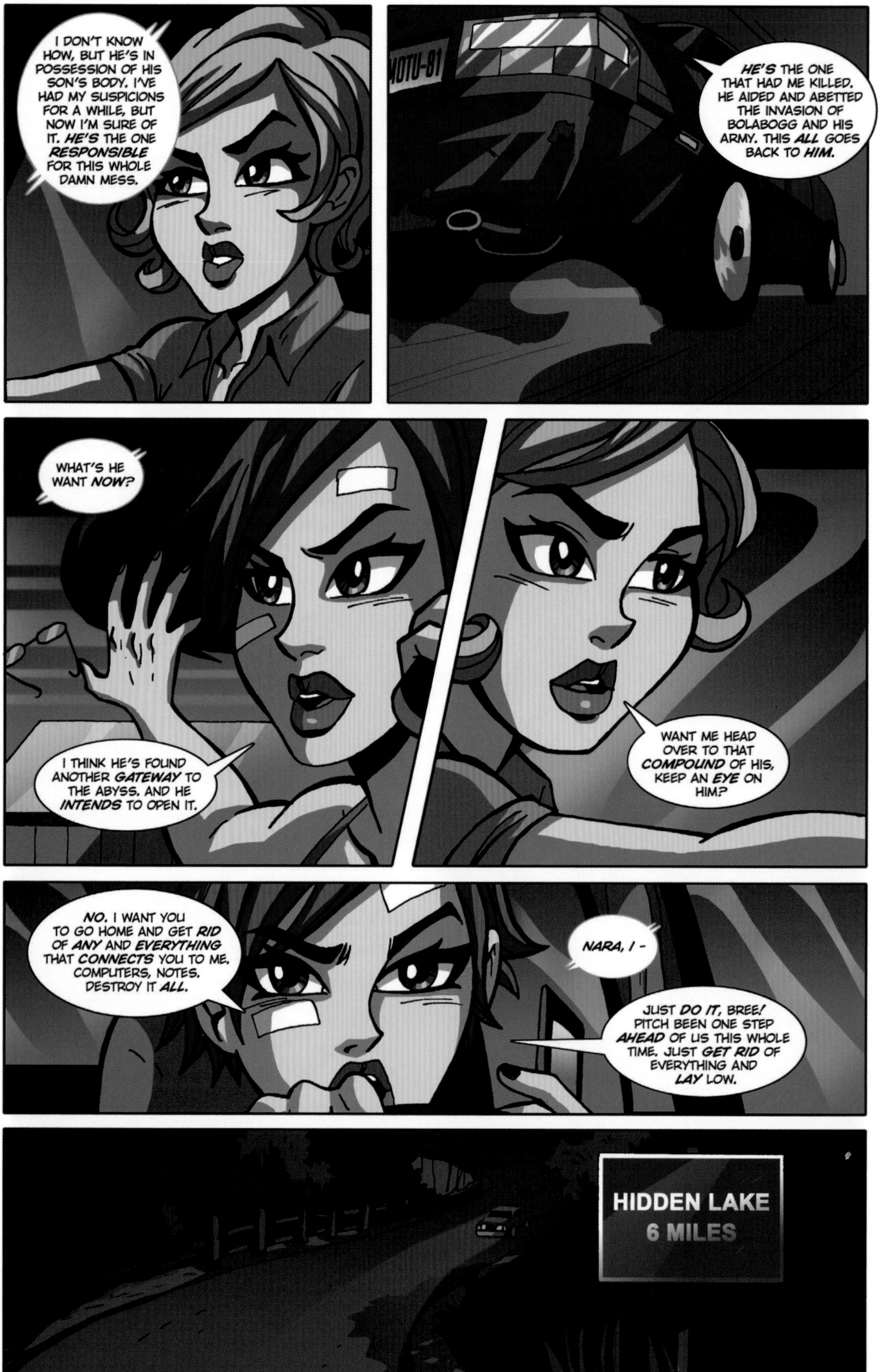
I DON'T KNOW HOW, BUT HE'S IN POSSESSION OF HIS SON'S BODY. I'VE HAD MY SUSPICIONS FOR A WHILE, BUT NOW I'M SURE OF IT. HE'S THE ONE RESPONSIBLE FOR THIS WHOLE DAMN MESS.
MOTU-81
HE'S THE ONE THAT HAD ME KILLED. HE AIDED AND ABETTED THE INVASION OF BOLABOGG AND HIS ARMY. THIS ALL GOES BACK TO HIM.
WHAT'S HE WANT NOW?
I THINK HE'S FOUND ANOTHER GATEWAY TO THE ABYSS. AND HE INTENDS TO OPEN IT.
WANT ME HEAD OVER TO THAT COMPOUND OF HIS, KEEP AN EYE ON HIM?
NO. I WANT YOU TO GO HOME AND GET RID OF ANY AND EVERYTHING THAT CONNECTS YOU TO ME. COMPUTERS, NOTES. DESTROY IT ALL.
NARA, I -
JUST DO IT, BREE! PITCH BEEN ONE STEP AHEAD OF US THIS WHOLE TIME. JUST GET RID OF EVERYTHING AND LAY LOW.
HIDDEN LAKE
6 MILES

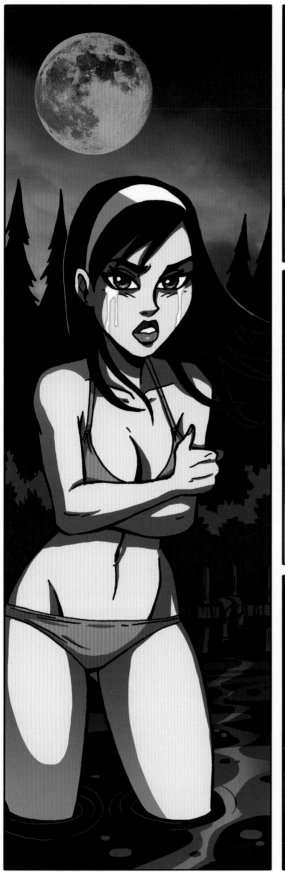

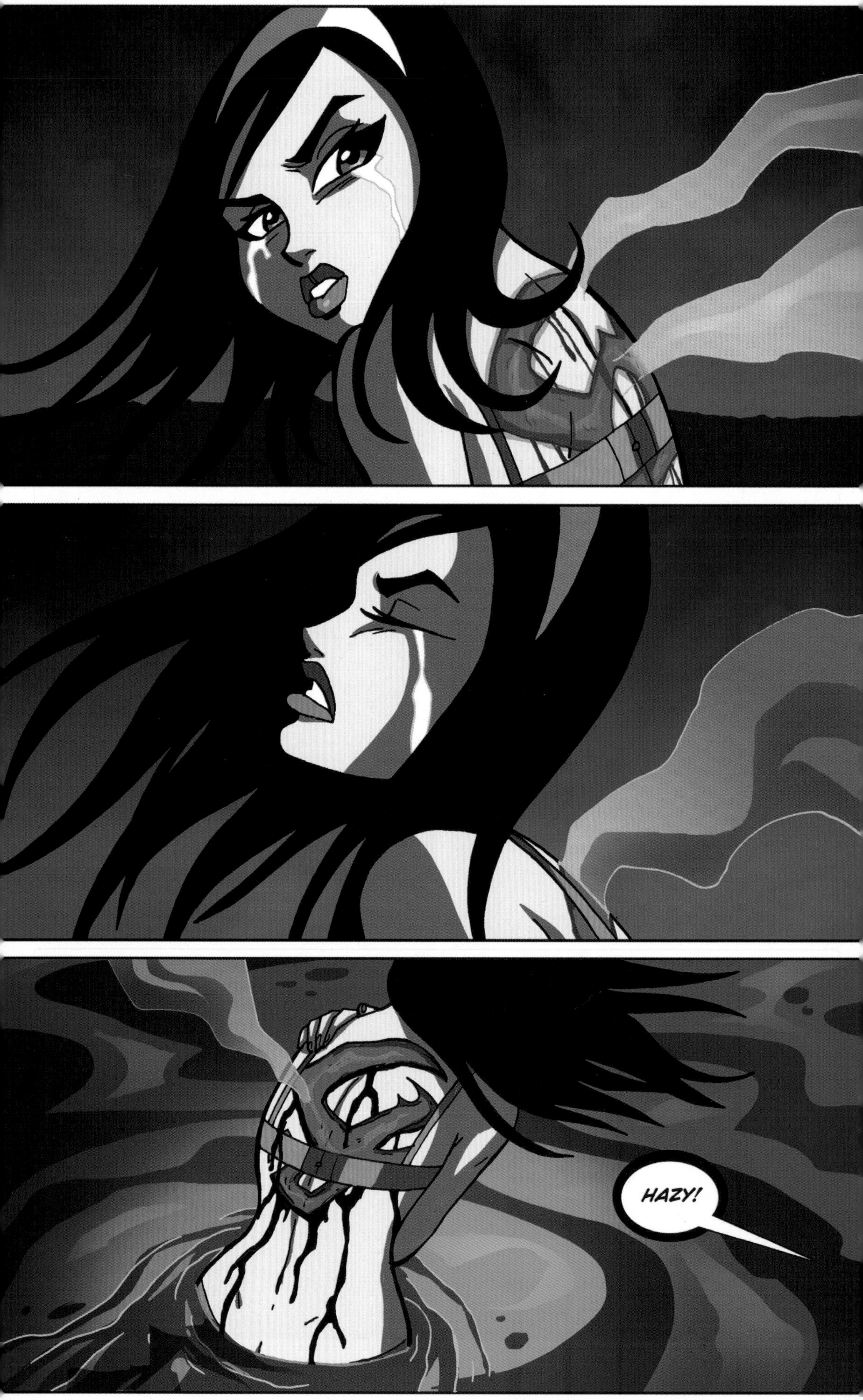
HAZY!

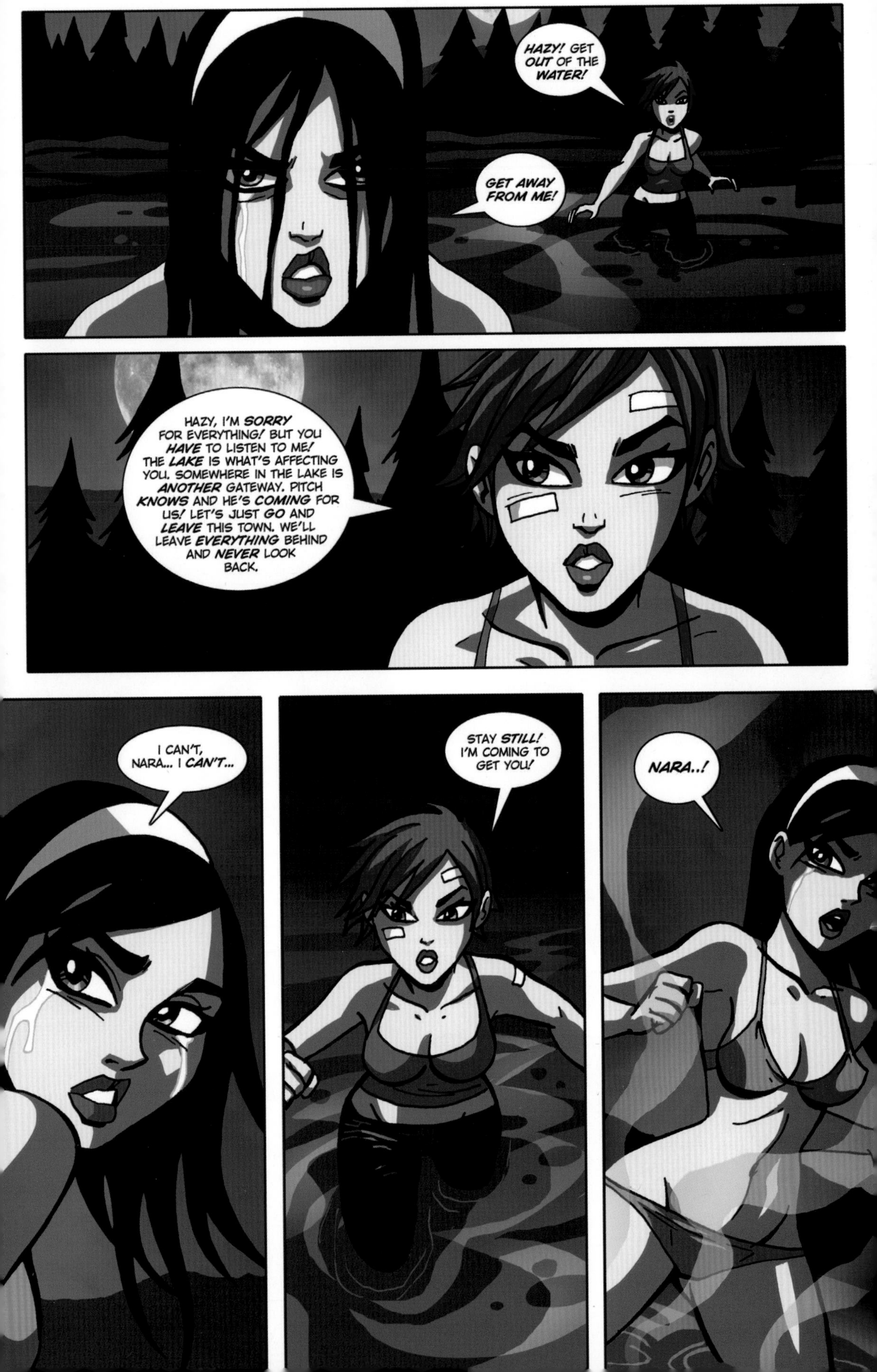
HAZY! GET OUT OF THE WATER!
GET AWAY FROM ME!
HAZY, I'M SORRY FOR EVERYTHING! BUT YOU HAVE TO LISTEN TO ME! THE LAKE IS WHAT'S AFFECTING YOU. SOMEWHERE IN THE LAKE IS ANOTHER GATEWAY. PITCH KNOWS AND HE'S COMING FOR US! LET'S JUST GO AND LEAVE THIS TOWN. WE'LL LEAVE EVERYTHING BEHIND AND NEVER LOOK BACK.
I CAN'T, NARA... I CAN'T...
STAY STILL! I'M COMING TO GET YOU!
NARA..!

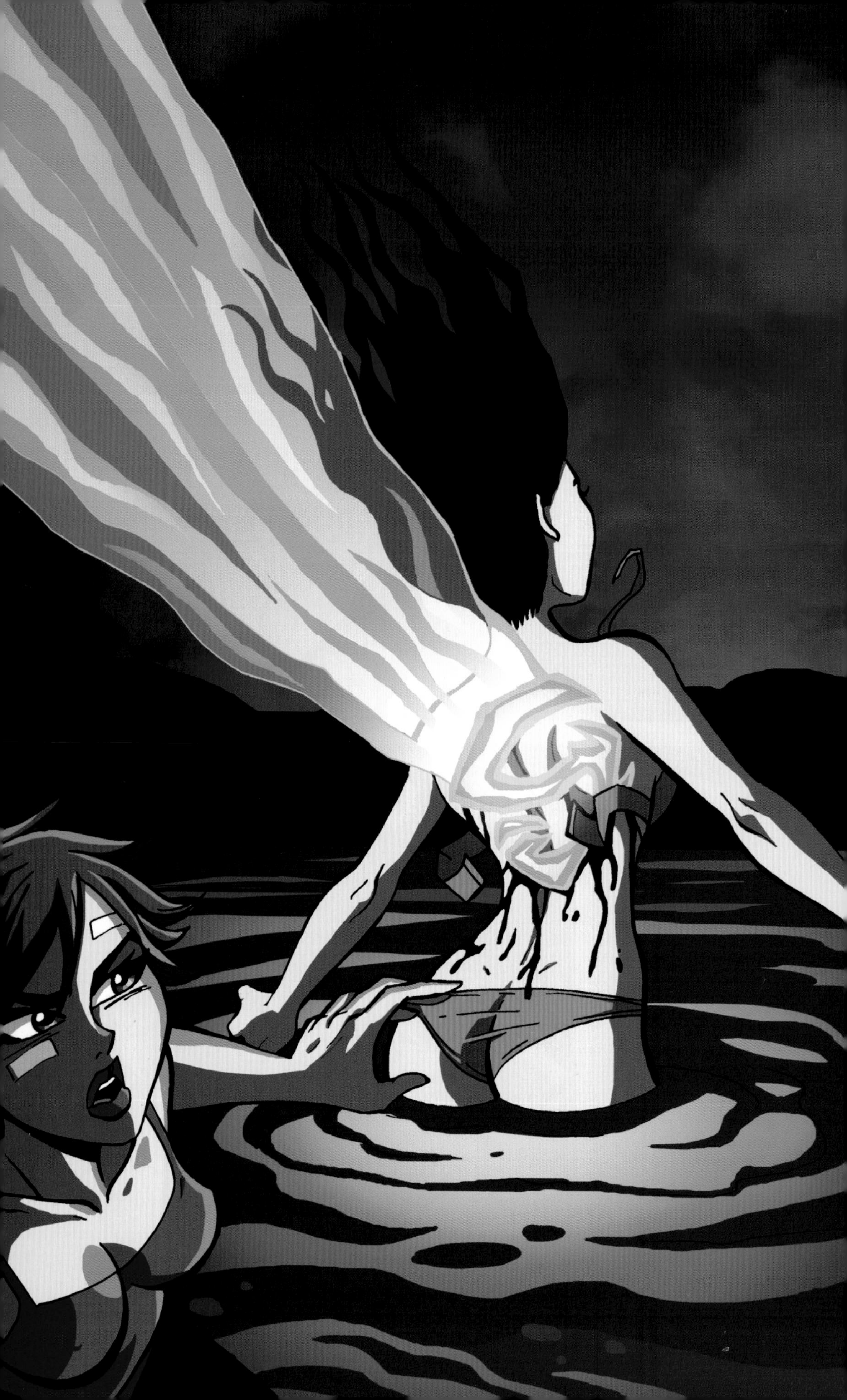

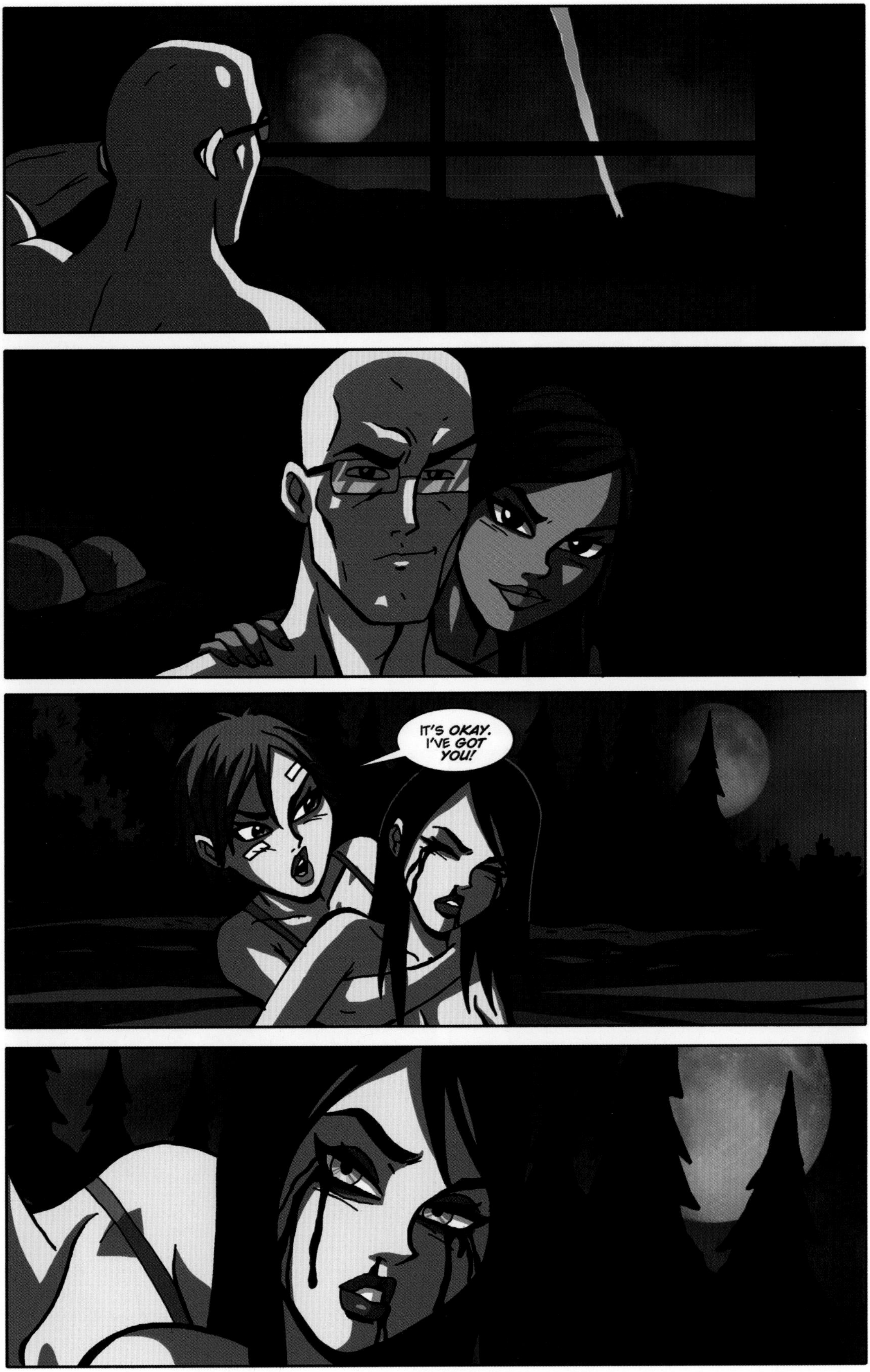
IT'S OKAY.
I'VE GOT
YOU!

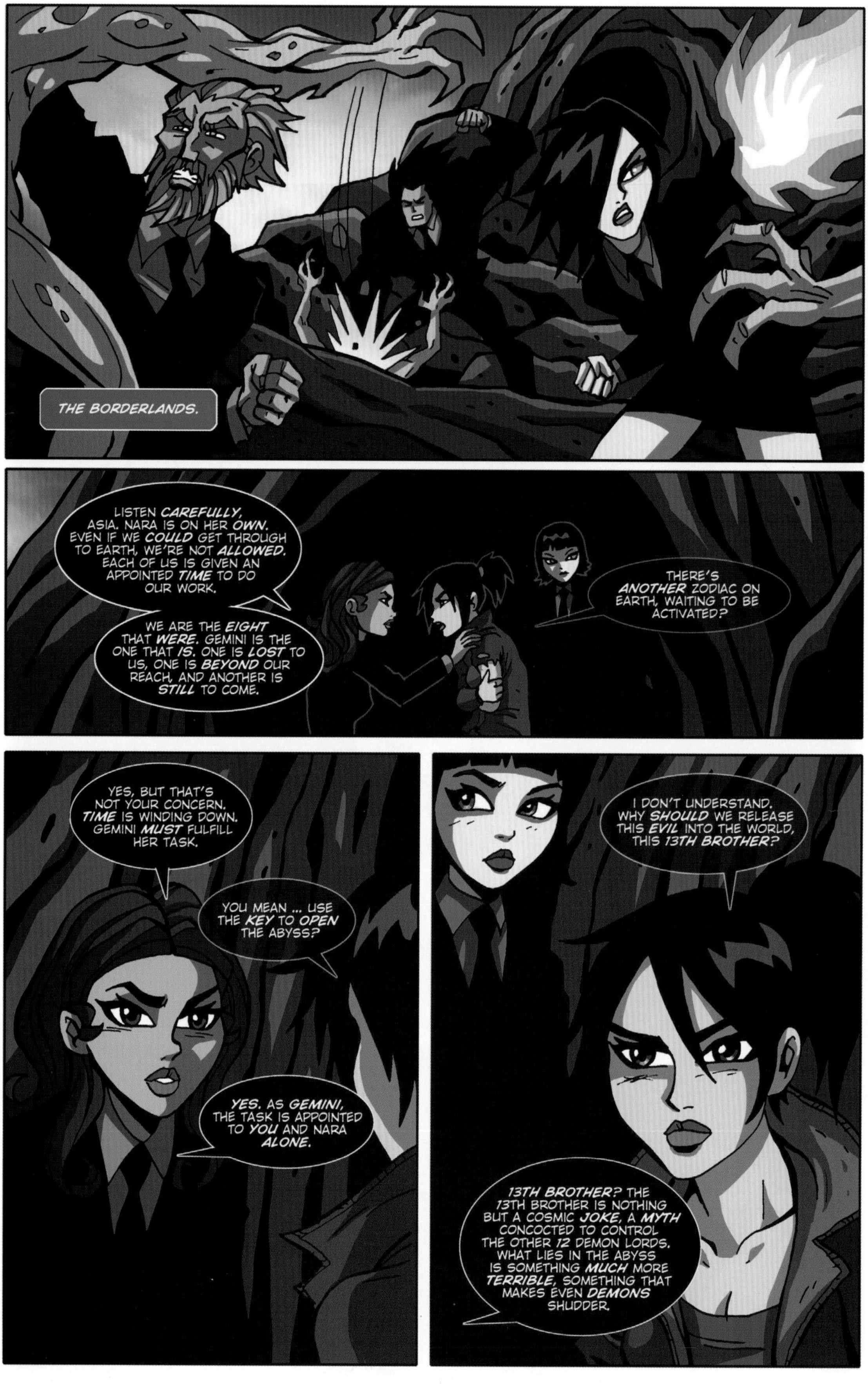
THE BORDERLANDS.
LISTEN CAREFULLY, ASIA. NARA IS ON HER OWN. EVEN IF WE COULD GET THROUGH TO EARTH, WE'RE NOT ALLOWED. EACH OF US IS GIVEN AN APPOINTED TIME TO DO OUR WORK.
WE ARE THE EIGHT THAT WERE. GEMINI IS THE ONE THAT IS. ONE IS LOST TO US, ONE IS BEYOND OUR REACH, AND ANOTHER IS STILL TO COME.
THERE'S ANOTHER ZODIAC ON EARTH, WAITING TO BE ACTIVATED?
YES, BUT THAT'S NOT YOUR CONCERN. TIME IS WINDING DOWN. GEMINI MUST FULFILL HER TASK.
YOU MEAN ... USE THE KEY TO OPEN THE ABYSS?
YES. AS GEMINI, THE TASK IS APPOINTED TO YOU AND NARA ALONE.
I DON'T UNDERSTAND. WHY SHOULD WE RELEASE THIS EVIL INTO THE WORLD, THIS 13TH BROTHER?
13TH BROTHER? THE 13TH BROTHER IS NOTHING BUT A COSMIC JOKE, A MYTH CONCOCTED TO CONTROL THE OTHER 12 DEMON LORDS. WHAT LIES IN THE ABYSS IS SOMETHING MUCH MORE TERRIBLE, SOMETHING THAT MAKES EVEN DEMONS SHUDDER.

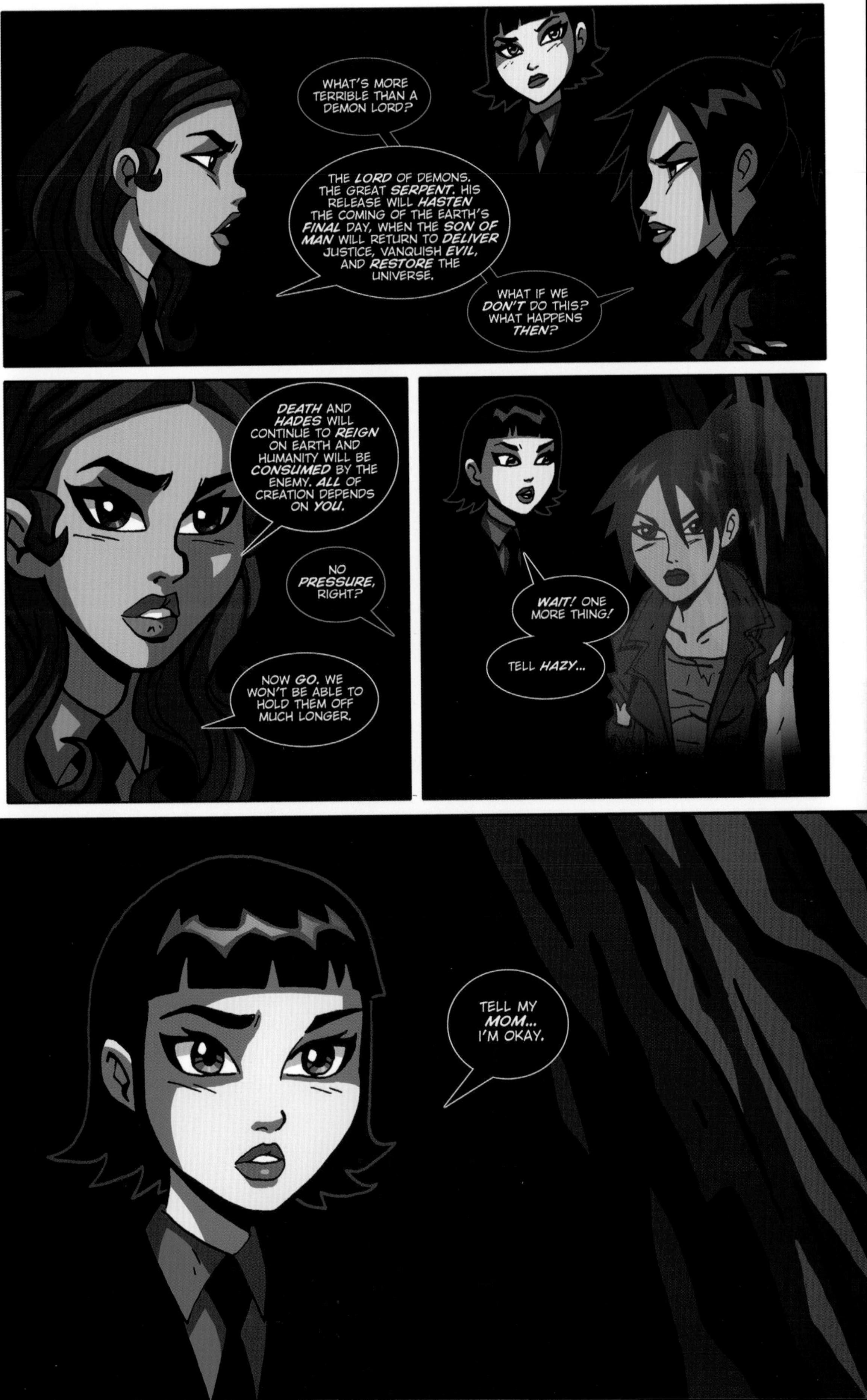
WHAT'S MORE TERRIBLE THAN A DEMON LORD?
THE LORD OF DEMONS. THE GREAT SERPENT. HIS RELEASE WILL HASTEN THE COMING OF THE EARTH'S FINAL DAY, WHEN THE SON OF MAN WILL RETURN TO DELIVER JUSTICE, VANQUISH EVIL, AND RESTORE THE UNIVERSE.
WHAT IF WE DON'T DO THIS? WHAT HAPPENS THEN?
DEATH AND HADES WILL CONTINUE TO REIGN ON EARTH AND HUMANITY WILL BE CONSUMED BY THE ENEMY. ALL OF CREATION DEPENDS ON YOU.
NO PRESSURE, RIGHT?
NOW GO. WE WON'T BE ABLE TO HOLD THEM OFF MUCH LONGER.
WAIT! ONE MORE THING!
TELL HAZY...
TELL MY MOM... I'M OKAY.

CHAPTER THREE

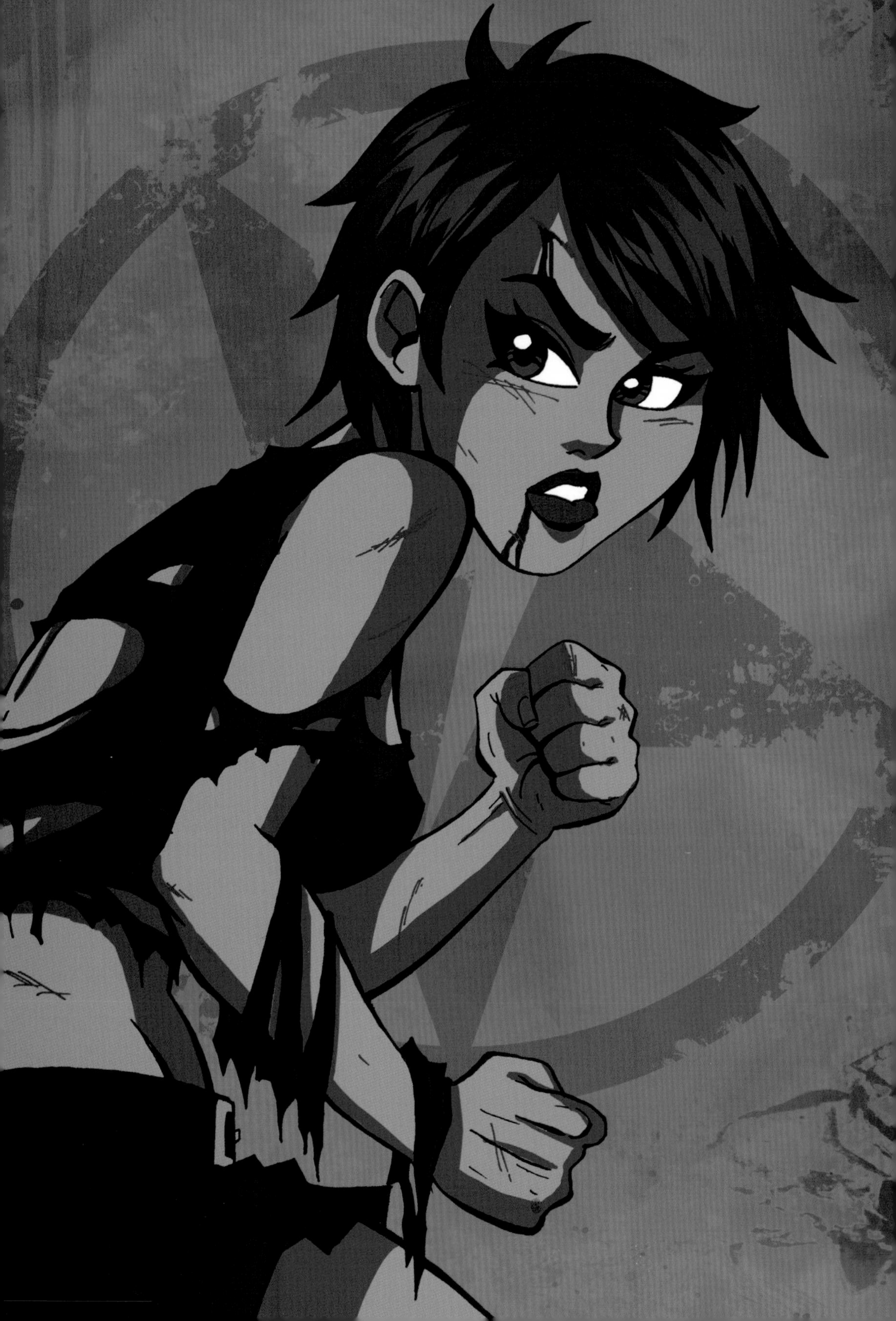

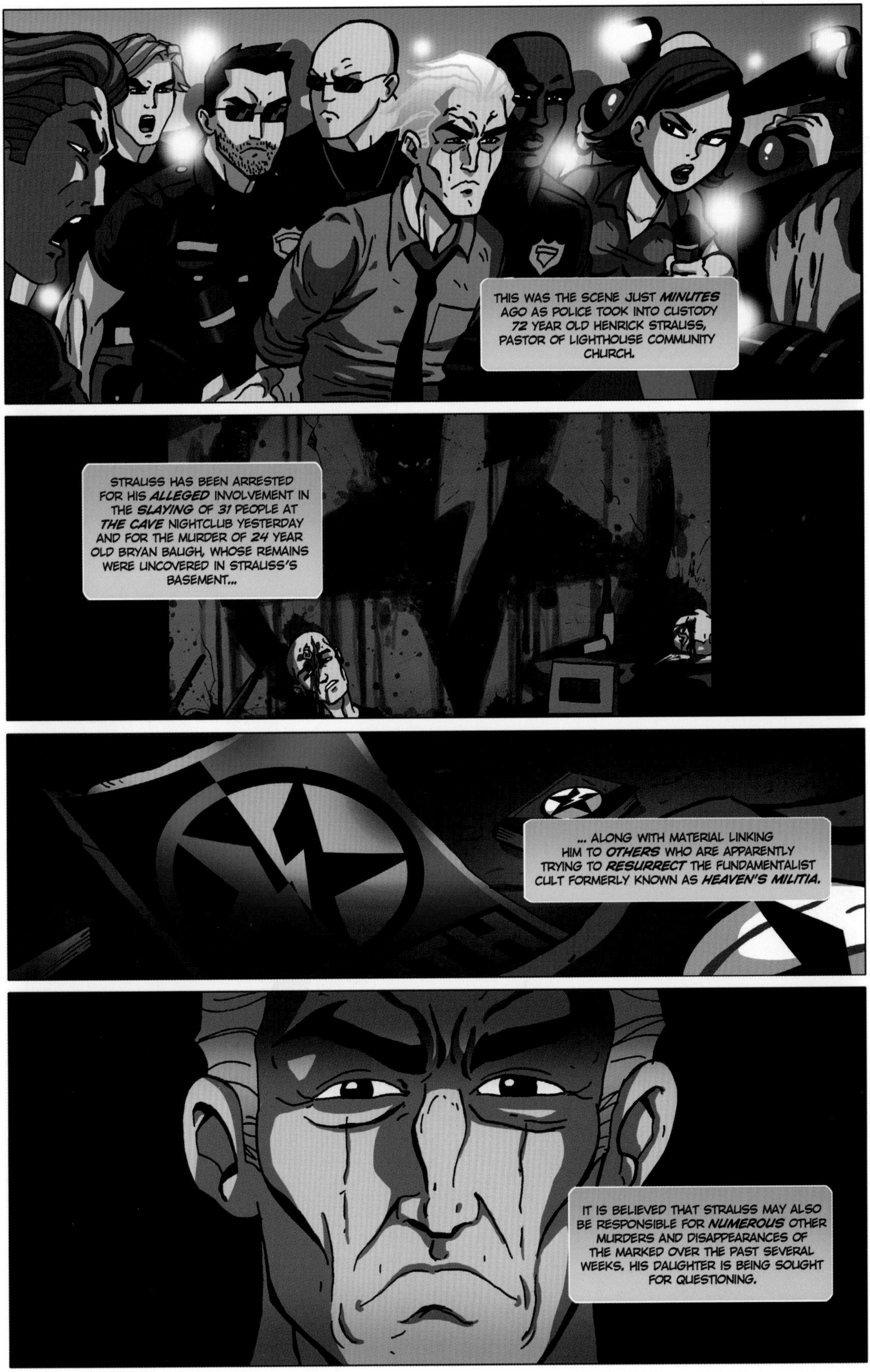
THIS WAS THE SCENE JUST *MINUTES* AGO AS POLICE TOOK INTO CUSTODY *72* YEAR OLD HENRICK STRAUSS, PASTOR OF LIGHTHOUSE COMMUNITY CHURCH.
STRAUSS HAS BEEN ARRESTED FOR HIS *ALLEGED* INVOLVEMENT IN THE *SLAYING* OF *31* PEOPLE AT *THE CAVE* NIGHTCLUB YESTERDAY AND FOR THE MURDER OF *24* YEAR OLD BRYAN BAUGH, WHOSE REMAINS WERE UNCOVERED IN STRAUSS'S BASEMENT...
... ALONG WITH MATERIAL LINKING HIM TO *OTHERS* WHO ARE APPARENTLY TRYING TO *RESURRECT* THE FUNDAMENTALIST CULT FORMERLY KNOWN AS *HEAVEN'S MILITIA*.
IT IS BELIEVED THAT STRAUSS MAY ALSO BE RESPONSIBLE FOR *NUMEROUS* OTHER MURDERS AND DISAPPEARANCES OF THE MARKED OVER THE PAST SEVERAL WEEKS. HIS DAUGHTER IS BEING SOUGHT FOR QUESTIONING.

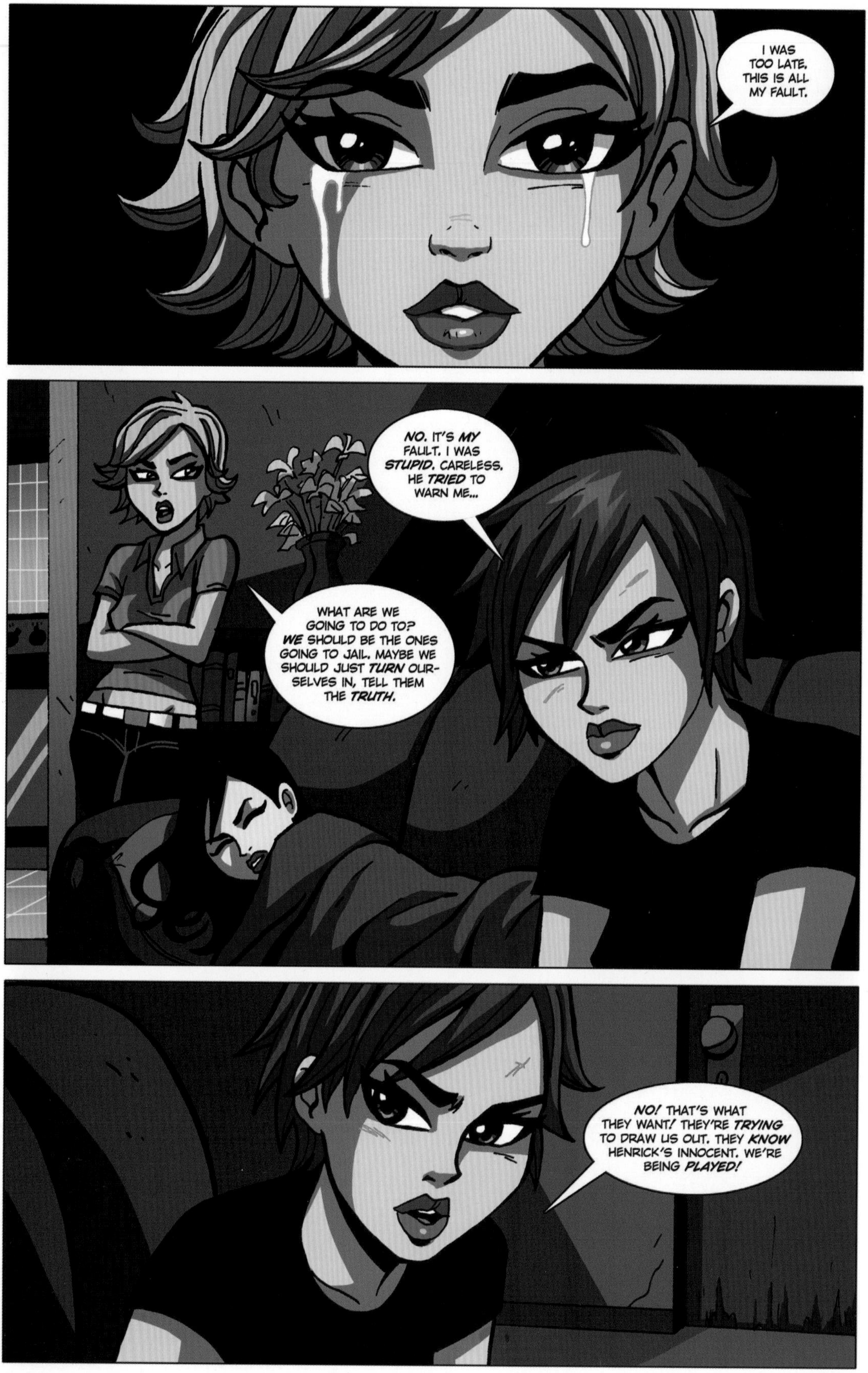
I WAS TOO LATE. THIS IS ALL MY FAULT.
NO. IT'S MY FAULT. I WAS STUPID. CARELESS. HE TRIED TO WARN ME...
WHAT ARE WE GOING TO DO TO? WE SHOULD BE THE ONES GOING TO JAIL. MAYBE WE SHOULD JUST TURN OURSELVES IN, TELL THEM THE TRUTH.
NO! THAT'S WHAT THEY WANT! THEY'RE TRYING TO DRAW US OUT. THEY KNOW HENRICK'S INNOCENT. WE'RE BEING PLAYED!

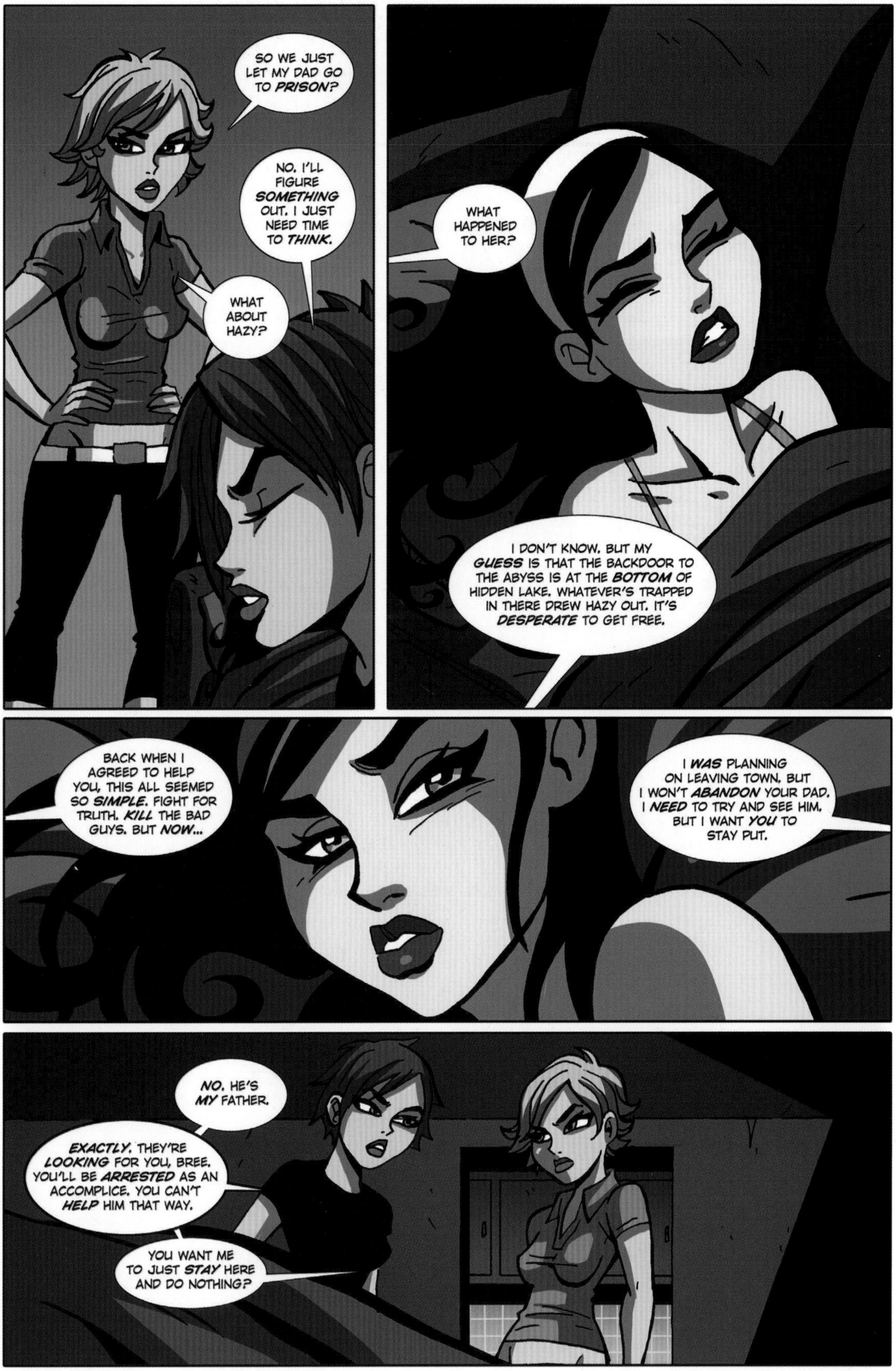
SO WE JUST LET MY DAD GO TO PRISON?
NO. I'LL FIGURE SOMETHING OUT. I JUST NEED TIME TO THINK.
WHAT ABOUT HAZY?
WHAT HAPPENED TO HER?
I DON'T KNOW. BUT MY GUESS IS THAT THE BACKDOOR TO THE ABYSS IS AT THE BOTTOM OF HIDDEN LAKE. WHATEVER'S TRAPPED IN THERE DREW HAZY OUT. IT'S DESPERATE TO GET FREE.
BACK WHEN I AGREED TO HELP YOU, THIS ALL SEEMED SO SIMPLE. FIGHT FOR TRUTH. KILL THE BAD GUYS. BUT NOW...
I WAS PLANNING ON LEAVING TOWN, BUT I WON'T ABANDON YOUR DAD. I NEED TO TRY AND SEE HIM. BUT I WANT YOU TO STAY PUT.
NO. HE'S MY FATHER.
EXACTLY. THEY'RE LOOKING FOR YOU, BREE. YOU'LL BE ARRESTED AS AN ACCOMPLICE. YOU CAN'T HELP HIM THAT WAY.
YOU WANT ME TO JUST STAY HERE AND DO NOTHING?

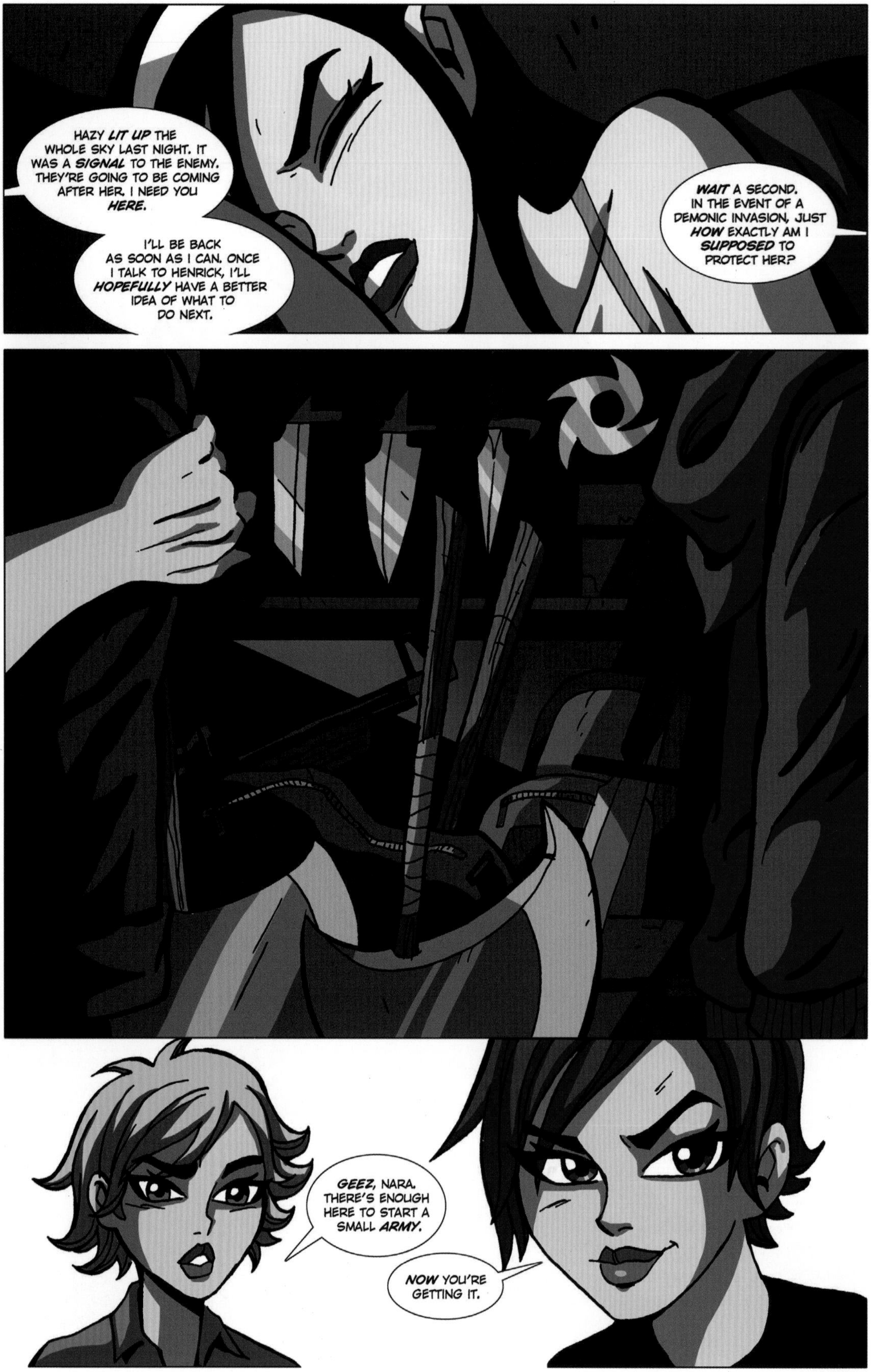
HAZY LIT UP THE WHOLE SKY LAST NIGHT. IT WAS A SIGNAL TO THE ENEMY. THEY'RE GOING TO BE COMING AFTER HER. I NEED YOU HERE.
I'LL BE BACK AS SOON AS I CAN. ONCE I TALK TO HENRICK, I'LL HOPEFULLY HAVE A BETTER IDEA OF WHAT TO DO NEXT.
WAIT A SECOND. IN THE EVENT OF A DEMONIC INVASION, JUST HOW EXACTLY AM I SUPPOSED TO PROTECT HER?
GEEZ, NARA. THERE'S ENOUGH HERE TO START A SMALL ARMY.
NOW YOU'RE GETTING IT.

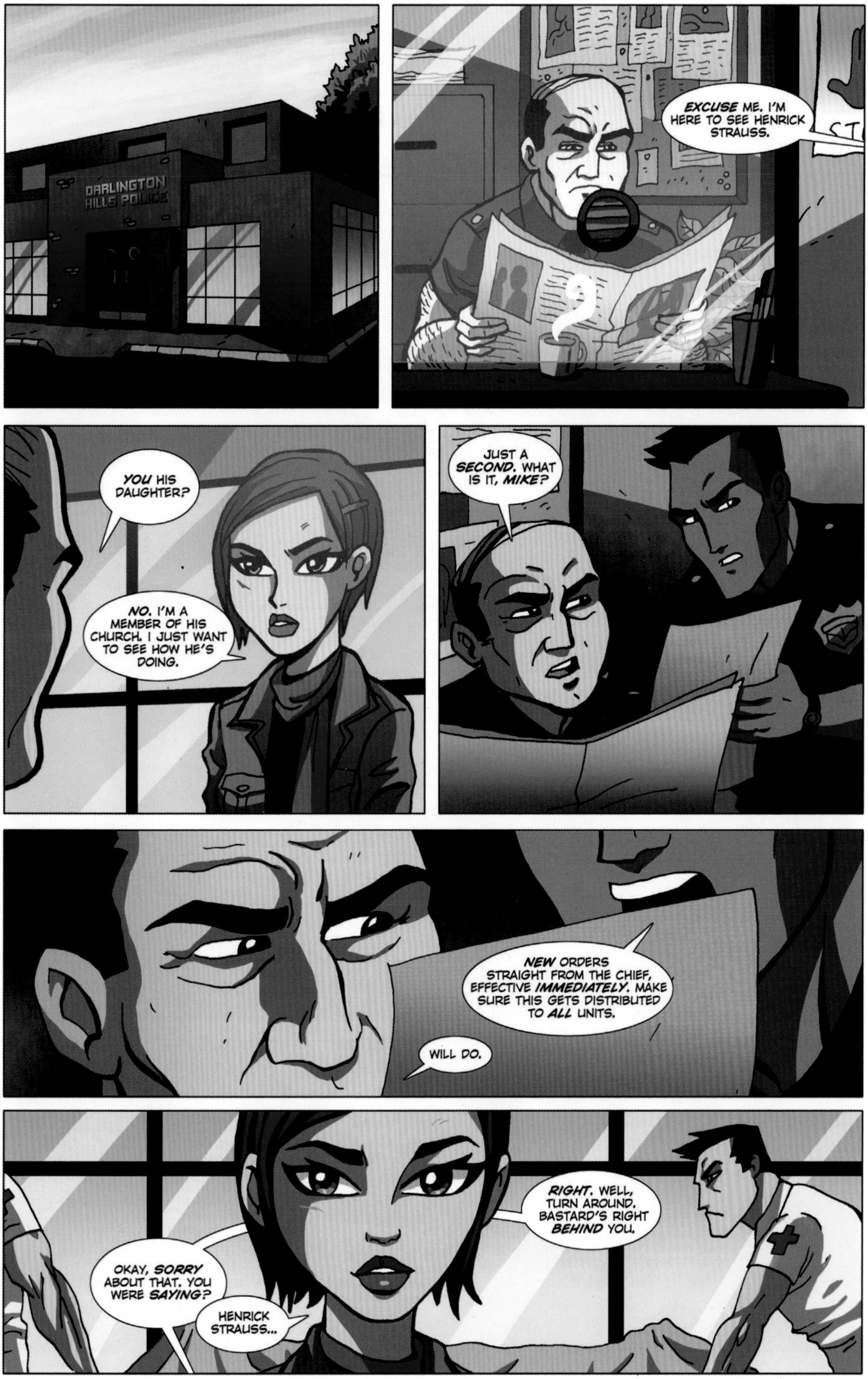
DARLINGTON HILLS POLICE
EXCUSE ME. I'M HERE TO SEE HENRICK STRAUSS.
YOU HIS DAUGHTER?
NO. I'M A MEMBER OF HIS CHURCH. I JUST WANT TO SEE HOW HE'S DOING.
JUST A SECOND. WHAT IS IT, MIKE?
NEW ORDERS STRAIGHT FROM THE CHIEF, EFFECTIVE IMMEDIATELY. MAKE SURE THIS GETS DISTRIBUTED TO ALL UNITS.
WILL DO.
OKAY, SORRY ABOUT THAT. YOU WERE SAYING?
HENRICK STRAUSS...
RIGHT. WELL, TURN AROUND. BASTARD'S RIGHT BEHIND YOU.

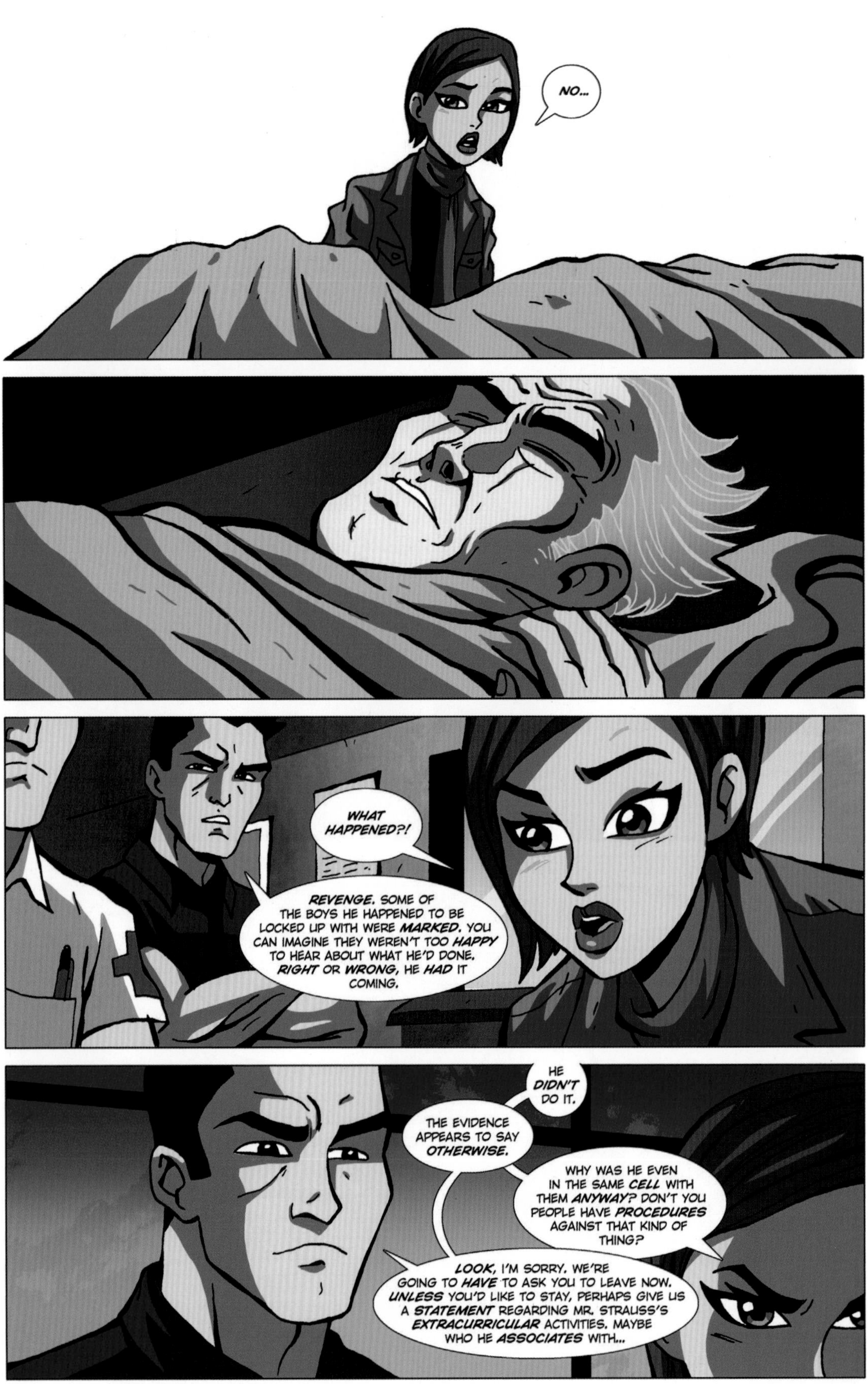
NO...
WHAT HAPPENED?!
REVENGE. SOME OF THE BOYS HE HAPPENED TO BE LOCKED UP WITH WERE MARKED. YOU CAN IMAGINE THEY WEREN'T TOO HAPPY TO HEAR ABOUT WHAT HE'D DONE. RIGHT OR WRONG, HE HAD IT COMING.
HE DIDN'T DO IT.
THE EVIDENCE APPEARS TO SAY OTHERWISE.
WHY WAS HE EVEN IN THE SAME CELL WITH THEM ANYWAY? DON'T YOU PEOPLE HAVE PROCEDURES AGAINST THAT KIND OF THING?
LOOK, I'M SORRY. WE'RE GOING TO HAVE TO ASK YOU TO LEAVE NOW. UNLESS YOU'D LIKE TO STAY, PERHAPS GIVE US A STATEMENT REGARDING MR. STRAUSS'S EXTRACURRICULAR ACTIVITIES. MAYBE WHO HE ASSOCIATES WITH...

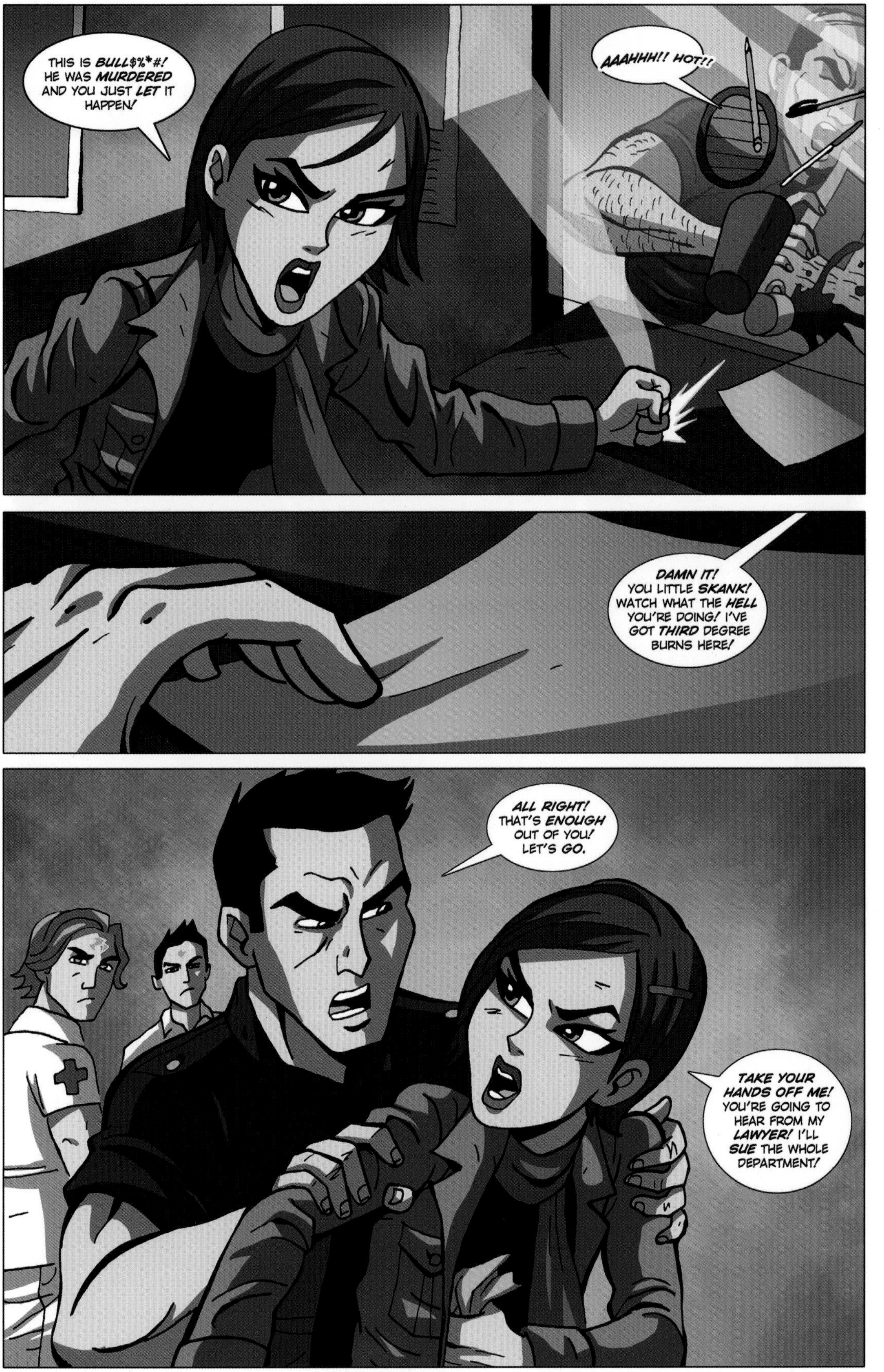
THIS IS BULL$%*#! HE WAS MURDERED AND YOU JUST LET IT HAPPEN!
AAAHHH!! HOT!!
DAMN IT! YOU LITTLE SKANK! WATCH WHAT THE HELL YOU'RE DOING! I'VE GOT THIRD DEGREE BURNS HERE!
ALL RIGHT! THAT'S ENOUGH OUT OF YOU! LET'S GO.
TAKE YOUR HANDS OFF ME! YOU'RE GOING TO HEAR FROM MY LAWYER! I'LL SUE THE WHOLE DEPARTMENT!

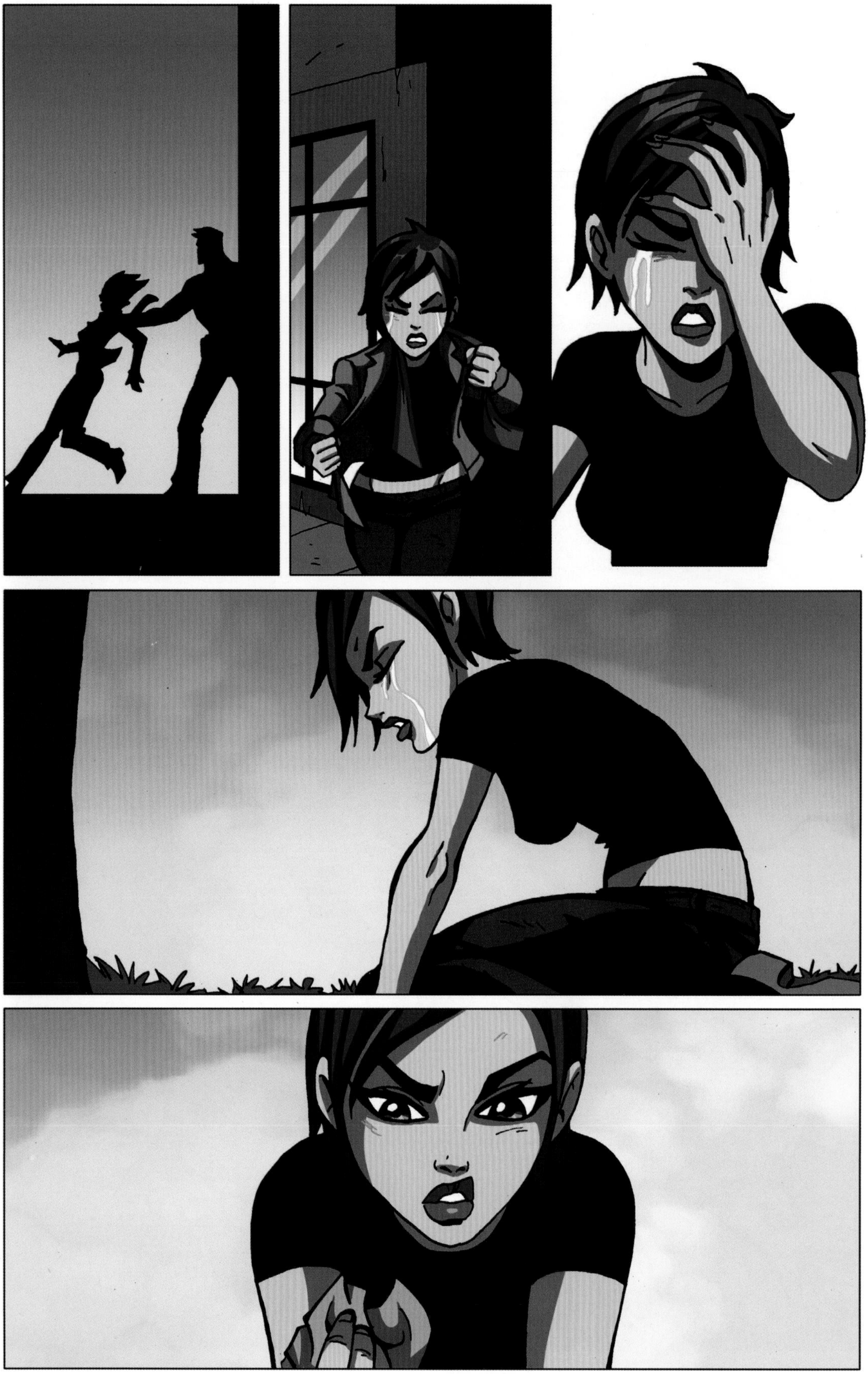

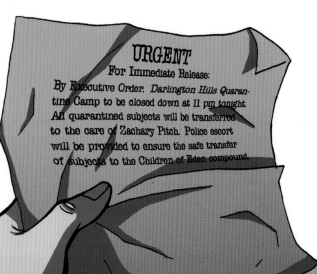

URGENT

For Immediate Release:

By Executive Order, Darlington Hills Quarantine Camp to be closed down at 11 pm tonight. All quarantined subjects will be transferred to the care of Zachary Pitch. Police escort will be provided to ensure the safe transfer of subjects to the Children of Eden compound.

I'VE *GOT* YOU *NOW*, YOU SON OF A *BITCH*.

THE *FIFTH* ANGEL SOUNDED HIS TRUMPET, AND I SAW A *STAR* THAT HAD FALLEN FROM THE SKY TO THE EARTH. THE STAR WAS GIVEN THE *KEY* TO THE ABYSS.

WHEN THE ABYSS WAS *OPENED*, SMOKE *ROSE* FROM IT LIKE SMOKE FROM A GIGANTIC FURNACE. THE SUN AND SKY WERE *DARKENED* BY THE SMOKE.

AND OUT OF THE SMOKE CAME *LOCUSTS* ...THEY HAD A *KING* OVER THEM, THE ANGEL OF THE ABYSS... THE *DESTROYER*.

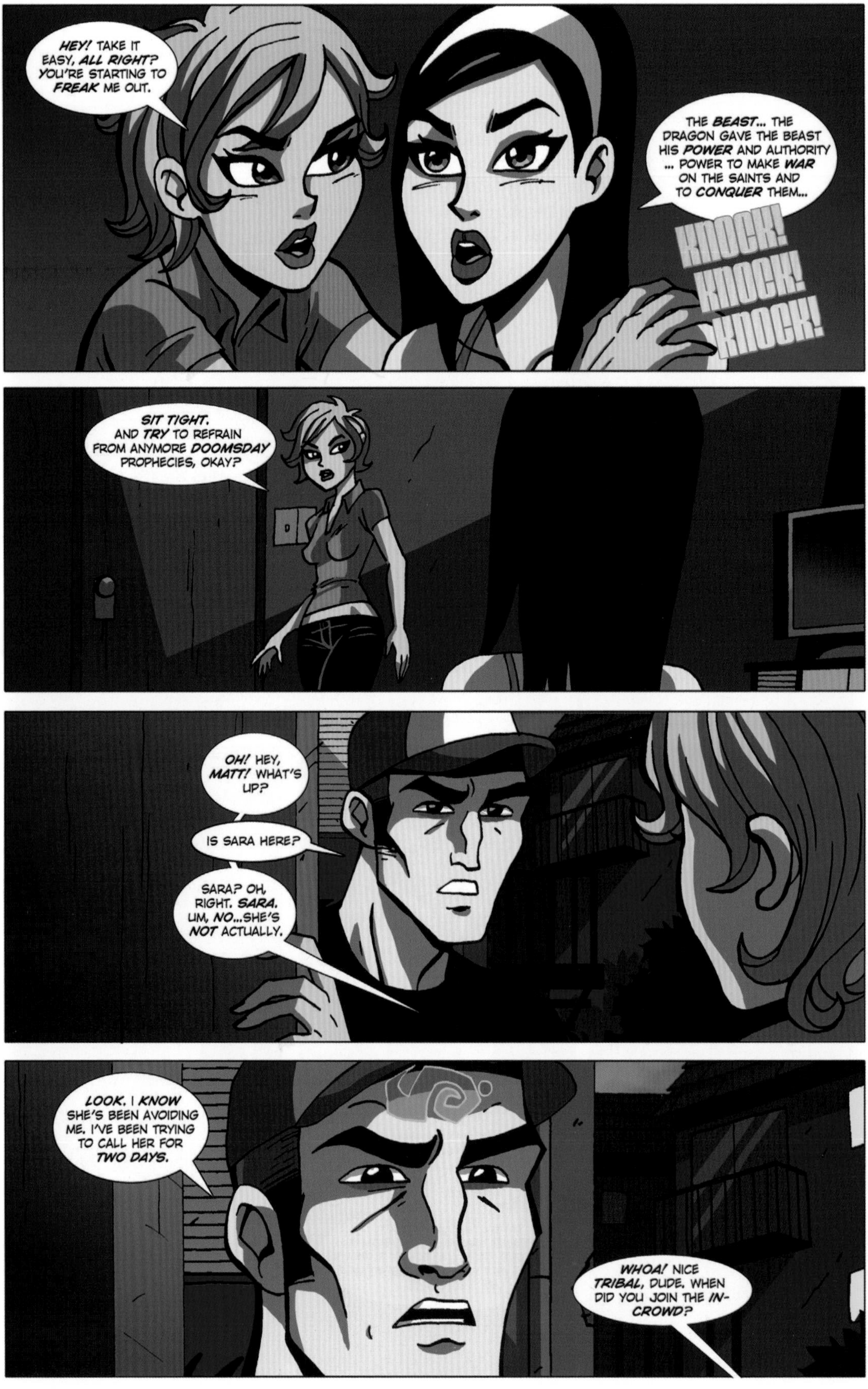
HEY! TAKE IT EASY, ALL RIGHT? YOU'RE STARTING TO FREAK ME OUT.
THE BEAST... THE DRAGON GAVE THE BEAST HIS POWER AND AUTHORITY ... POWER TO MAKE WAR ON THE SAINTS AND TO CONQUER THEM...
KNOCK! KNOCK! KNOCK!
SIT TIGHT. AND TRY TO REFRAIN FROM ANYMORE DOOMSDAY PROPHECIES, OKAY?
OH! HEY, MATT! WHAT'S UP?
IS SARA HERE?
SARA? OH, RIGHT. SARA. UM, NO...SHE'S NOT ACTUALLY.
LOOK. I KNOW SHE'S BEEN AVOIDING ME. I'VE BEEN TRYING TO CALL HER FOR TWO DAYS.
WHOA! NICE TRIBAL, DUDE. WHEN DID YOU JOIN THE IN-CROWD?

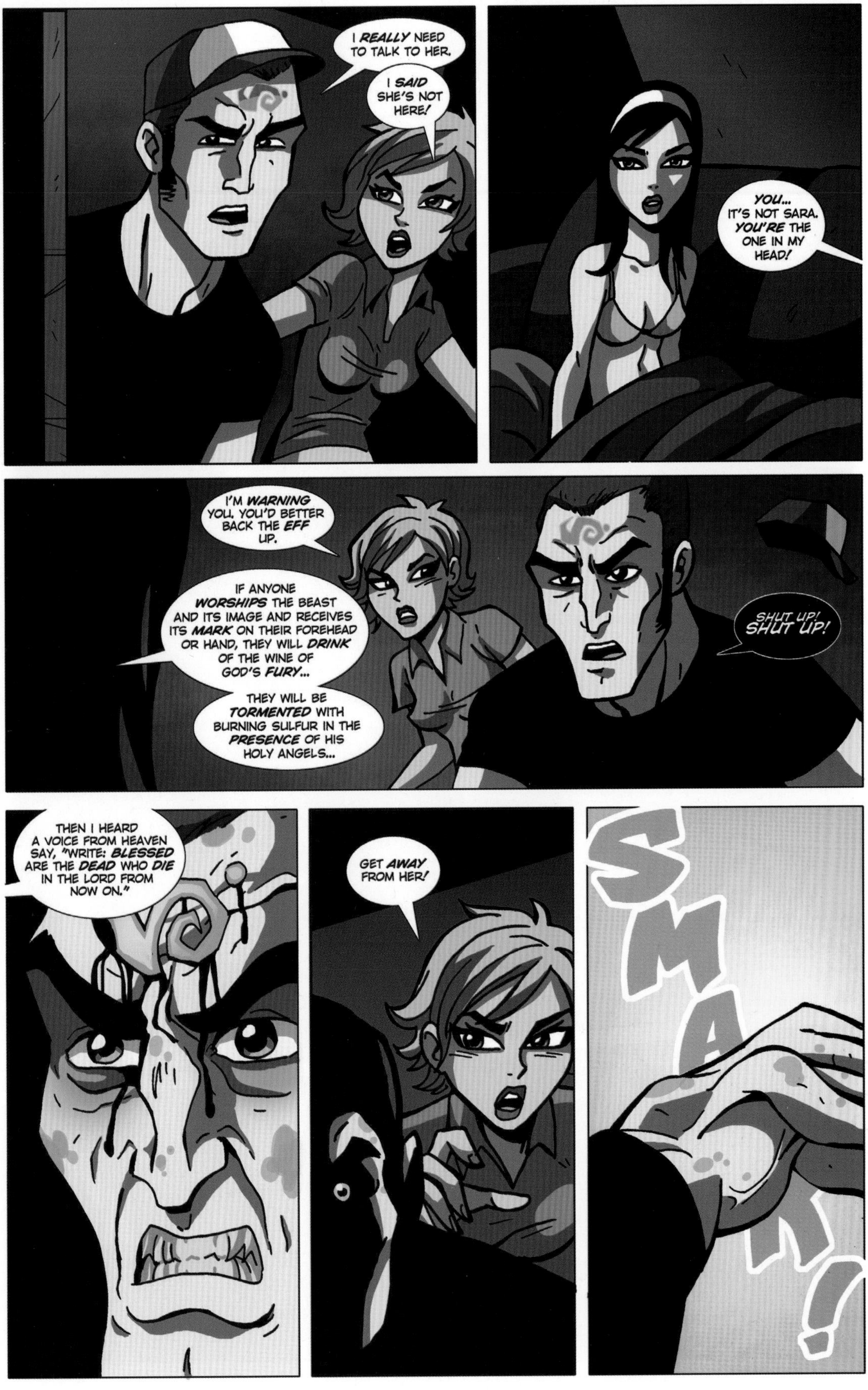
I REALLY NEED TO TALK TO HER.
I SAID SHE'S NOT HERE!
YOU... IT'S NOT SARA. YOU'RE THE ONE IN MY HEAD!
I'M WARNING YOU. YOU'D BETTER BACK THE EFF UP.
IF ANYONE WORSHIPS THE BEAST AND ITS IMAGE AND RECEIVES ITS MARK ON THEIR FOREHEAD OR HAND, THEY WILL DRINK OF THE WINE OF GOD'S FURY...
THEY WILL BE TORMENTED WITH BURNING SULFUR IN THE PRESENCE OF HIS HOLY ANGELS...
SHUT UP! SHUT UP!
THEN I HEARD A VOICE FROM HEAVEN SAY, "WRITE: BLESSED ARE THE DEAD WHO DIE IN THE LORD FROM NOW ON."
GET AWAY FROM HER!
SMAK!

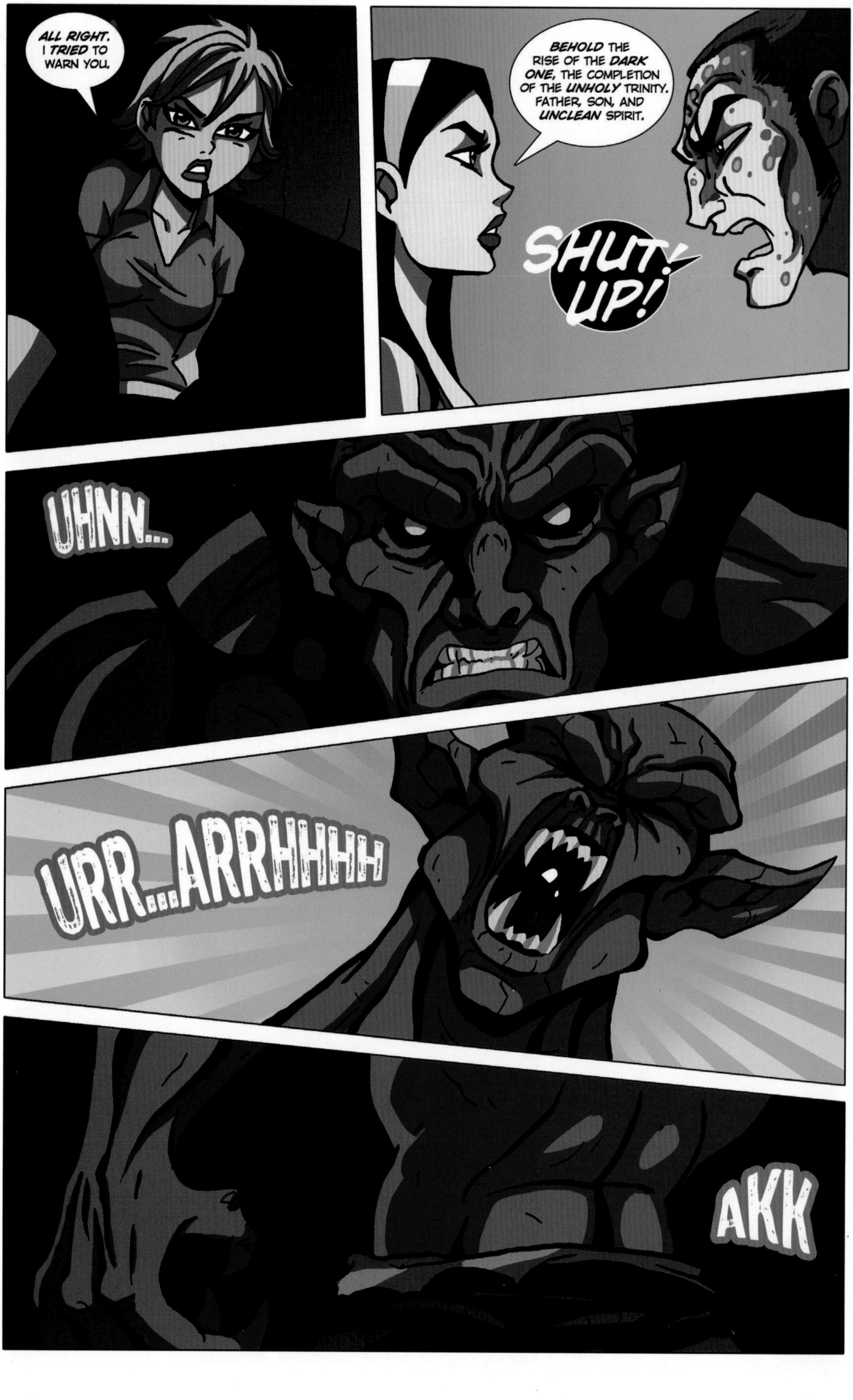
ALL RIGHT. I TRIED TO WARN YOU.
BEHOLD THE RISE OF THE DARK ONE, THE COMPLETION OF THE UNHOLY TRINITY. FATHER, SON, AND UNCLEAN SPIRIT.
SHUT UP!
UHNN...
URR...ARRHHHH
AKK

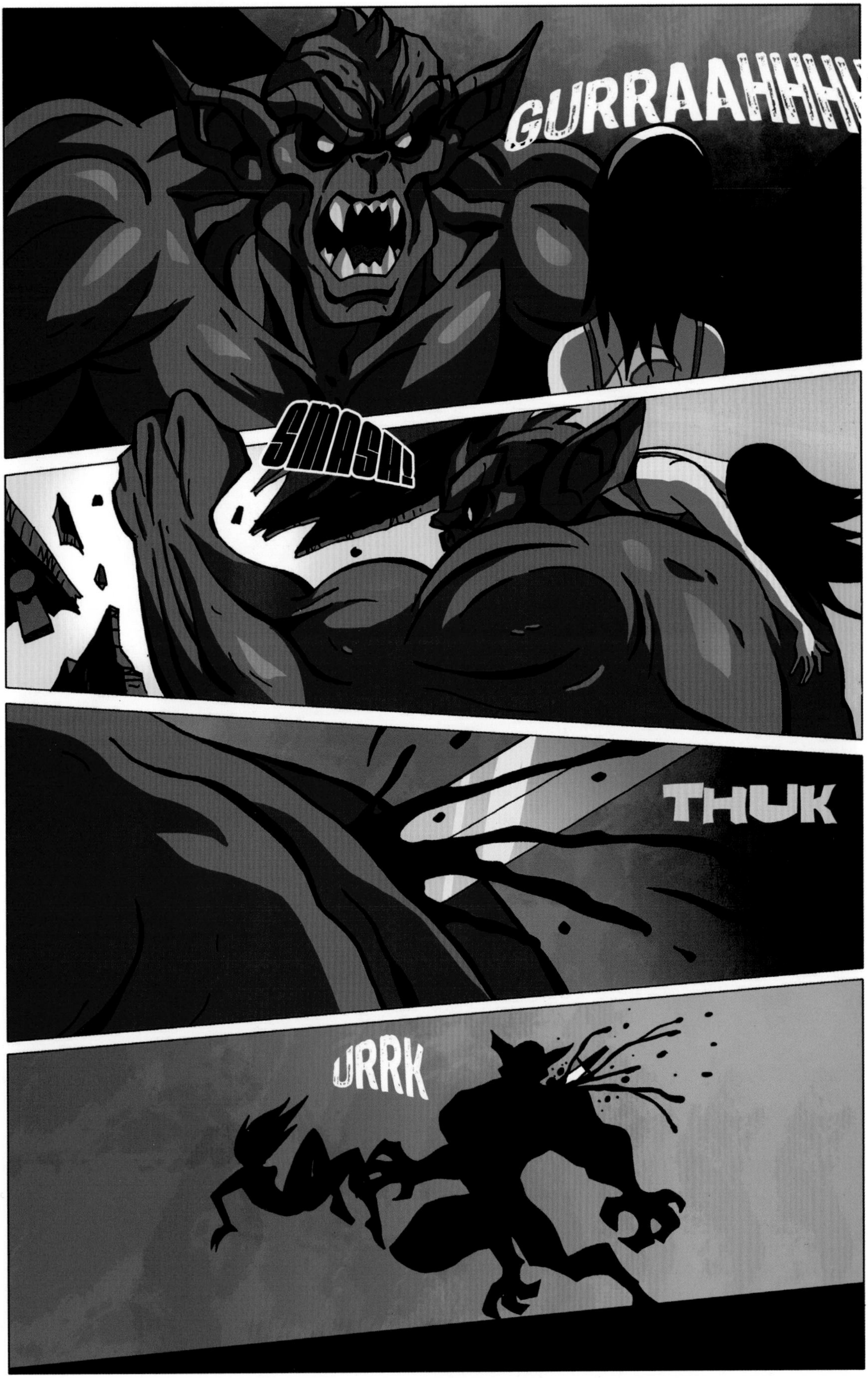
GURRAAHHHH
SMASH!
THUK
URRK

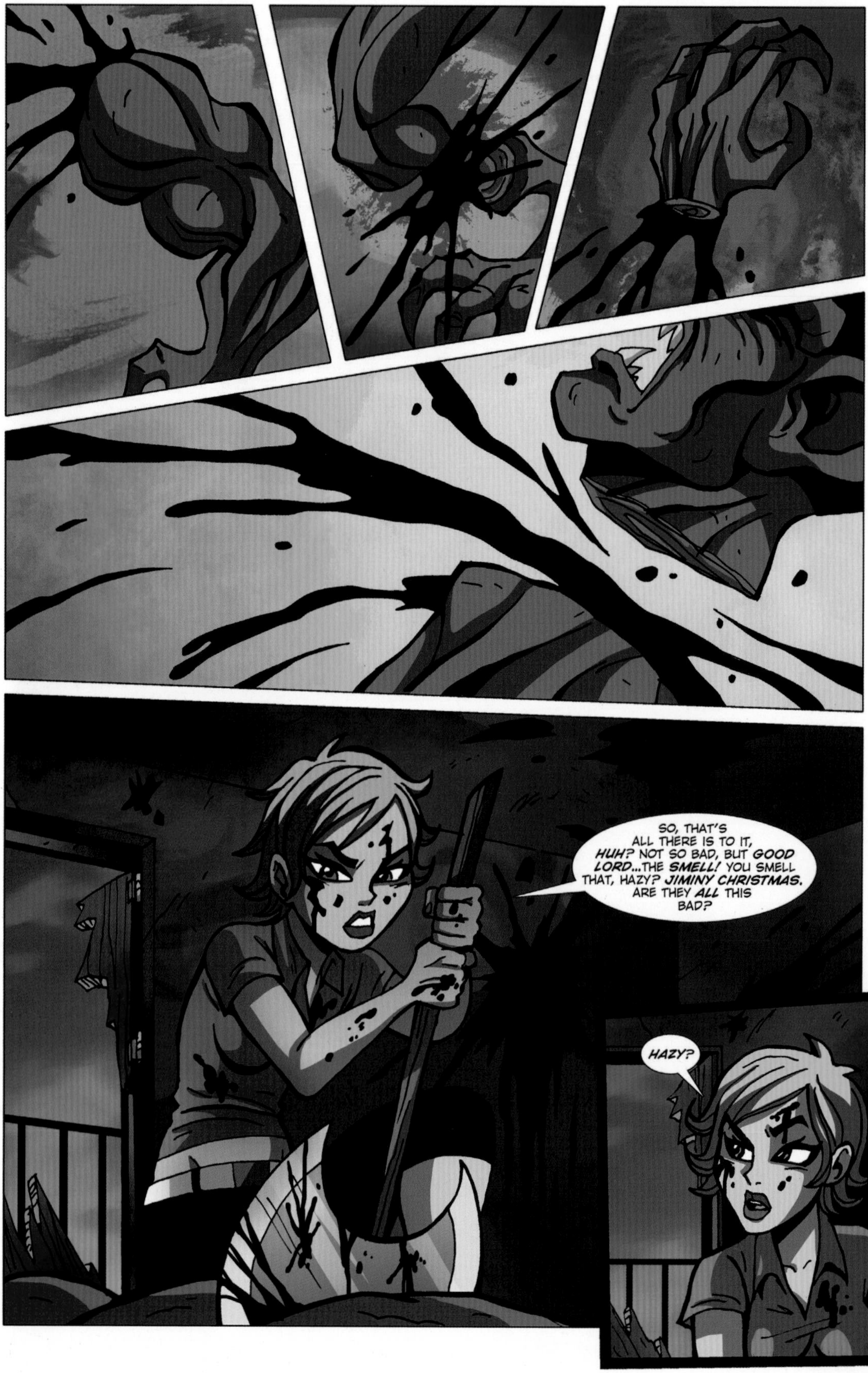
SO, THAT'S ALL THERE IS TO IT, HUH? NOT SO BAD, BUT GOOD LORD...THE SMELL! YOU SMELL THAT, HAZY? JIMINY CHRISTMAS. ARE THEY ALL THIS BAD?
HAZY?

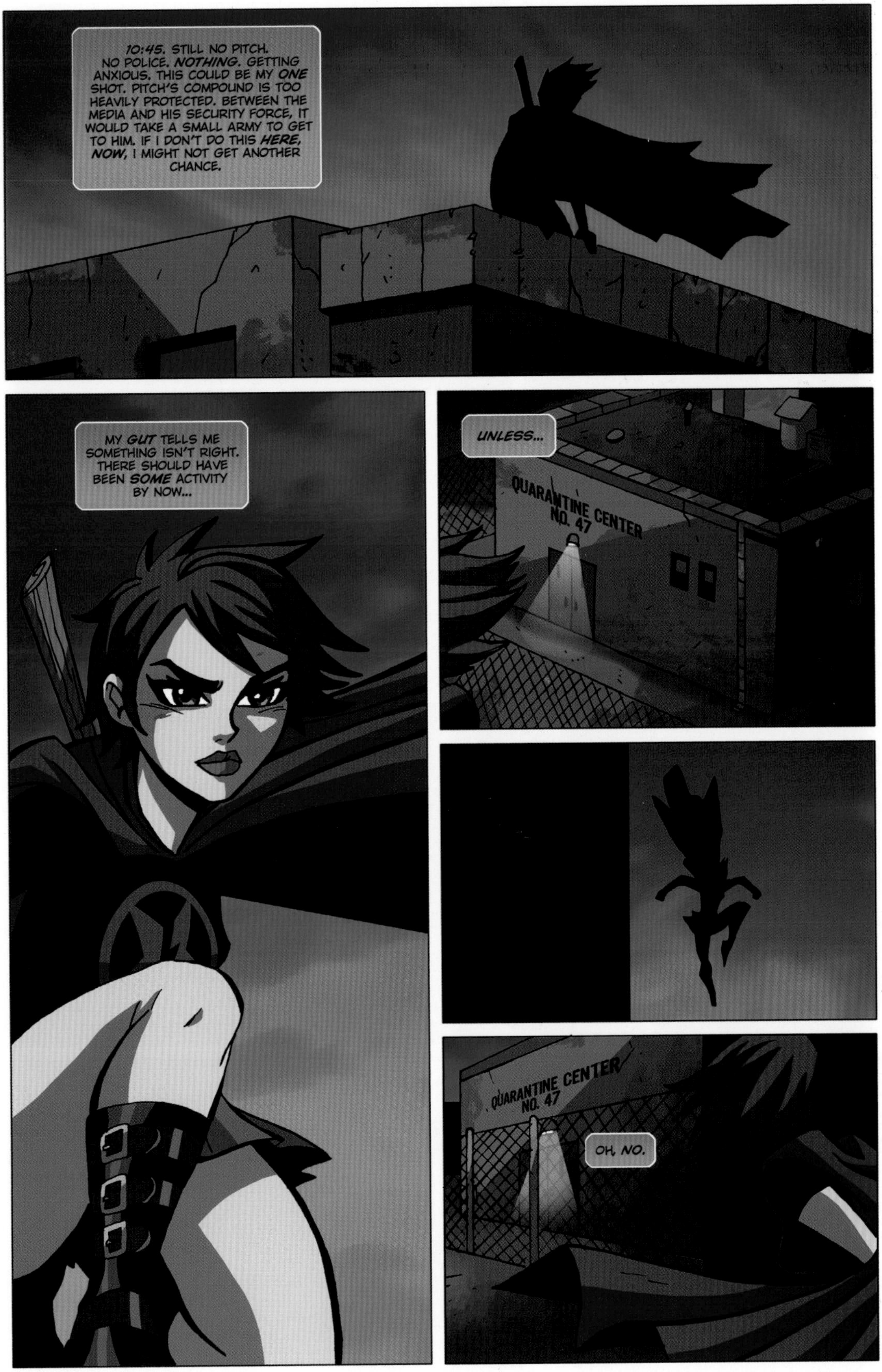
10:45. STILL NO PITCH. NO POLICE. NOTHING. GETTING ANXIOUS. THIS COULD BE MY ONE SHOT. PITCH'S COMPOUND IS TOO HEAVILY PROTECTED. BETWEEN THE MEDIA AND HIS SECURITY FORCE, IT WOULD TAKE A SMALL ARMY TO GET TO HIM. IF I DON'T DO THIS HERE, NOW, I MIGHT NOT GET ANOTHER CHANCE.
MY GUT TELLS ME SOMETHING ISN'T RIGHT. THERE SHOULD HAVE BEEN SOME ACTIVITY BY NOW...
UNLESS...
QUARANTINE CENTER NO. 47
QUARANTINE CENTER NO. 47
OH, NO.

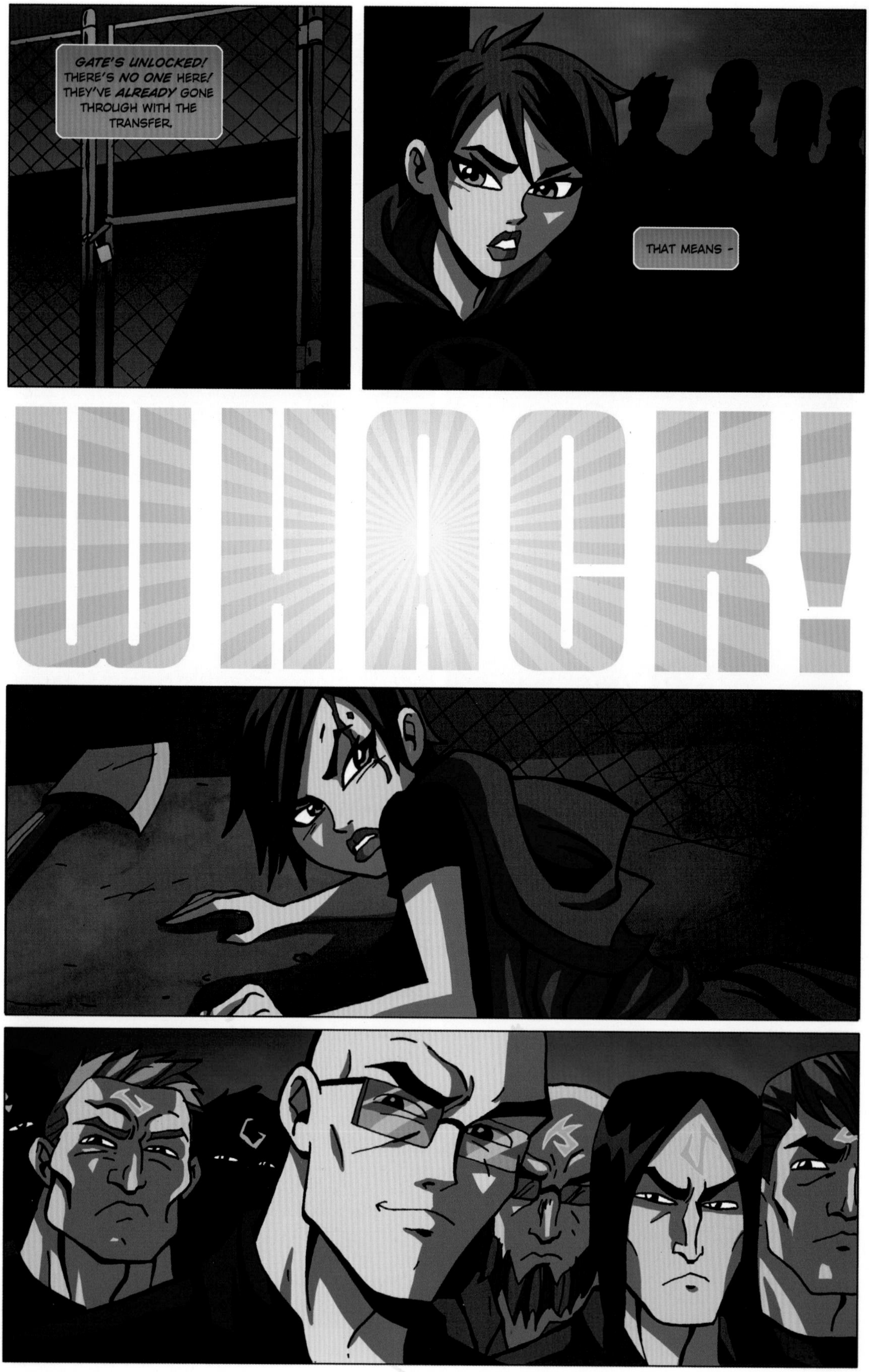
GATE'S UNLOCKED! THERE'S NO ONE HERE! THEY'VE ALREADY GONE THROUGH WITH THE TRANSFER.
THAT MEANS -
WHACK!

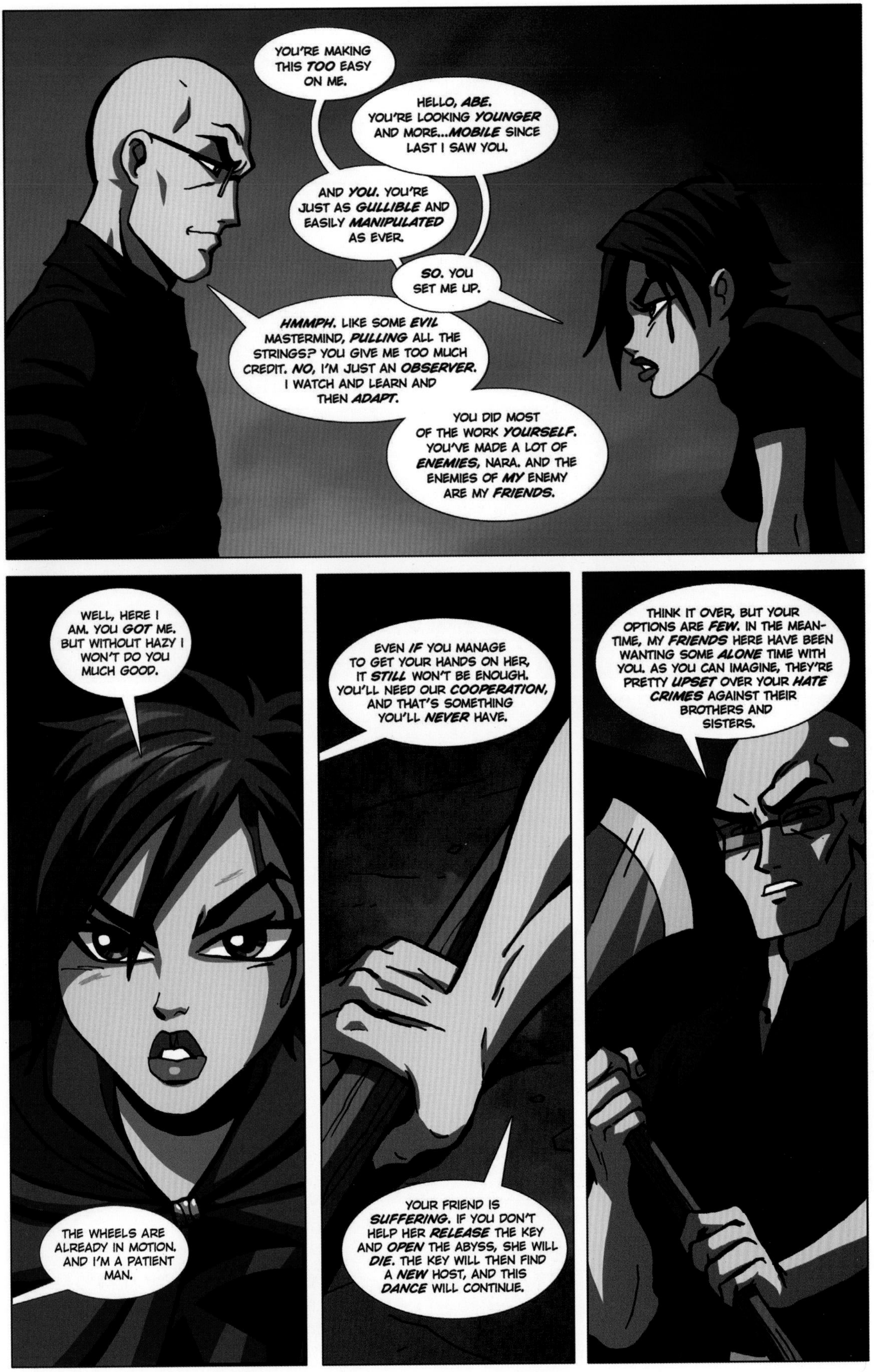
YOU'RE MAKING THIS TOO EASY ON ME.
HELLO, ABE. YOU'RE LOOKING YOUNGER AND MORE...MOBILE SINCE LAST I SAW YOU.
AND YOU. YOU'RE JUST AS GULLIBLE AND EASILY MANIPULATED AS EVER.
SO. YOU SET ME UP.
HMMPH. LIKE SOME EVIL MASTERMIND, PULLING ALL THE STRINGS? YOU GIVE ME TOO MUCH CREDIT. NO, I'M JUST AN OBSERVER. I WATCH AND LEARN AND THEN ADAPT.
YOU DID MOST OF THE WORK YOURSELF. YOU'VE MADE A LOT OF ENEMIES, NARA. AND THE ENEMIES OF MY ENEMY ARE MY FRIENDS.
WELL, HERE I AM. YOU GOT ME. BUT WITHOUT HAZY I WON'T DO YOU MUCH GOOD.
THE WHEELS ARE ALREADY IN MOTION. AND I'M A PATIENT MAN.
EVEN IF YOU MANAGE TO GET YOUR HANDS ON HER, IT STILL WON'T BE ENOUGH. YOU'LL NEED OUR COOPERATION, AND THAT'S SOMETHING YOU'LL NEVER HAVE.
YOUR FRIEND IS SUFFERING. IF YOU DON'T HELP HER RELEASE THE KEY AND OPEN THE ABYSS, SHE WILL DIE. THE KEY WILL THEN FIND A NEW HOST, AND THIS DANCE WILL CONTINUE.
THINK IT OVER, BUT YOUR OPTIONS ARE FEW. IN THE MEAN-TIME, MY FRIENDS HERE HAVE BEEN WANTING SOME ALONE TIME WITH YOU. AS YOU CAN IMAGINE, THEY'RE PRETTY UPSET OVER YOUR HATE CRIMES AGAINST THEIR BROTHERS AND SISTERS.

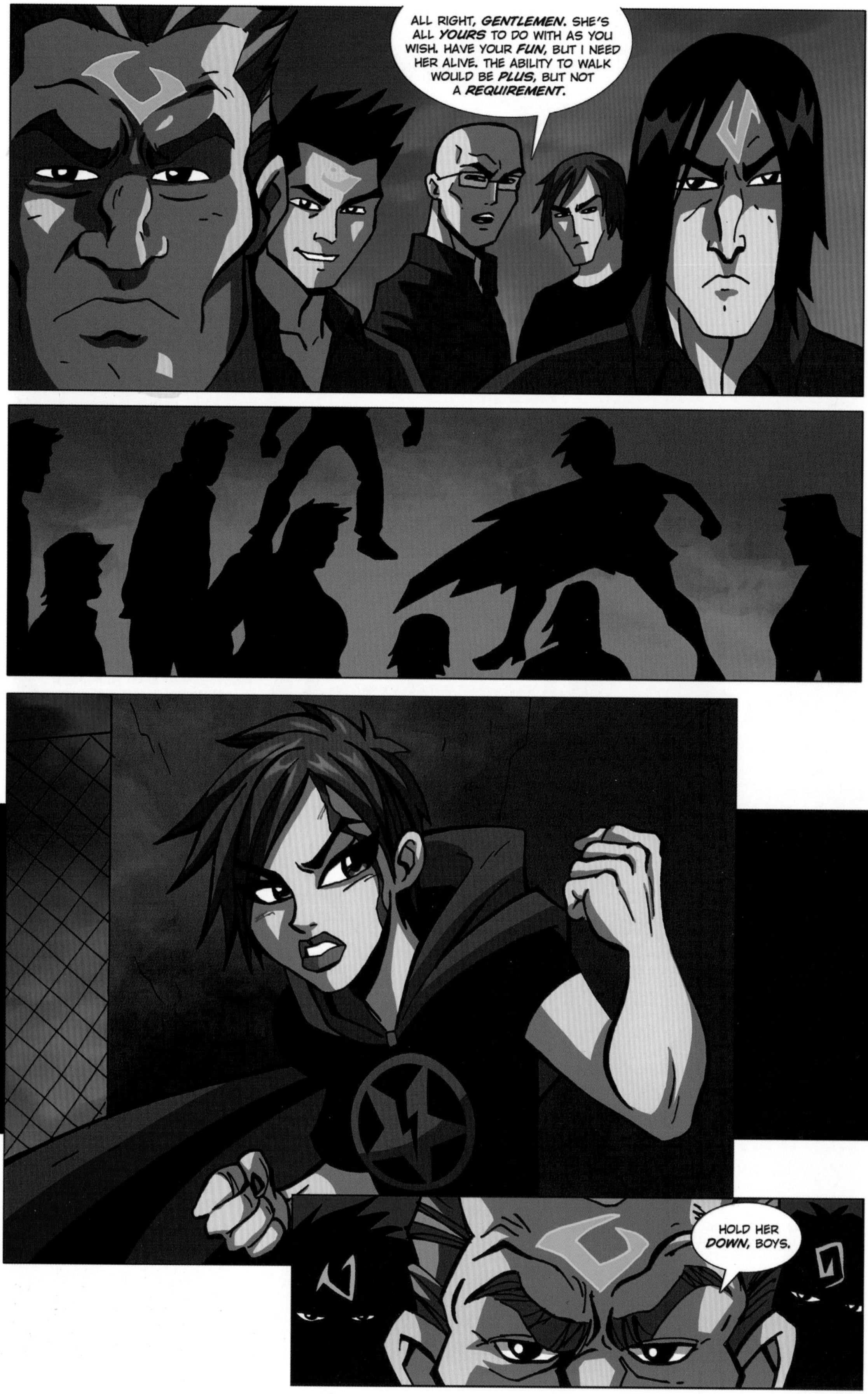
ALL RIGHT, GENTLEMEN. SHE'S ALL YOURS TO DO WITH AS YOU WISH. HAVE YOUR FUN, BUT I NEED HER ALIVE. THE ABILITY TO WALK WOULD BE PLUS, BUT NOT A REQUIREMENT.
HOLD HER DOWN, BOYS.

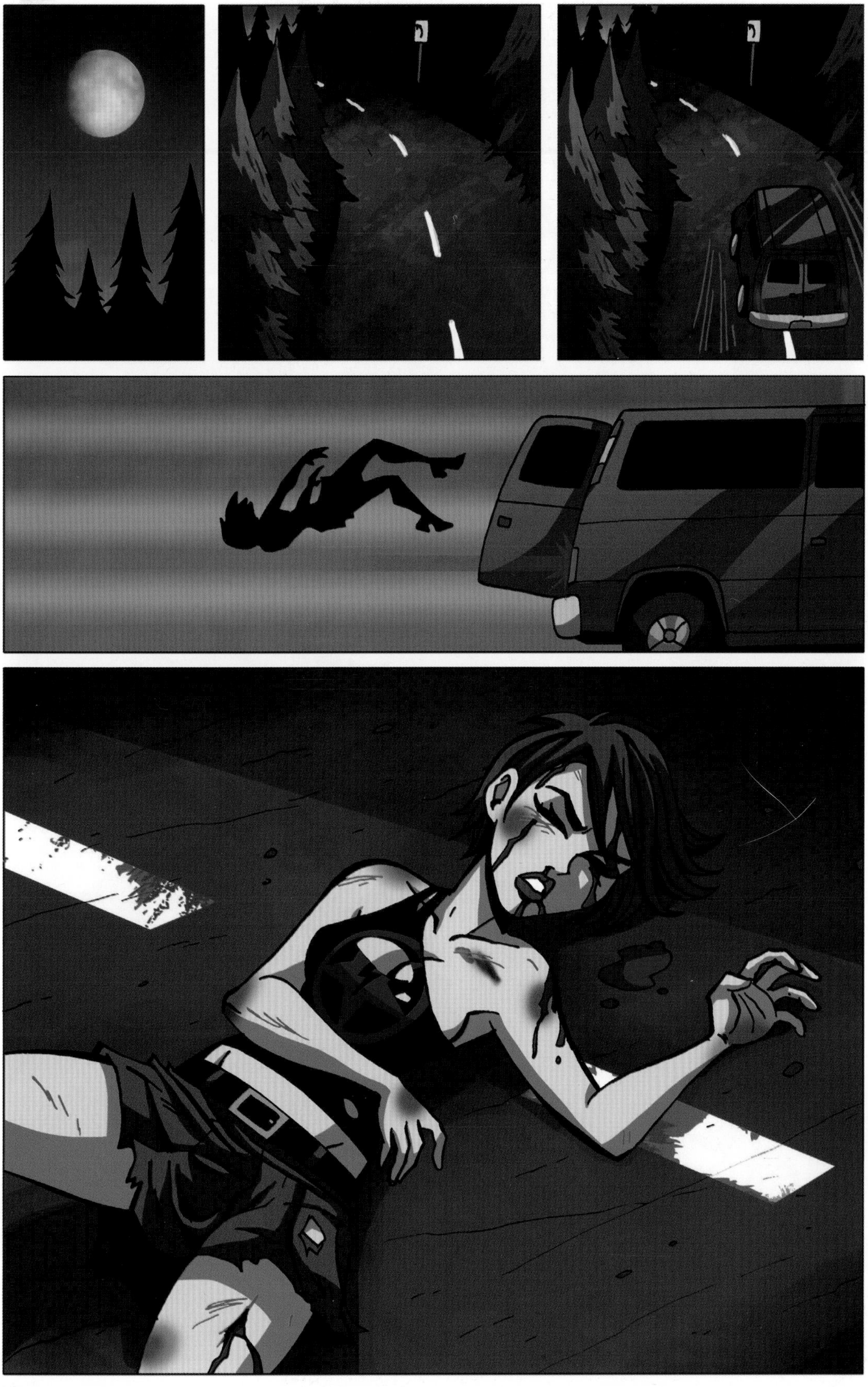

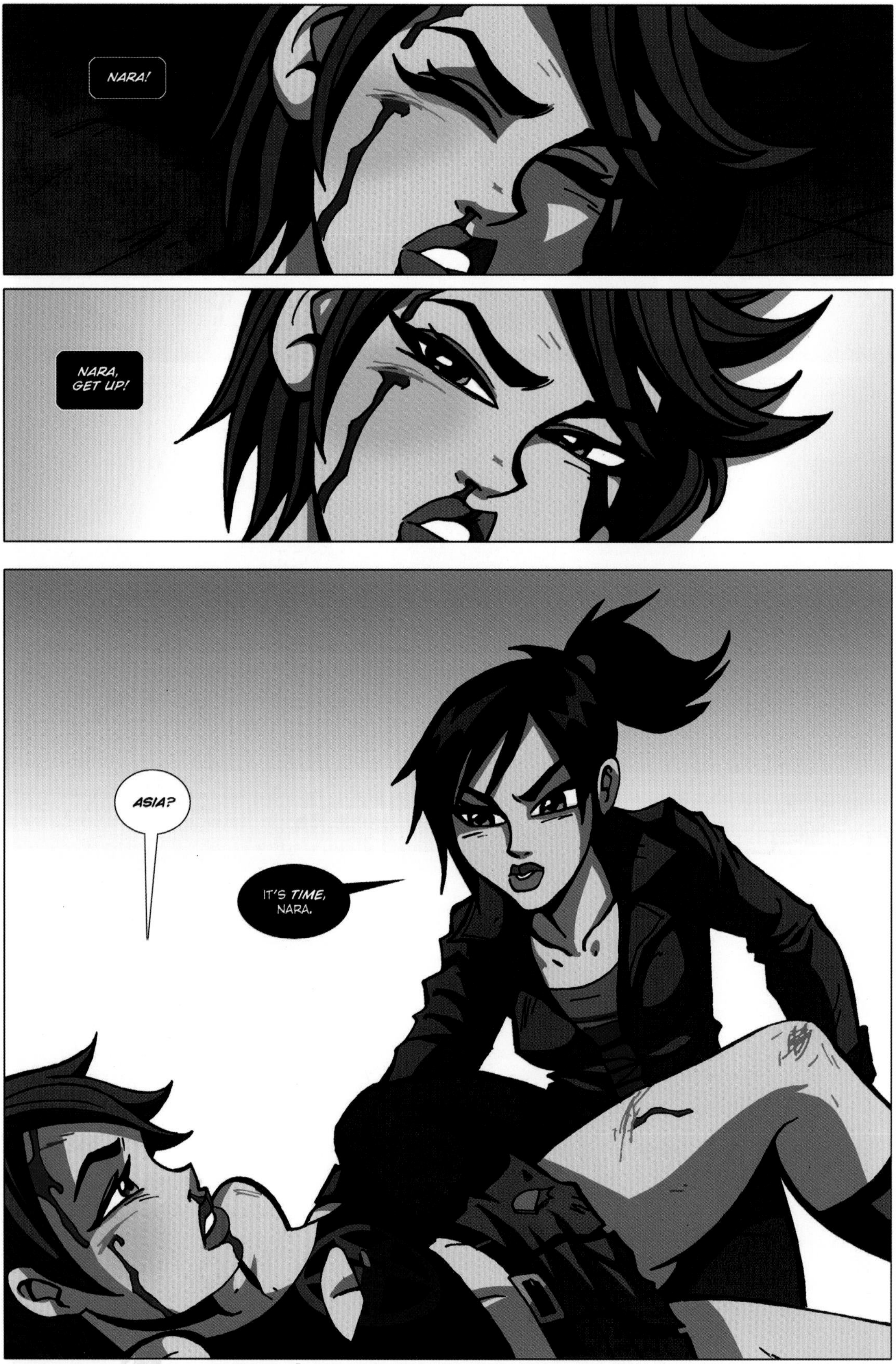
NARA!
NARA, GET UP!
ASIA?
IT'S *TIME*, NARA.

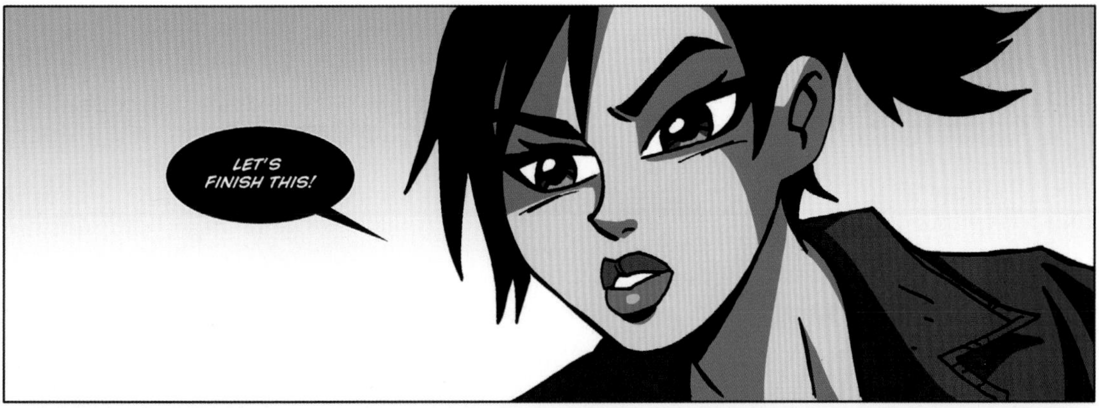
LET'S FINISH THIS!

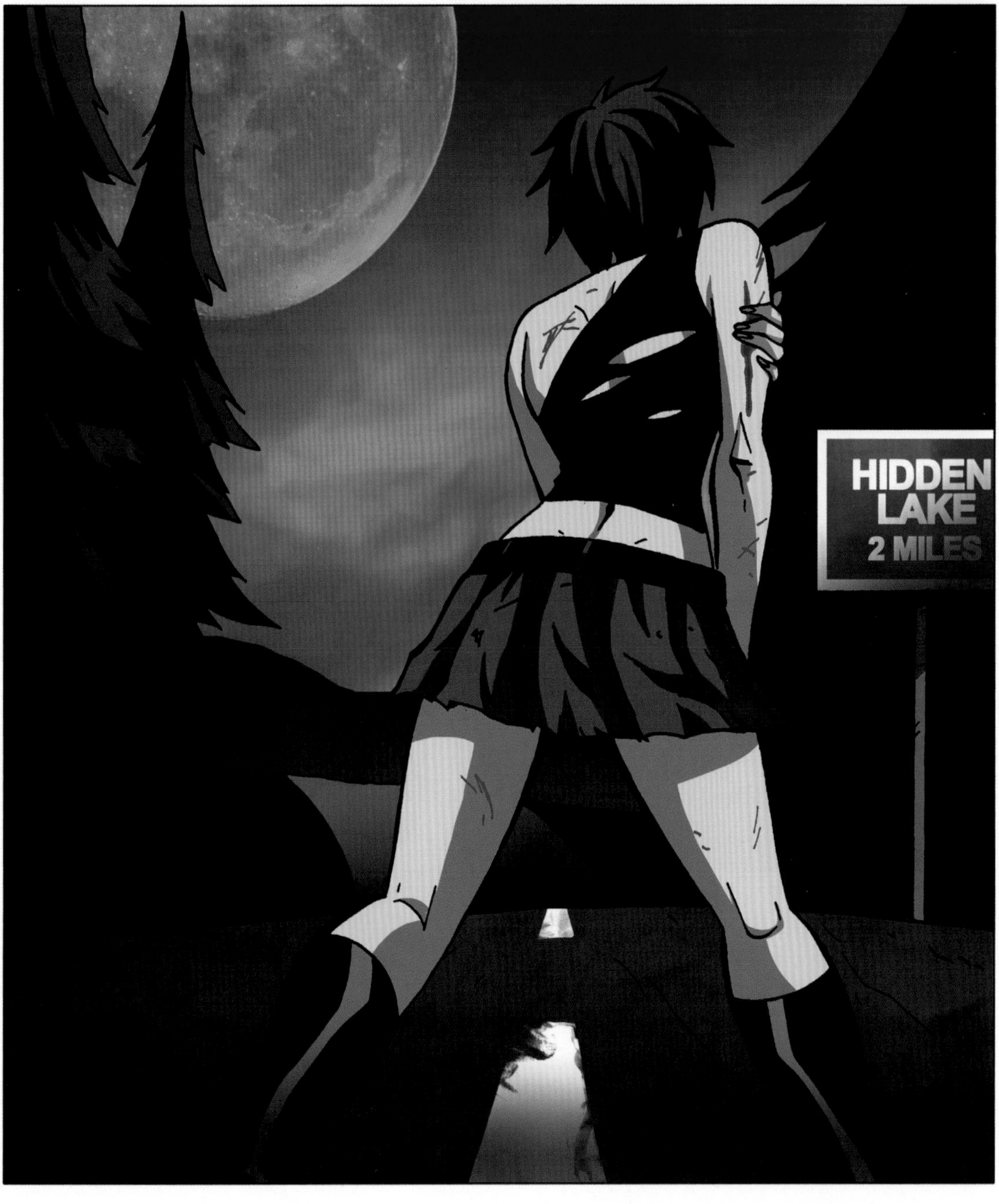
HIDDEN LAKE 2 MILES

CHAPTER FOUR

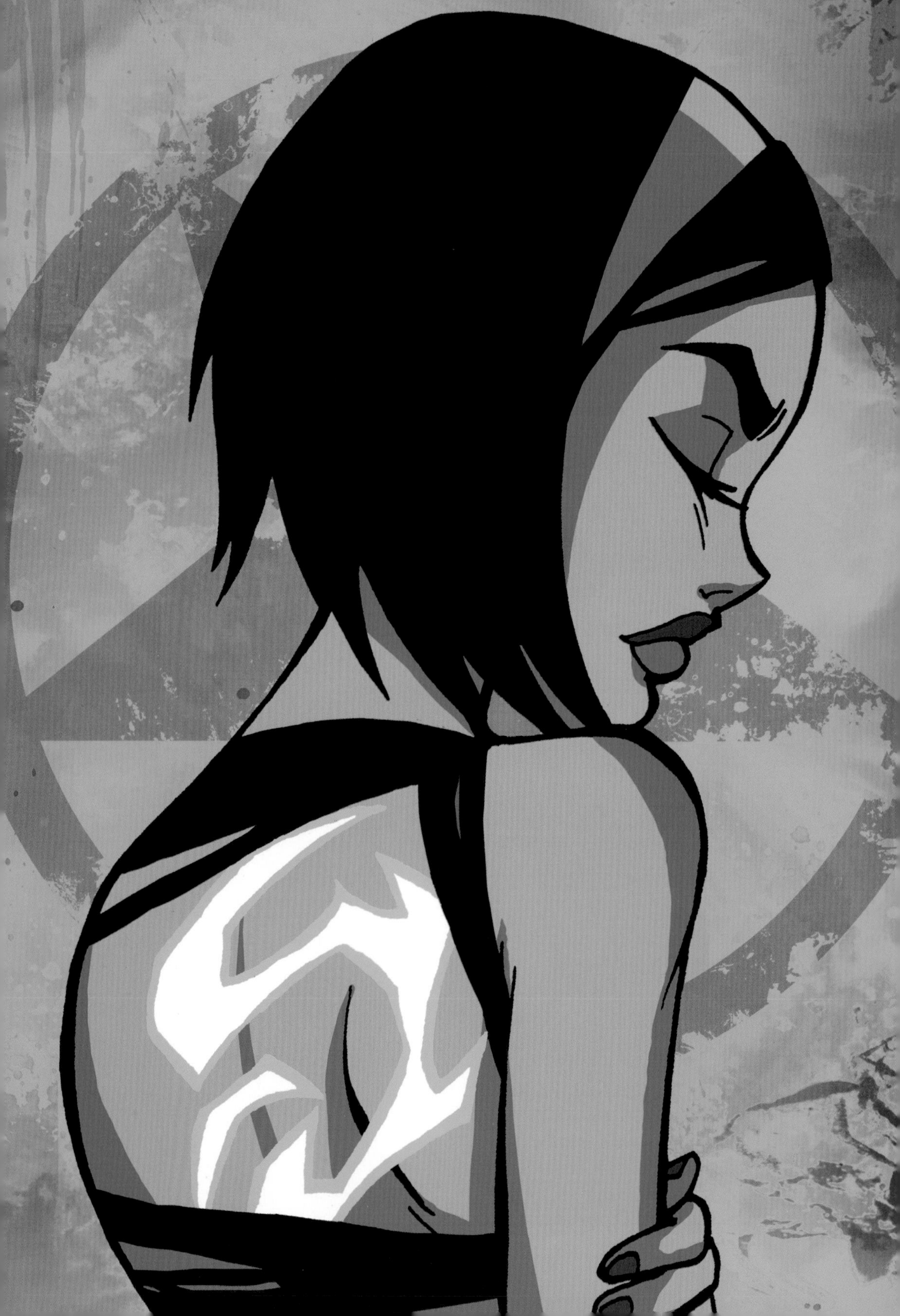

NARA, ARE YOU *SURE* ABOUT THIS? YOU SHOULD BE IN THE *HOSPITAL* RIGHT NOW, NOT PLOTTING YOUR *REVENGE.*

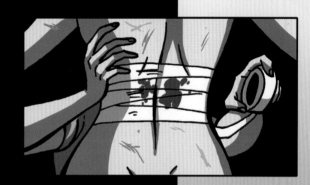

THIS *ISN'T* ABOUT REVENGE. BESIDES, WE'RE OUT OF TIME. THIS IS — *OUCH! TAKE IT EASY!*

SORRY! DO YOU WANT TO AT LEAST *TALK* ABOUT IT? WHAT THEY *DID* TO YOU —

I SAID *NO.*

FINE. BUT YOU CAN'T KEEP IT BOTTLED UP *FOREVER.* IT'LL *KILL* YOU.

I'VE BEEN DEAD BEFORE.

BREE, THERE *IS* SOMETHING I NEED TO TELL YOU. *I* -
I *KNOW*. IT'S ALL OVER TV. THEY'RE PRACTICALLY *CELEBRATING*.
I'M *SO* SORRY, BREE. I *WISH* I KNEW WHAT TO SAY. HE WOULD STILL BE *ALIVE* IF IT WASN'T FOR *ME*. IF I COULD DO IT ALL OVER...

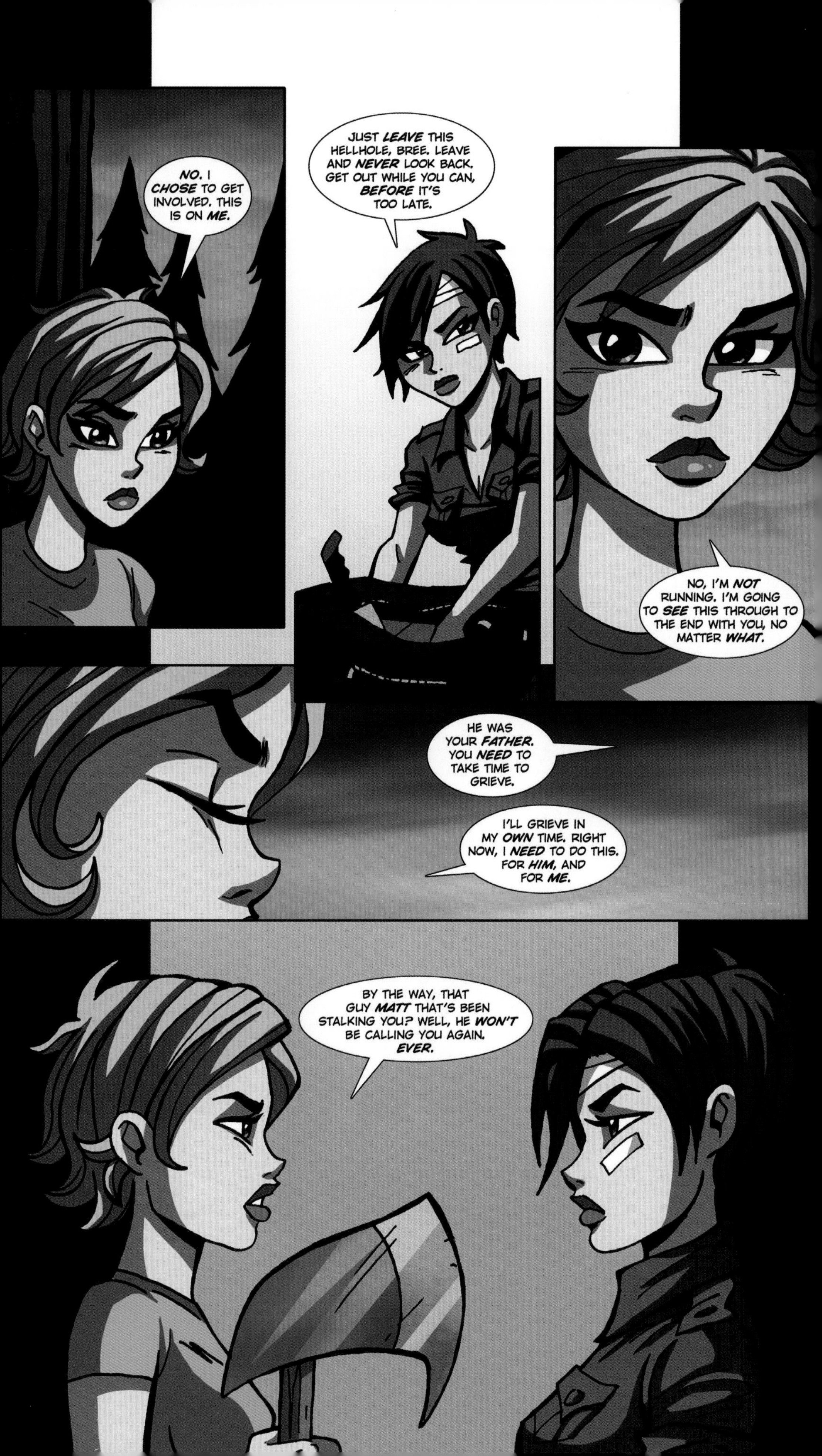
NO. I CHOSE TO GET INVOLVED. THIS IS ON ME.
JUST LEAVE THIS HELLHOLE, BREE. LEAVE AND NEVER LOOK BACK. GET OUT WHILE YOU CAN, BEFORE IT'S TOO LATE.
NO, I'M NOT RUNNING. I'M GOING TO SEE THIS THROUGH TO THE END WITH YOU, NO MATTER WHAT.
HE WAS YOUR FATHER. YOU NEED TO TAKE TIME TO GRIEVE.
I'LL GRIEVE IN MY OWN TIME. RIGHT NOW, I NEED TO DO THIS. FOR HIM, AND FOR ME.
BY THE WAY, THAT GUY MATT THAT'S BEEN STALKING YOU? WELL, HE WON'T BE CALLING YOU AGAIN. EVER.

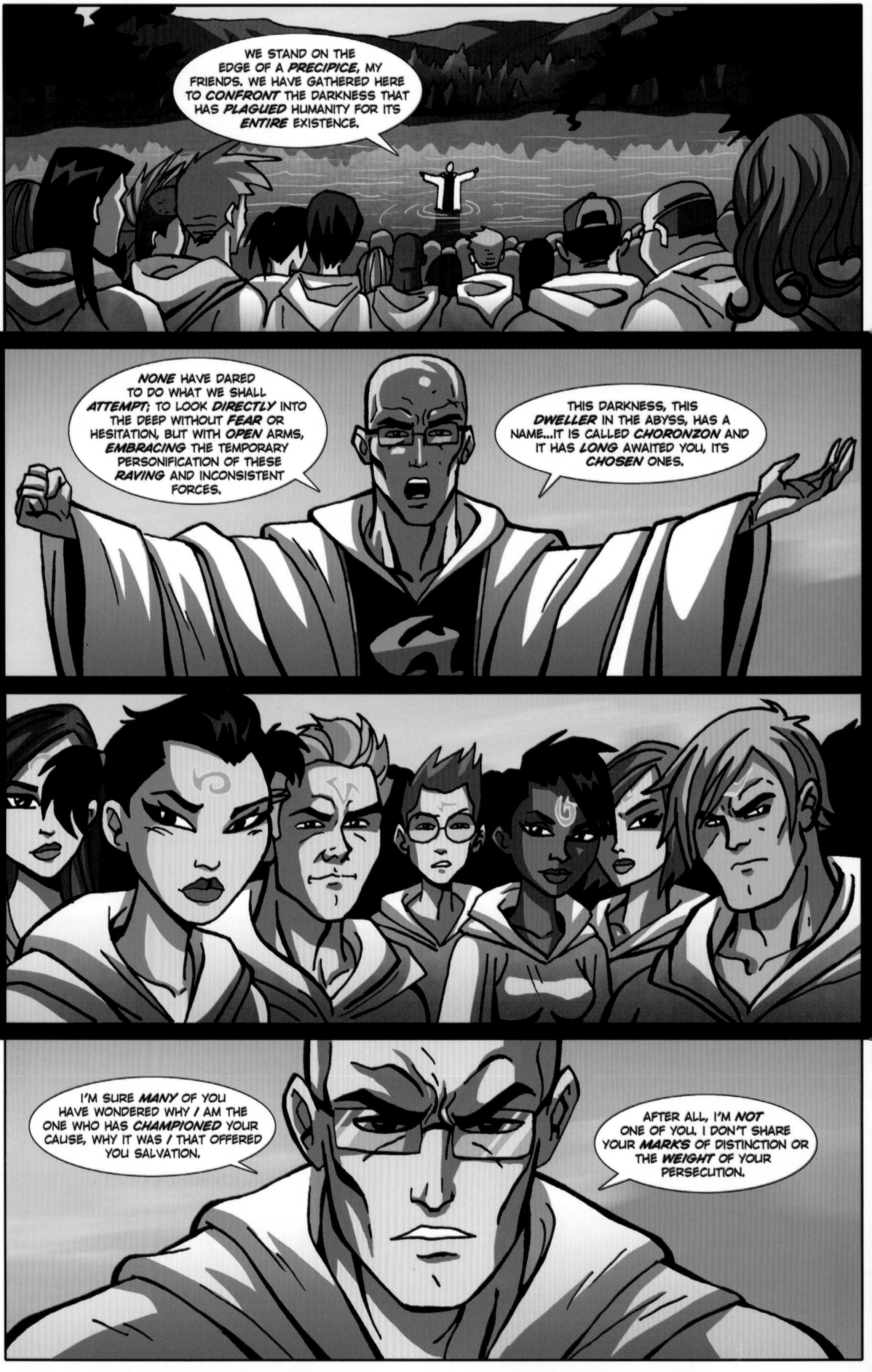

WE STAND ON THE EDGE OF A PRECIPICE, MY FRIENDS. WE HAVE GATHERED HERE TO CONFRONT THE DARKNESS THAT HAS PLAGUED HUMANITY FOR ITS ENTIRE EXISTENCE.
NONE HAVE DARED TO DO WHAT WE SHALL ATTEMPT; TO LOOK DIRECTLY INTO THE DEEP WITHOUT FEAR OR HESITATION, BUT WITH OPEN ARMS, EMBRACING THE TEMPORARY PERSONIFICATION OF THESE RAVING AND INCONSISTENT FORCES.
THIS DARKNESS, THIS DWELLER IN THE ABYSS, HAS A NAME...IT IS CALLED CHORONZON AND IT HAS LONG AWAITED YOU, ITS CHOSEN ONES.
I'M SURE MANY OF YOU HAVE WONDERED WHY I AM THE ONE WHO HAS CHAMPIONED YOUR CAUSE, WHY IT WAS I THAT OFFERED YOU SALVATION.
AFTER ALL, I'M NOT ONE OF YOU. I DON'T SHARE YOUR MARKS OF DISTINCTION OR THE WEIGHT OF YOUR PERSECUTION.

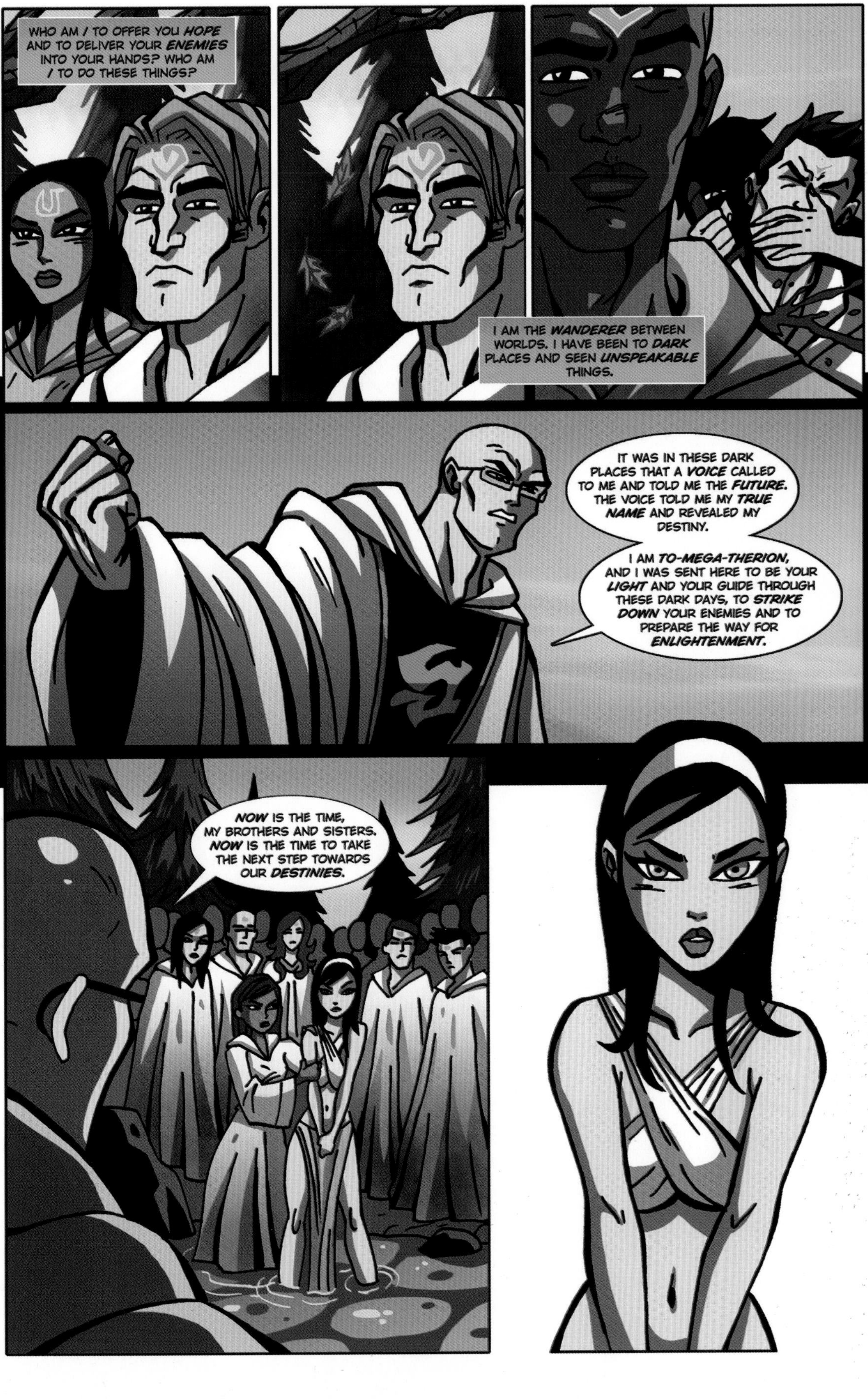

WHO AM *I* TO OFFER YOU *HOPE* AND TO DELIVER YOUR *ENEMIES* INTO YOUR HANDS? WHO AM *I* TO DO THESE THINGS?
I AM THE *WANDERER* BETWEEN WORLDS. I HAVE BEEN TO *DARK* PLACES AND SEEN *UNSPEAKABLE* THINGS.
IT WAS IN THESE DARK PLACES THAT A *VOICE* CALLED TO ME AND TOLD ME THE *FUTURE*. THE VOICE TOLD ME MY *TRUE NAME* AND REVEALED MY DESTINY.
I AM *TO-MEGA-THERION*, AND I WAS SENT HERE TO BE YOUR *LIGHT* AND YOUR GUIDE THROUGH THESE DARK DAYS, TO *STRIKE DOWN* YOUR ENEMIES AND TO PREPARE THE WAY FOR *ENLIGHTENMENT*.
NOW IS THE TIME, MY BROTHERS AND SISTERS. *NOW* IS THE TIME TO TAKE THE NEXT STEP TOWARDS OUR *DESTINIES*.

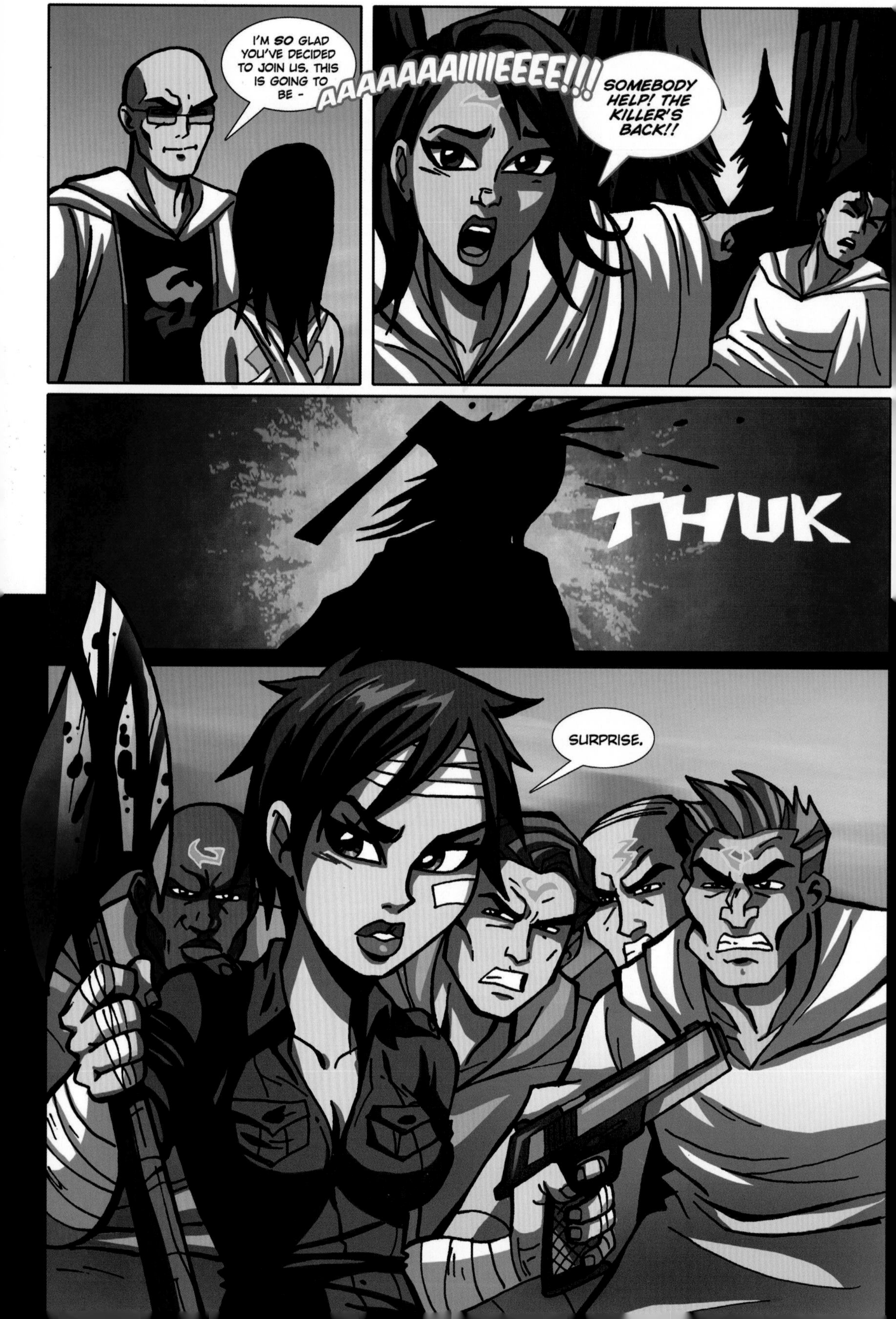
I'M SO GLAD YOU'VE DECIDED TO JOIN US. THIS IS GOING TO BE -
AAAAAAAIIIIIEEEE!!!
SOMEBODY HELP! THE KILLER'S BACK!!
THUK
SURPRISE.

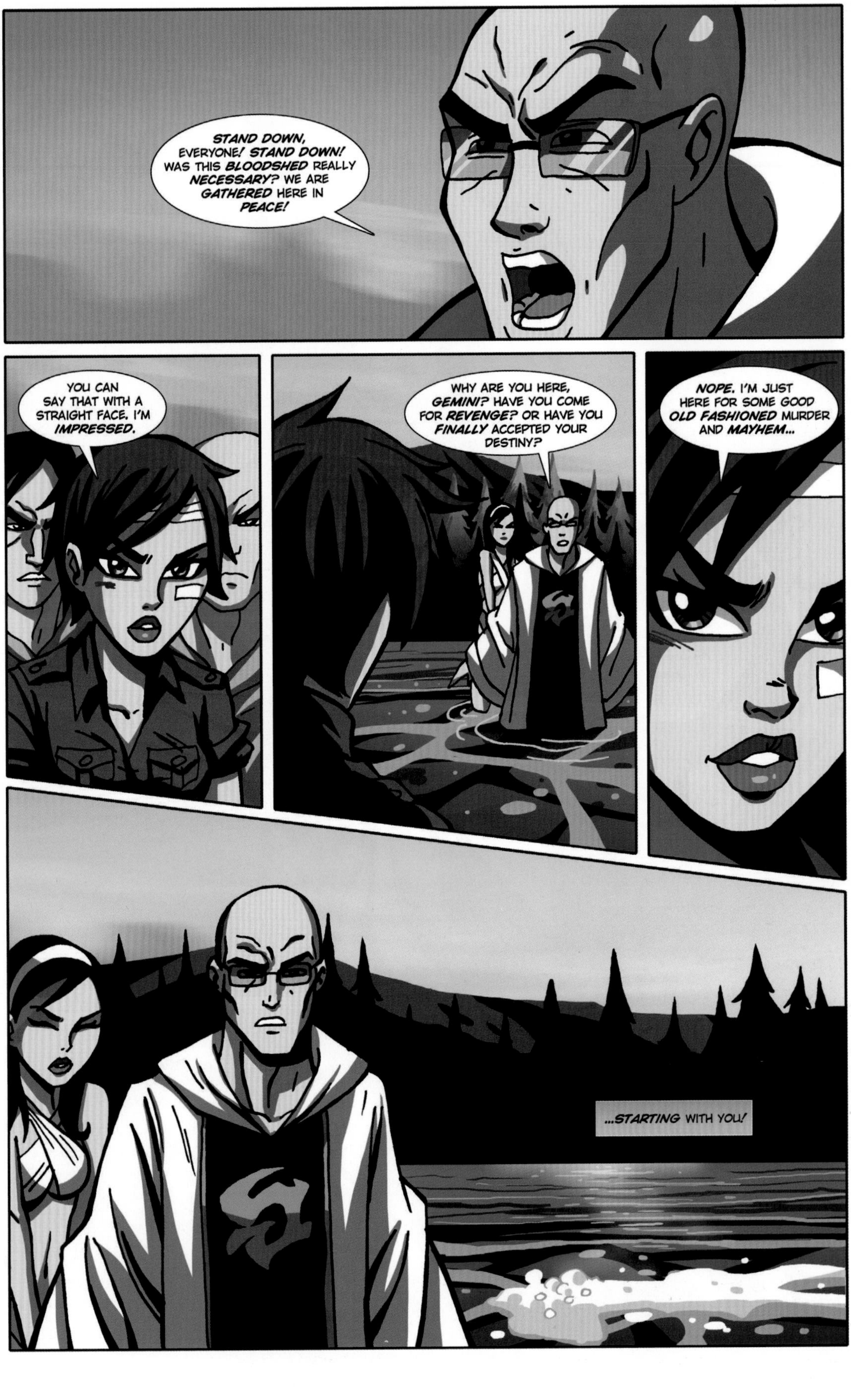
STAND DOWN, EVERYONE! STAND DOWN! WAS THIS BLOODSHED REALLY NECESSARY? WE ARE GATHERED HERE IN PEACE!
YOU CAN SAY THAT WITH A STRAIGHT FACE. I'M IMPRESSED.
WHY ARE YOU HERE, GEMINI? HAVE YOU COME FOR REVENGE? OR HAVE YOU FINALLY ACCEPTED YOUR DESTINY?
NOPE. I'M JUST HERE FOR SOME GOOD OLD FASHIONED MURDER AND MAYHEM...
...STARTING WITH YOU!

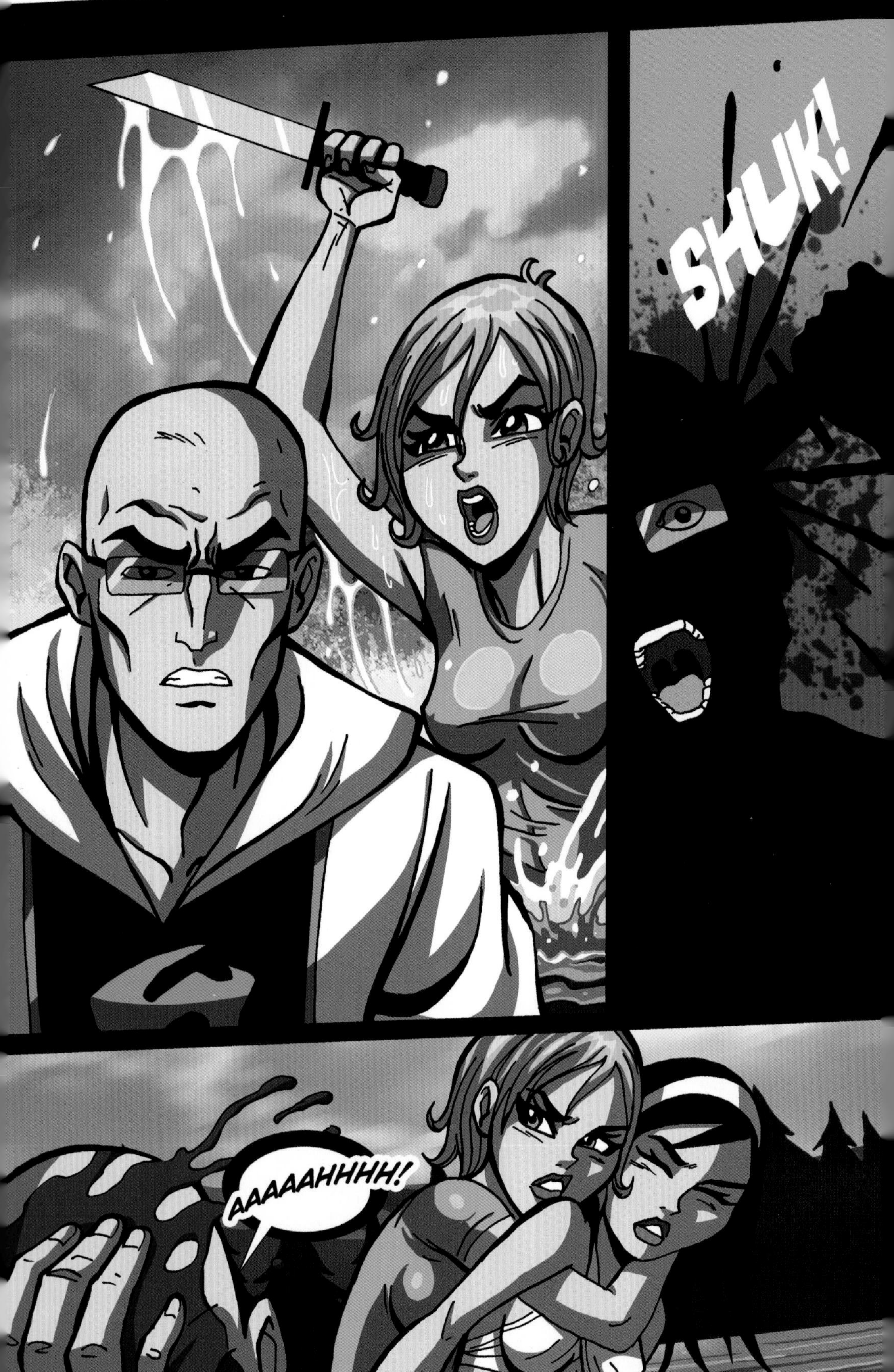
SHUK!
AAAAAHHHH!

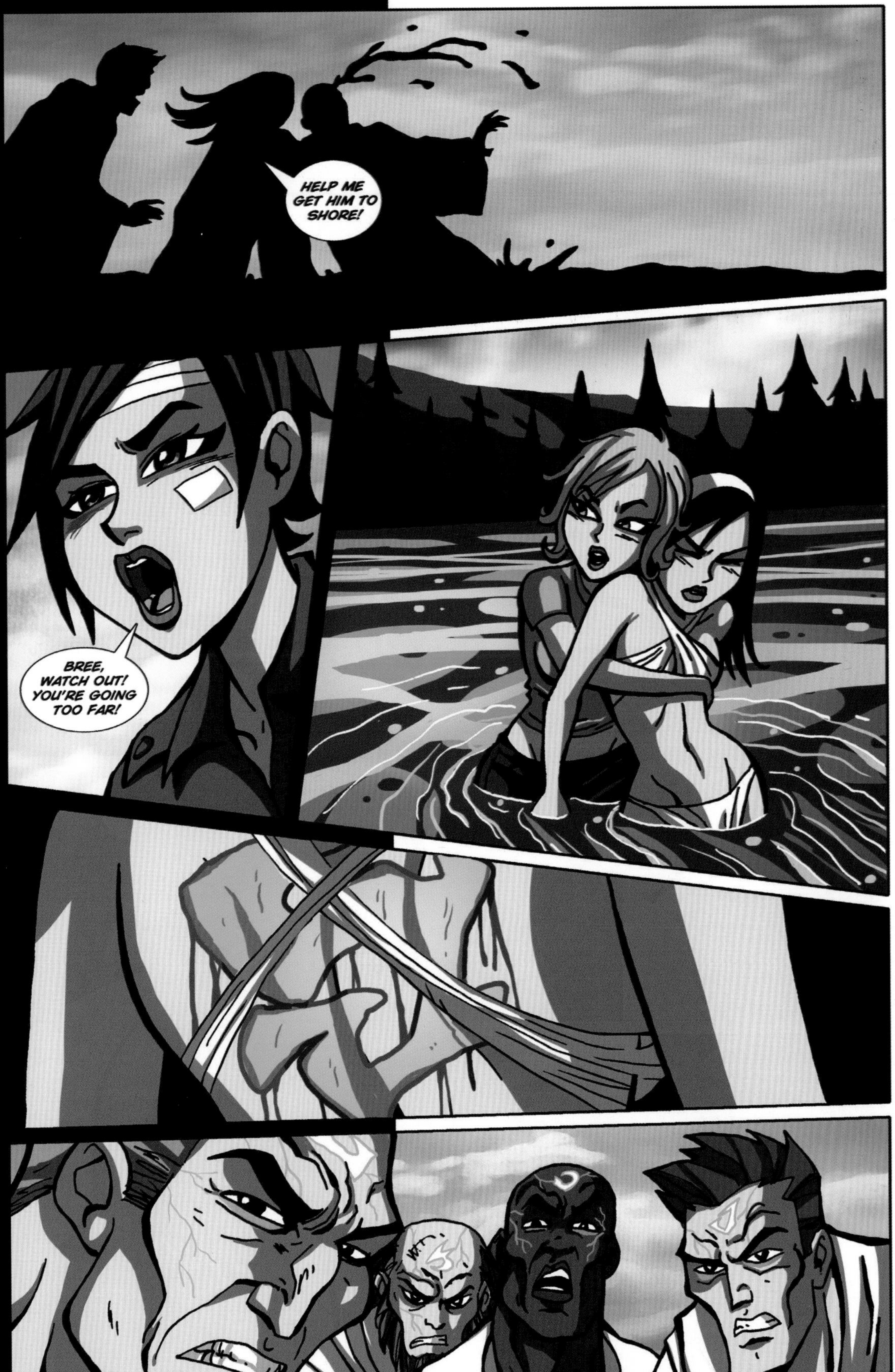
HELP ME GET HIM TO SHORE!
BREE, WATCH OUT! YOU'RE GOING TOO FAR!

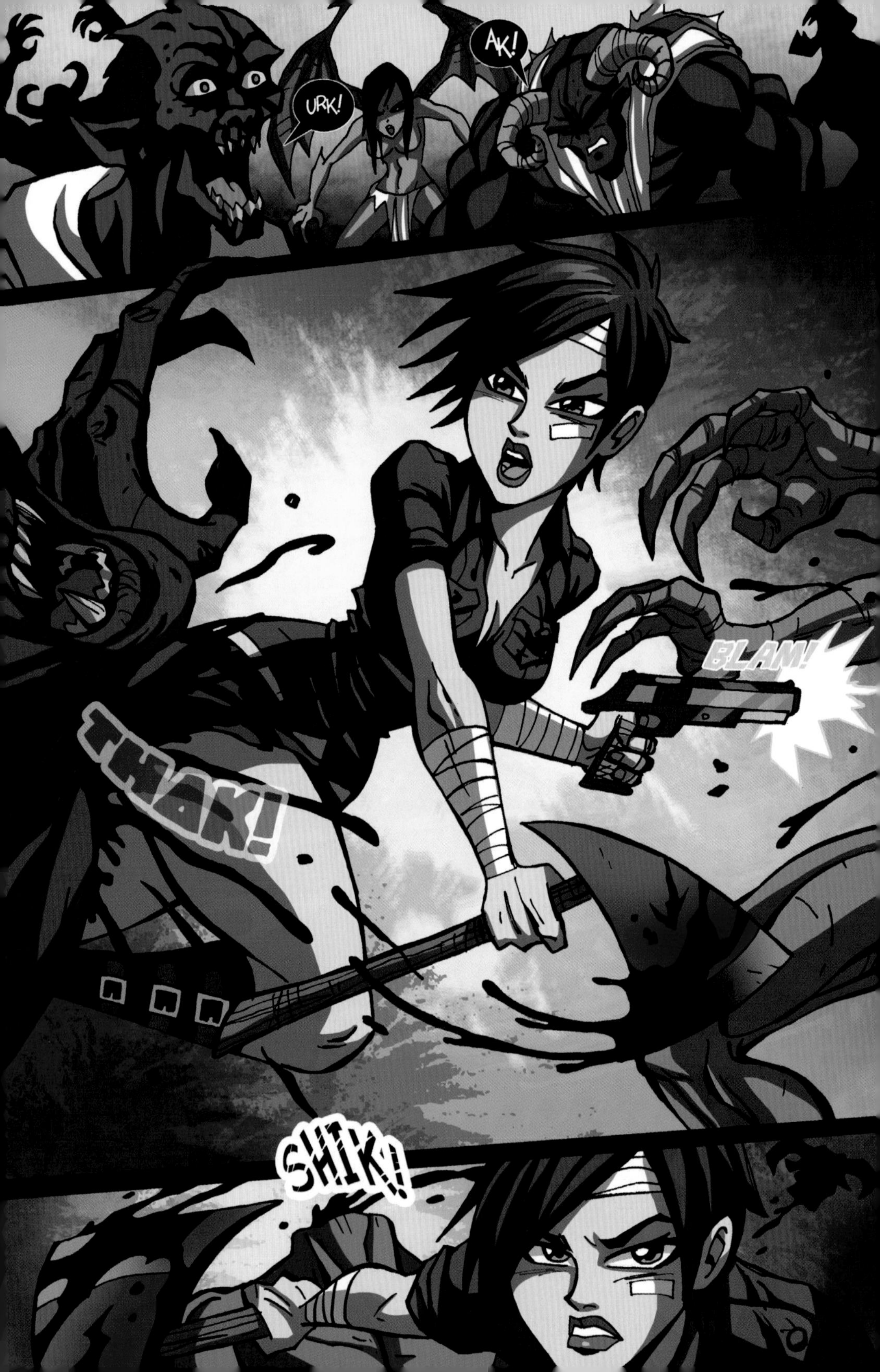
URK!
AK!
BLAM!
THAK!
SHIK!

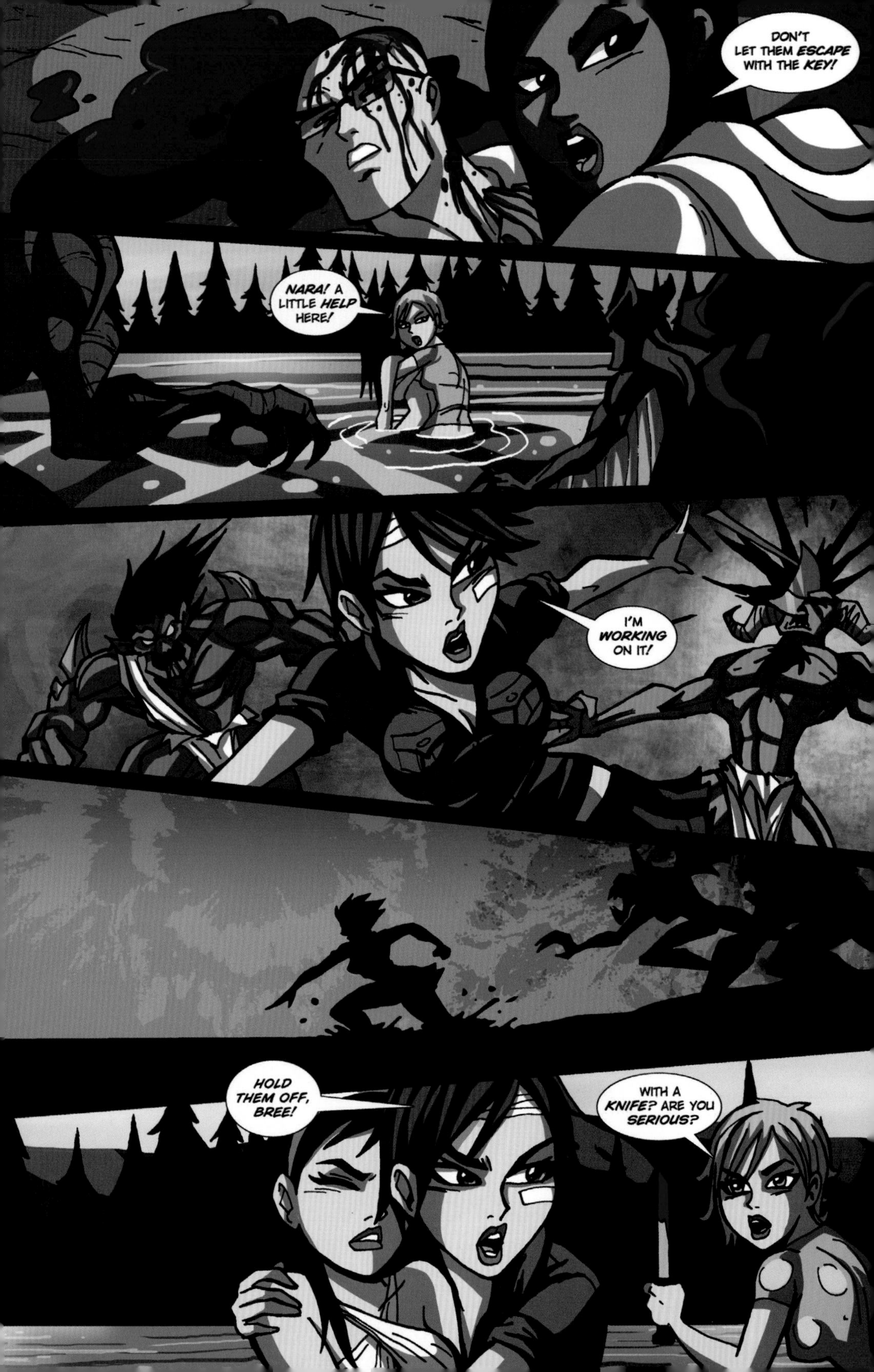
DON'T LET THEM ESCAPE WITH THE KEY!
NARA! A LITTLE HELP HERE!
I'M WORKING ON IT!
HOLD THEM OFF, BREE!
WITH A KNIFE? ARE YOU SERIOUS?

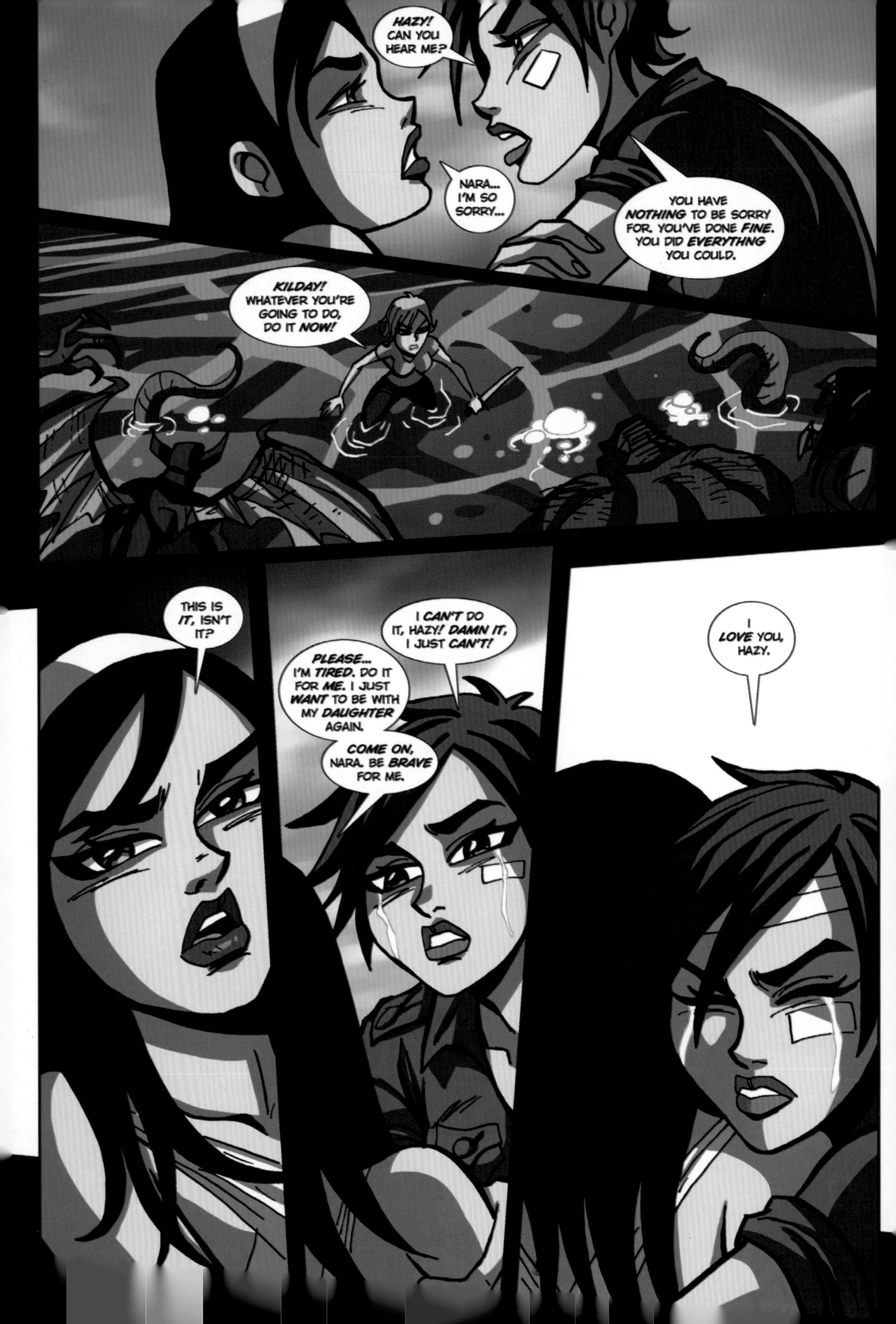

HAZY! CAN YOU HEAR ME?
NARA... I'M SO SORRY...
YOU HAVE NOTHING TO BE SORRY FOR. YOU'VE DONE FINE. YOU DID EVERYTHING YOU COULD.
KILDAY! WHATEVER YOU'RE GOING TO DO, DO IT NOW!
THIS IS IT, ISN'T IT?
I CAN'T DO IT, HAZY! DAMN IT, I JUST CAN'T!
PLEASE... I'M TIRED. DO IT FOR ME. I JUST WANT TO BE WITH MY DAUGHTER AGAIN.
COME ON, NARA. BE BRAVE FOR ME.
I LOVE YOU, HAZY.

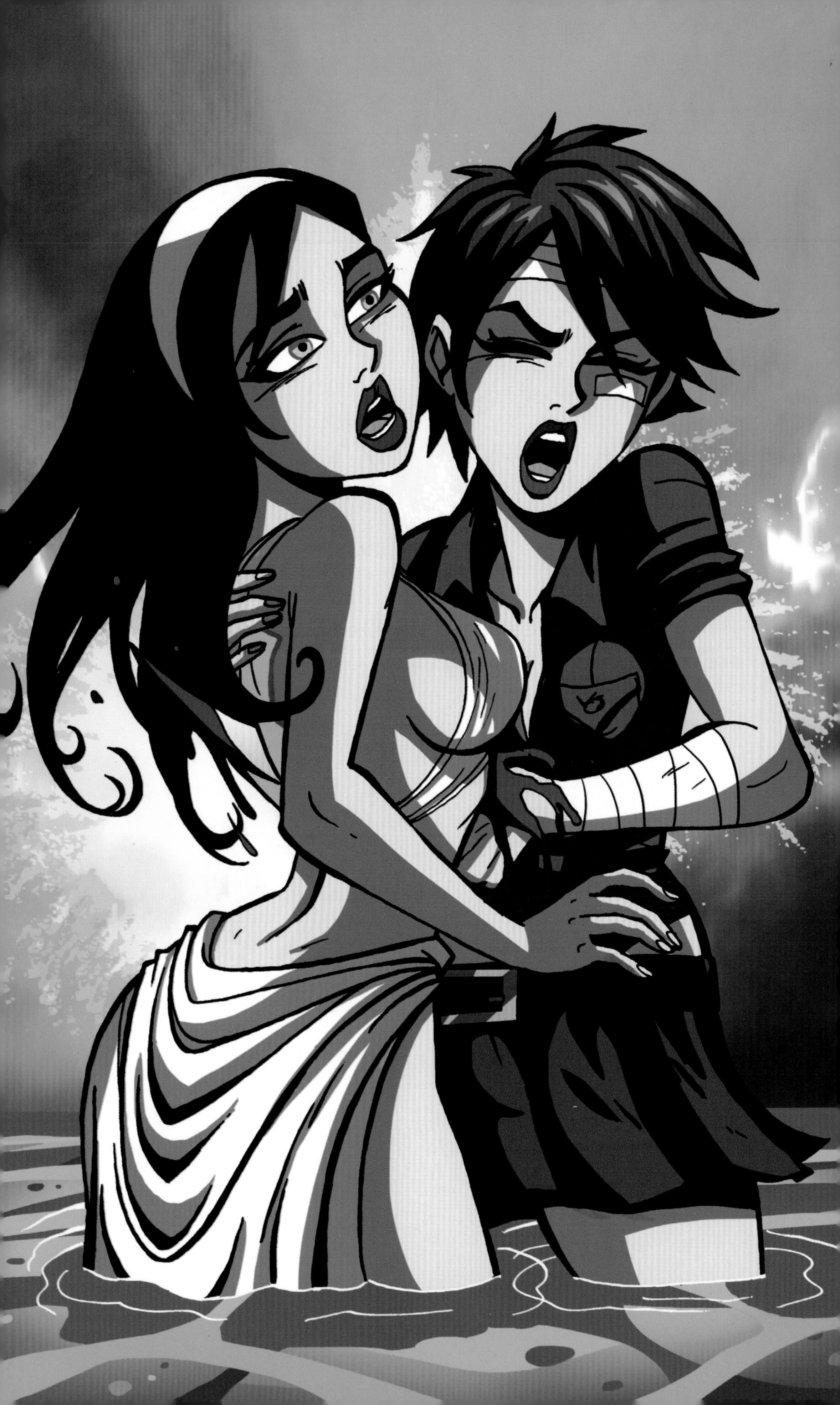

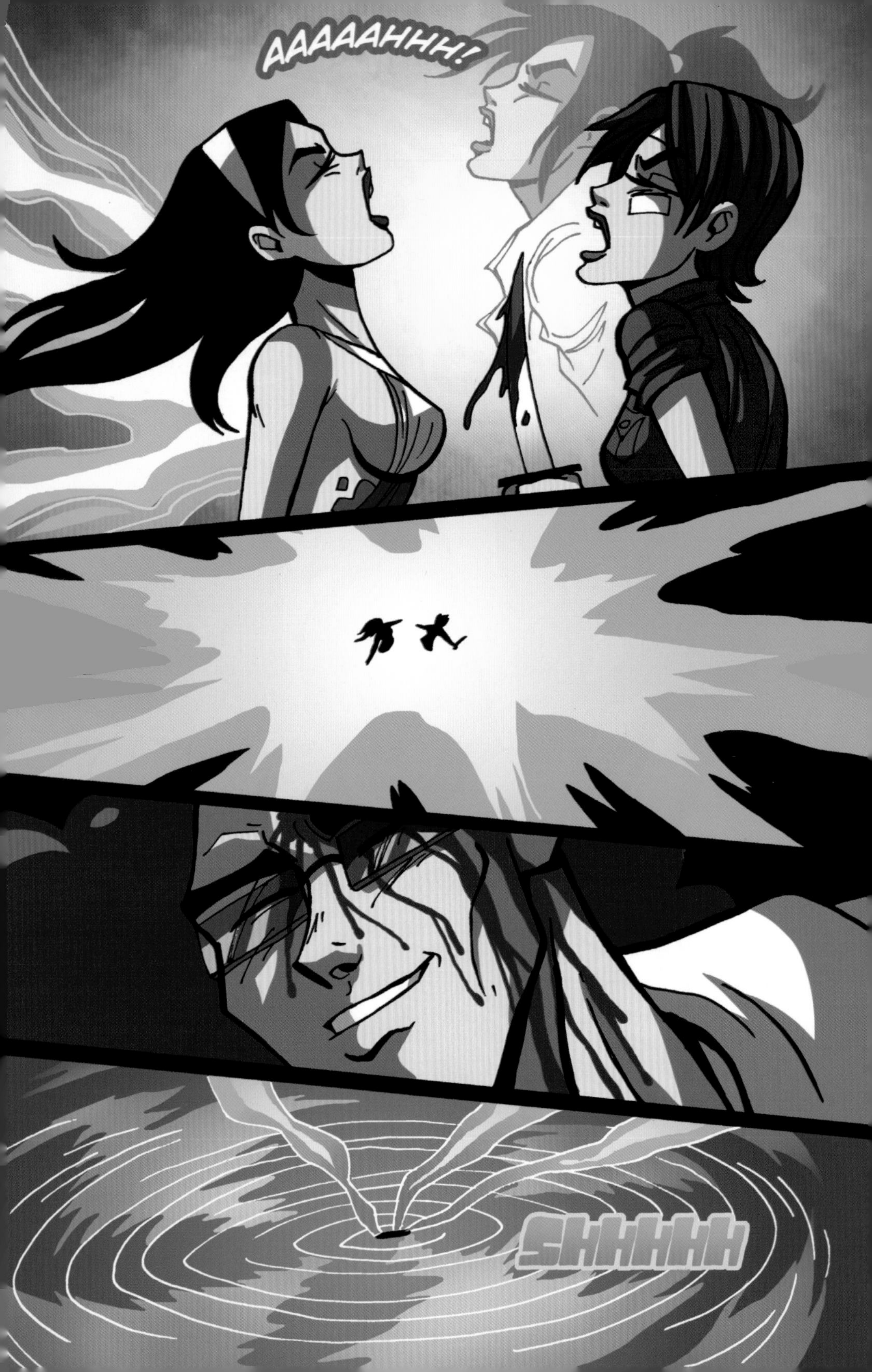
AAAAAHHH!
SHHHHH

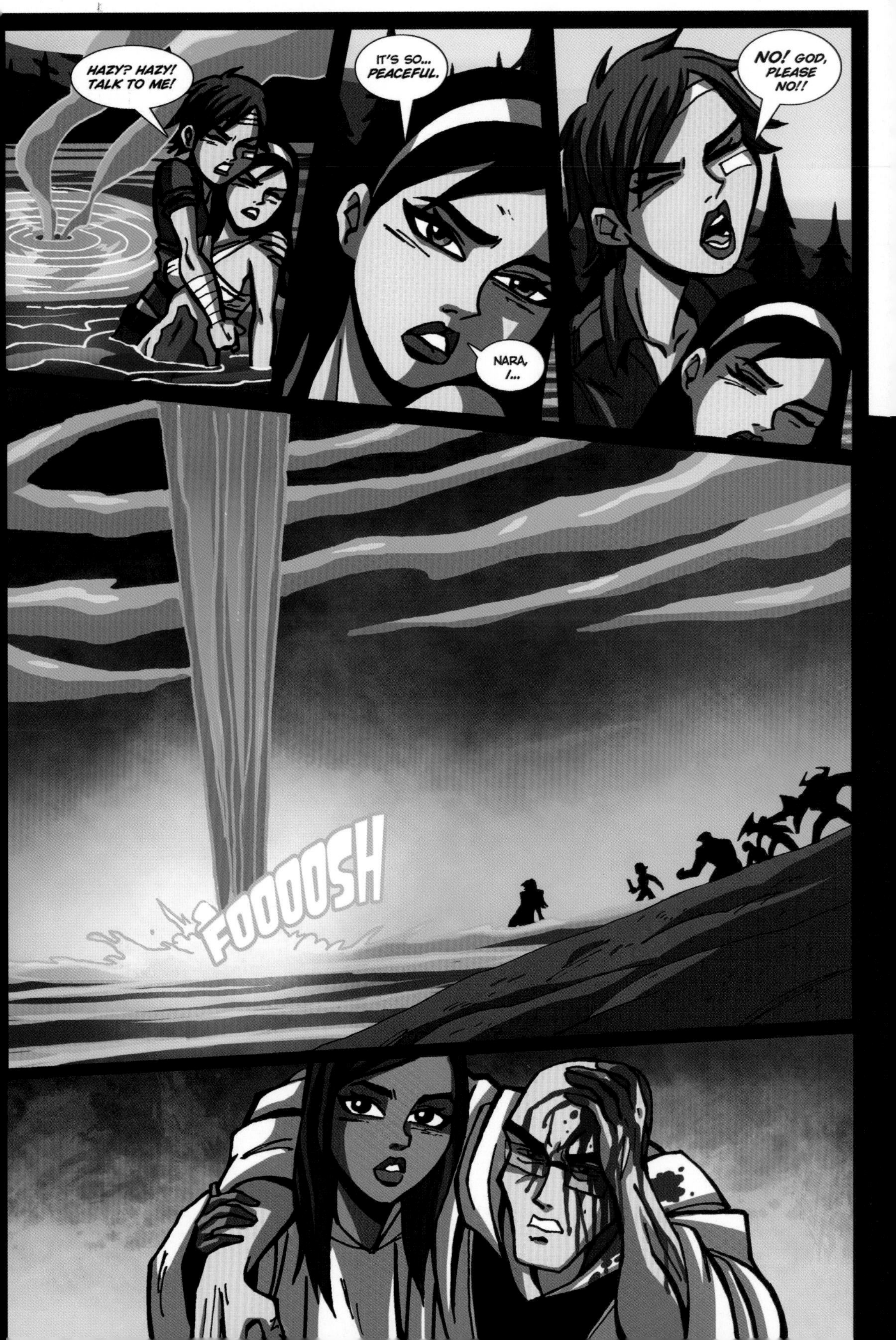
HAZY? HAZY! TALK TO ME!
IT'S SO... PEACEFUL.
NARA, I...
NO! GOD, PLEASE NO!!
FOOOOOSH

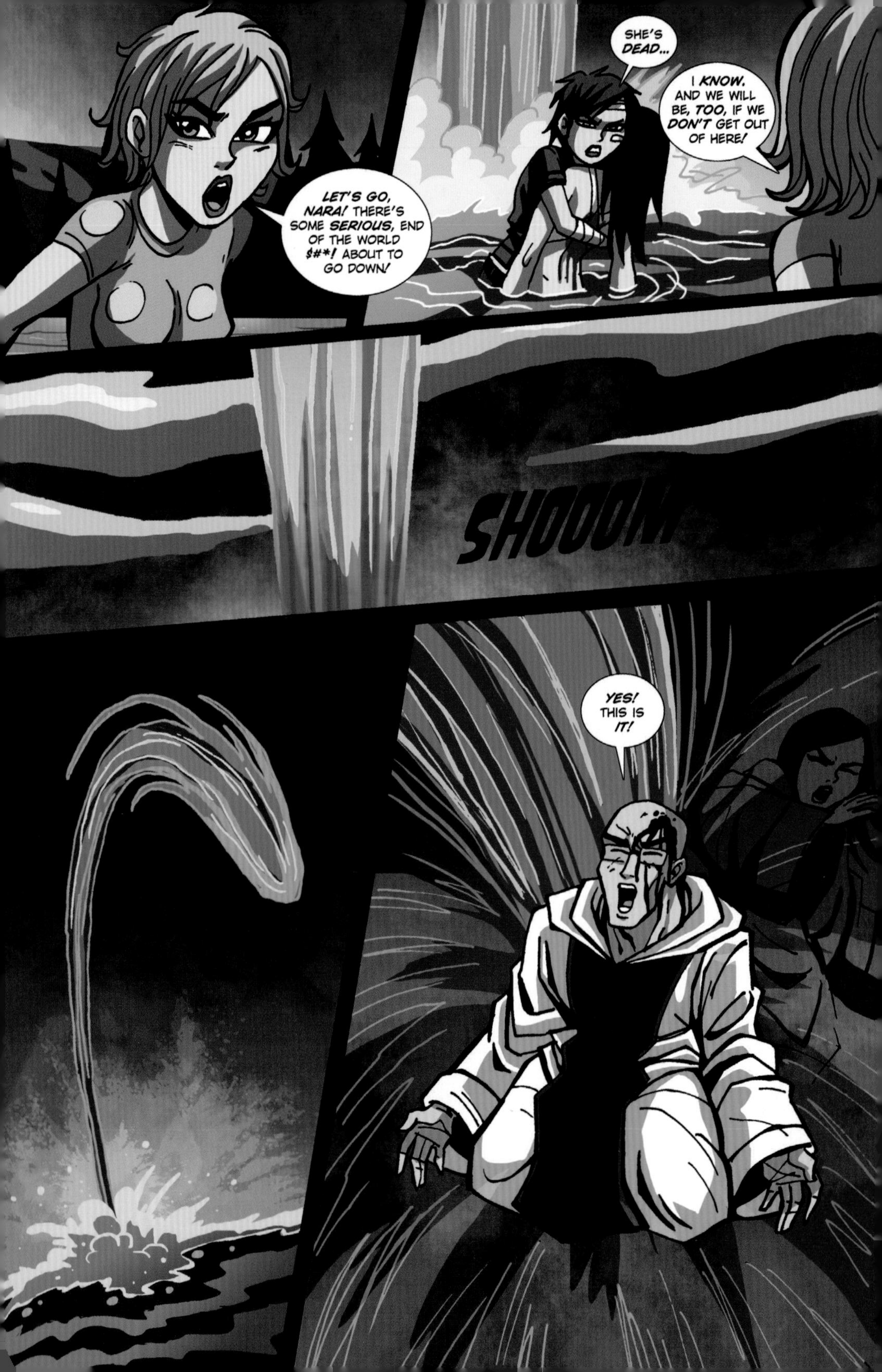
LET'S GO, NARA! THERE'S SOME SERIOUS, END OF THE WORLD $#*! ABOUT TO GO DOWN!
SHE'S DEAD...
I KNOW. AND WE WILL BE, TOO, IF WE DON'T GET OUT OF HERE!
SHOOOM
YES! THIS IS IT!

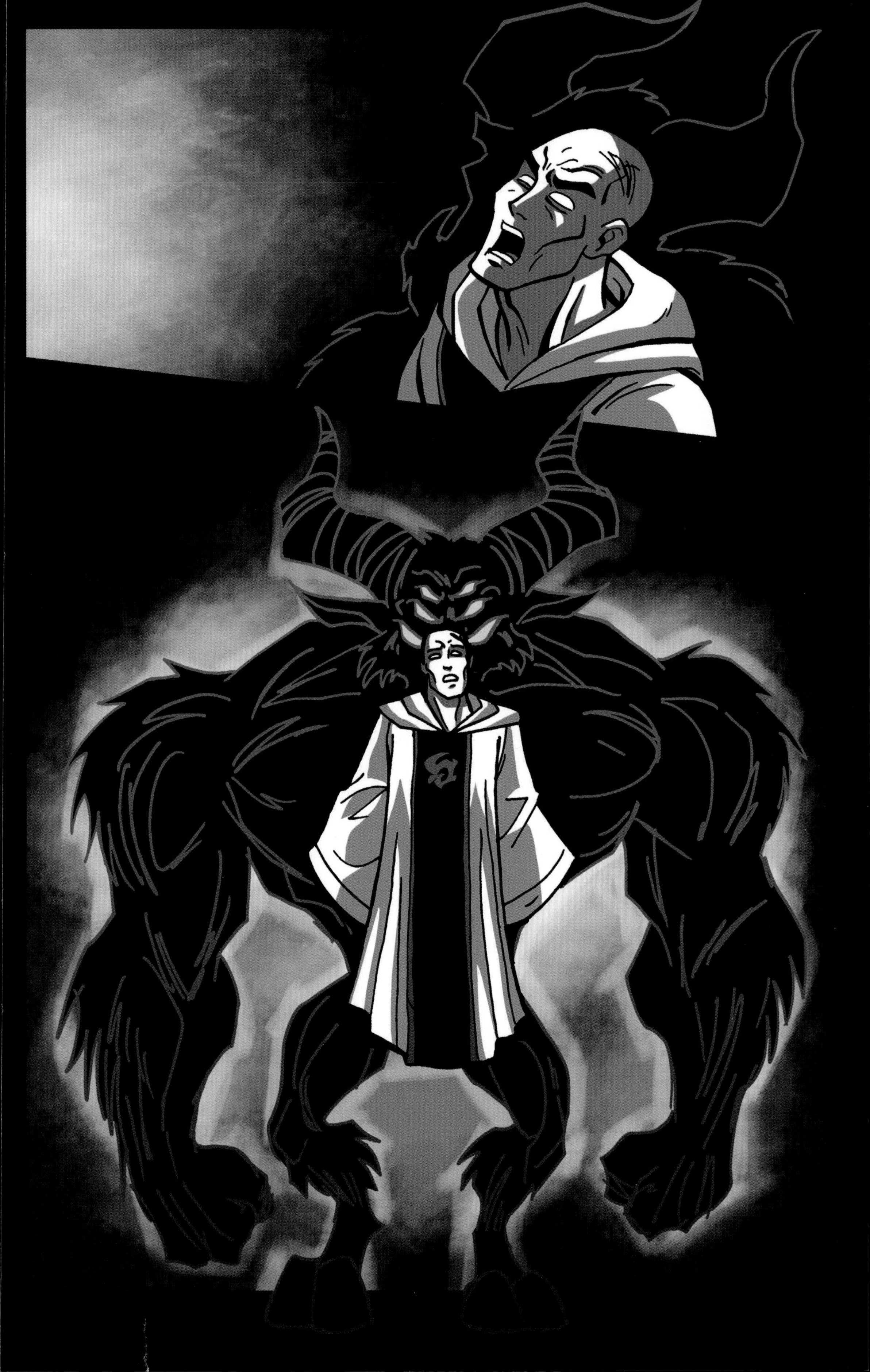

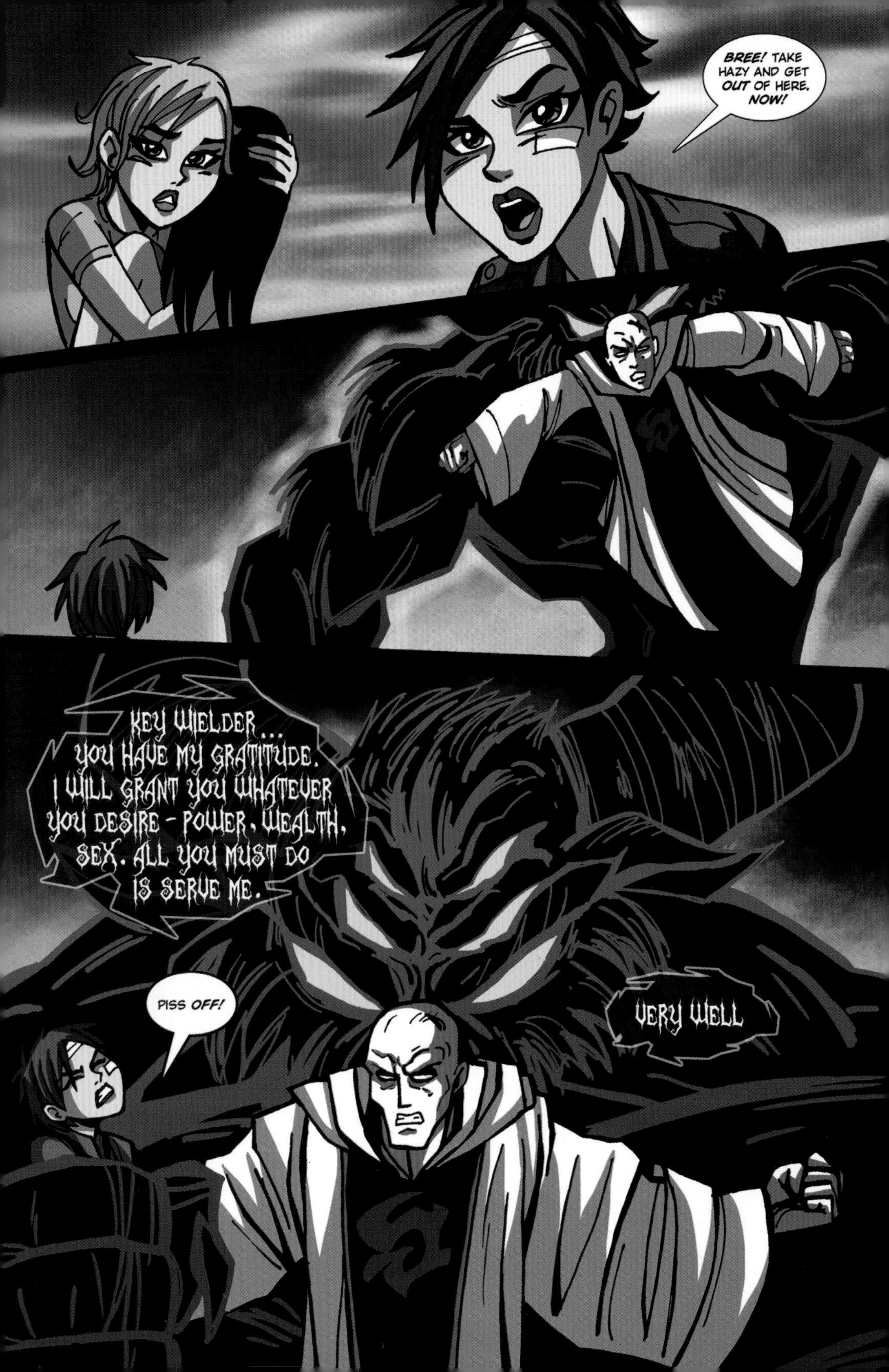
BREE! TAKE HAZY AND GET OUT OF HERE. NOW!
KEY WIELDER... YOU HAVE MY GRATITUDE. I WILL GRANT YOU WHATEVER YOU DESIRE - POWER, WEALTH, SEX. ALL YOU MUST DO IS SERVE ME.
PISS OFF!
VERY WELL

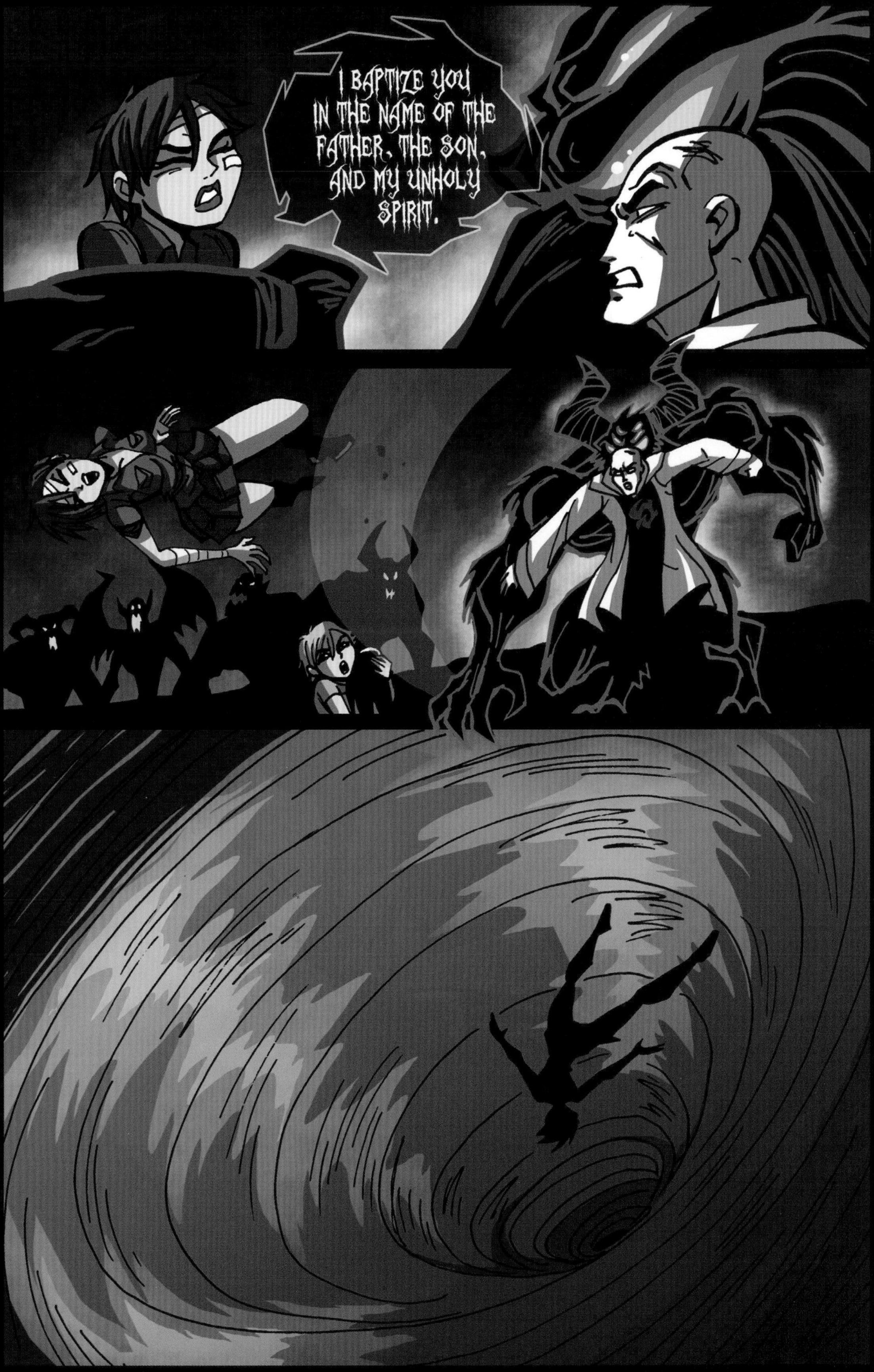
I BAPTIZE YOU IN THE NAME OF THE FATHER, THE SON, AND MY UNHOLY SPIRIT.

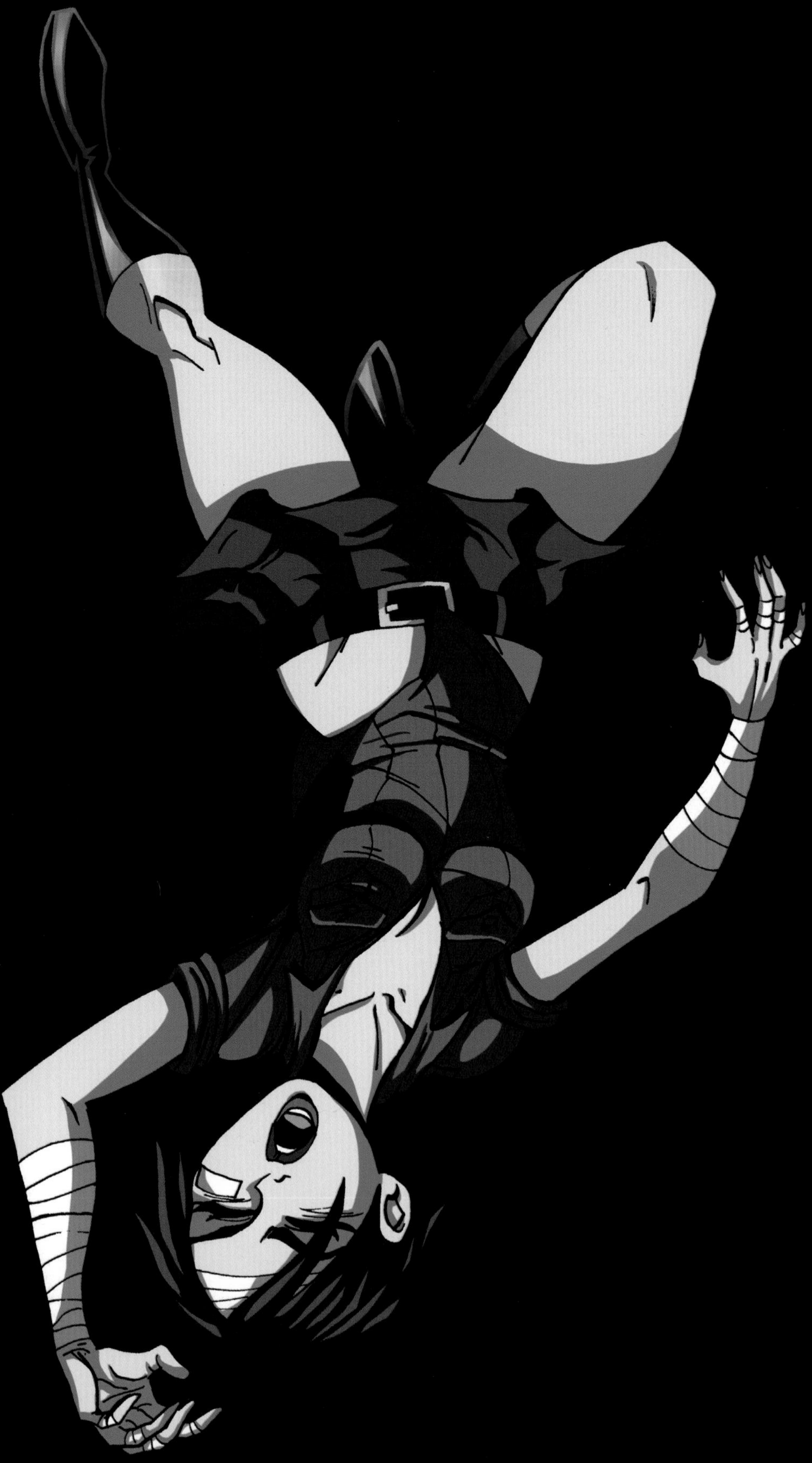

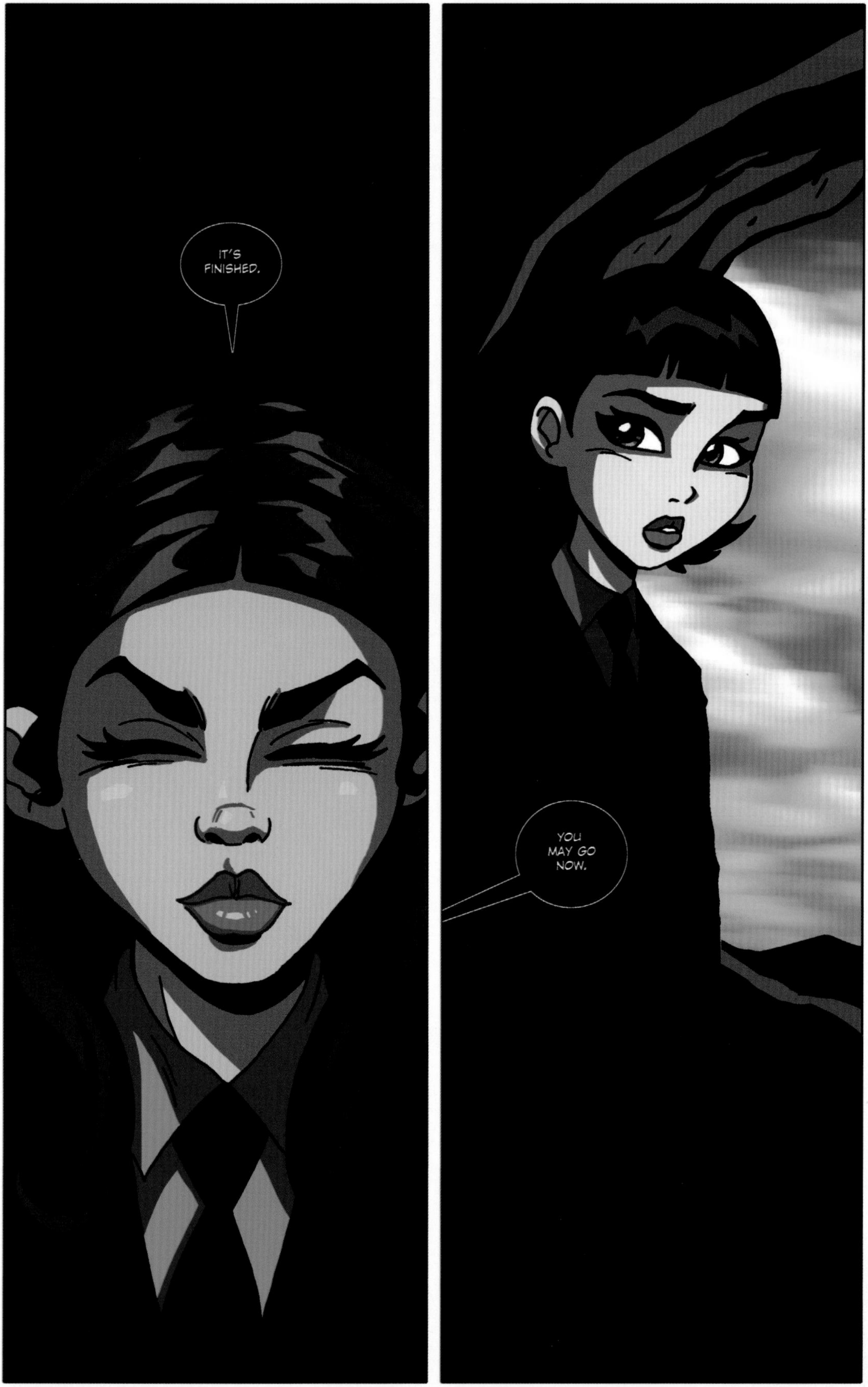
IT'S FINISHED.
YOU MAY GO NOW.

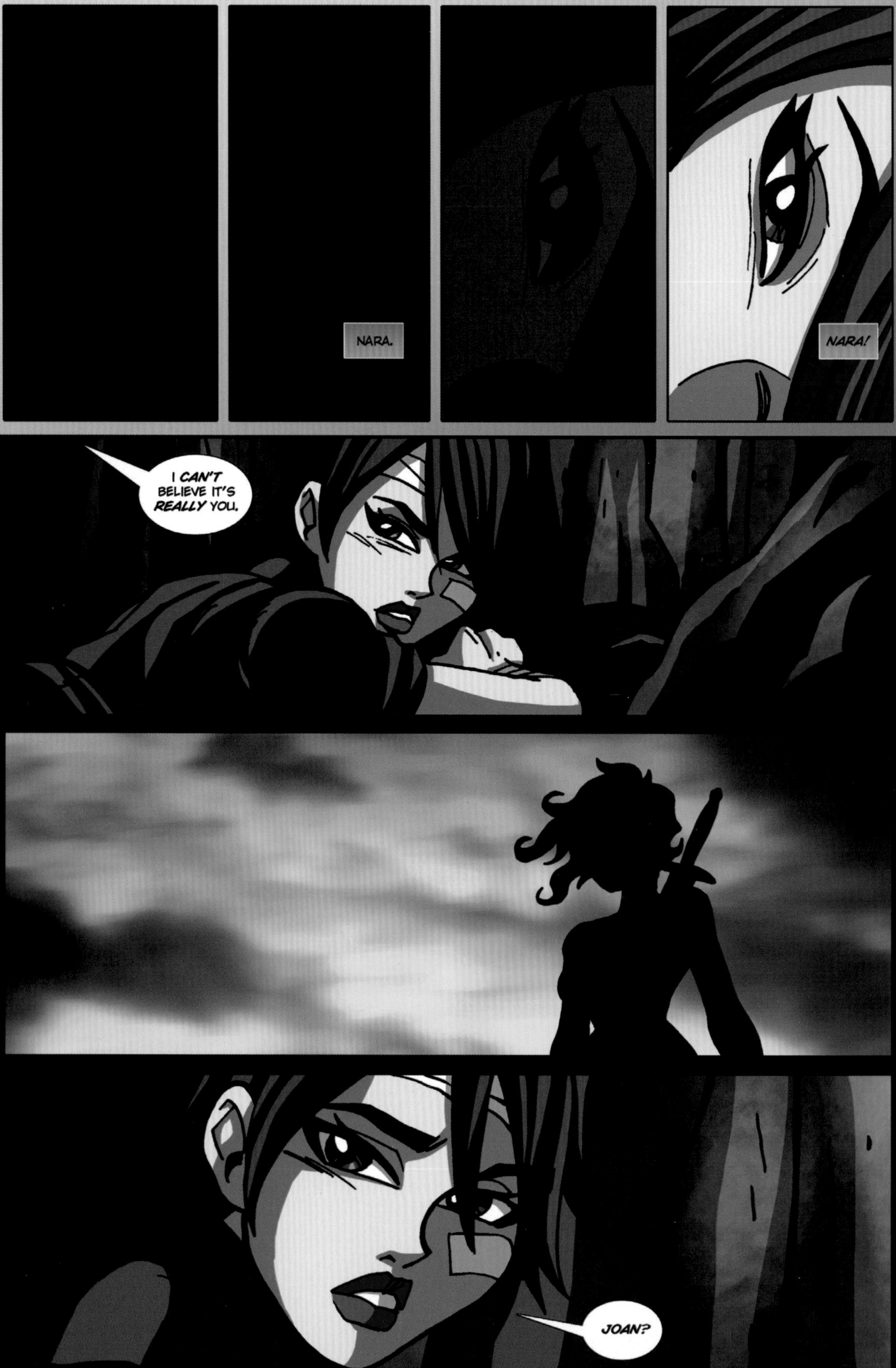
NARA.
NARA!
I CAN'T BELIEVE IT'S REALLY YOU.
JOAN?

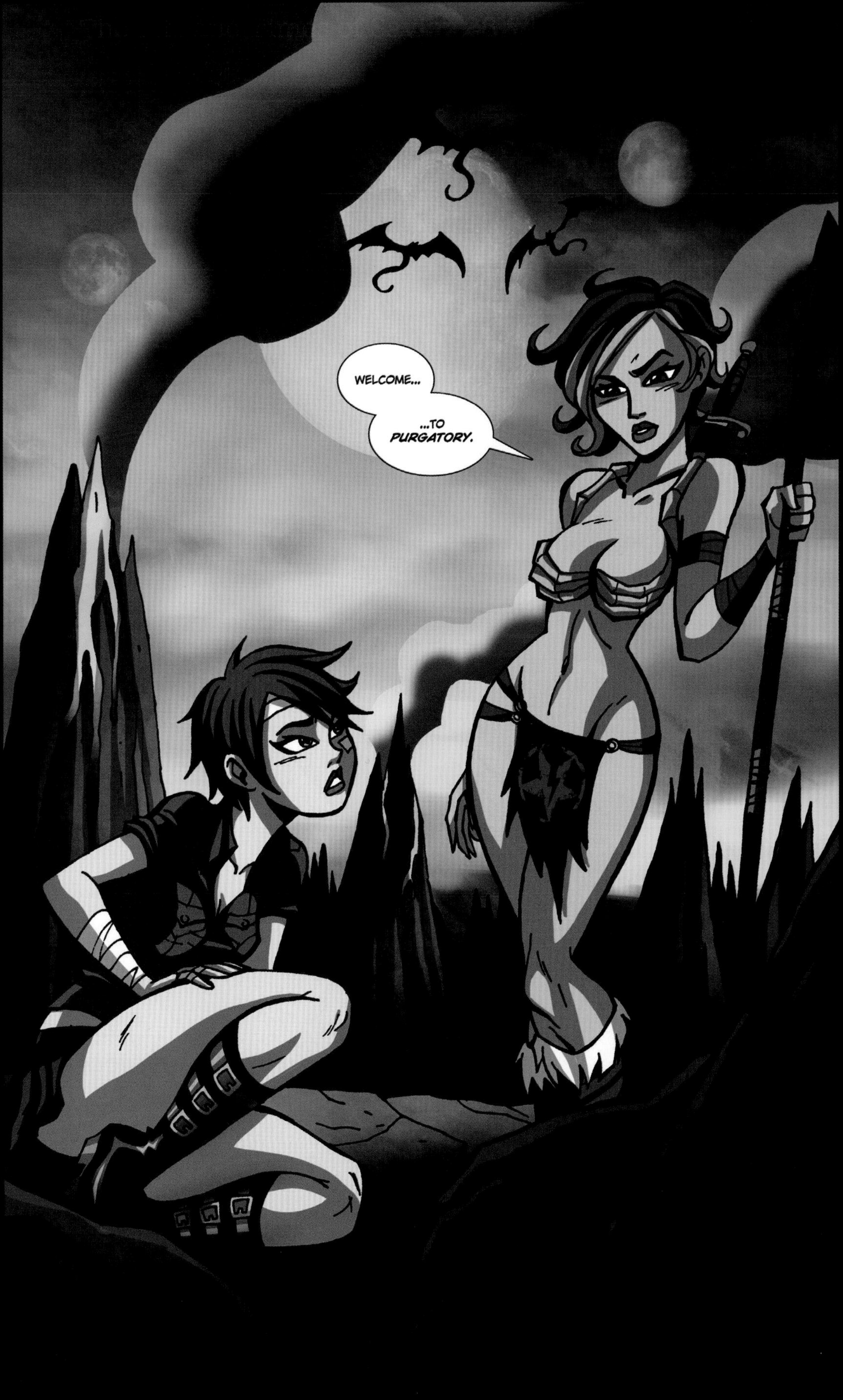
WELCOME...
...TO PURGATORY.

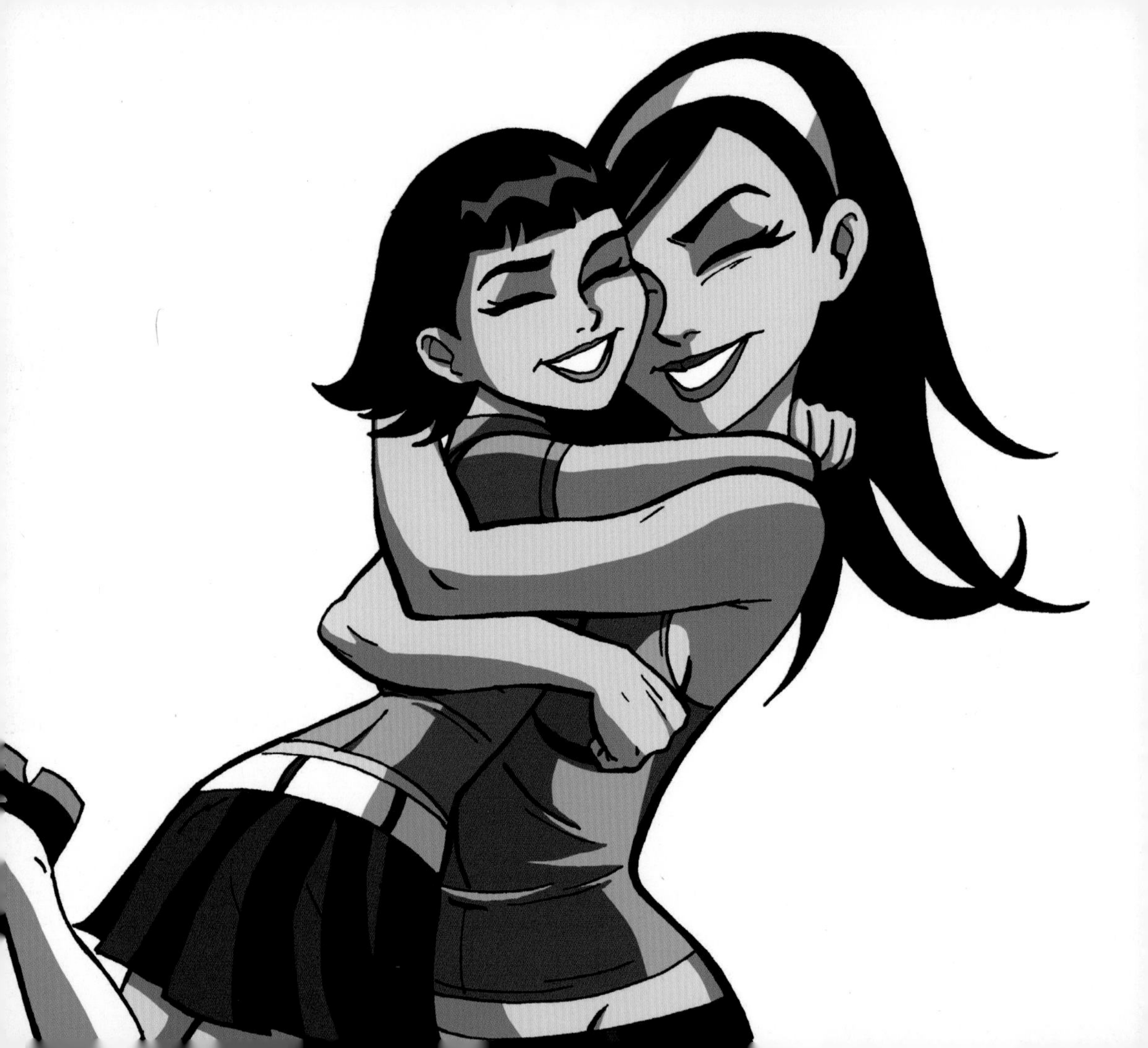

PIN UPS

ANTHONY COFFEY AMITYINK.COM

JESSE LABBE AMITYINK.COM

JASON MARTIN SUPERREALGRAPHICS.COM

BRIAN THOMPSON BRITOWN.COM

GUY LEMAY ANGELFIRE.COM/CA6/PINBALLCOMICS

CAL SLAYTON CALSLAYTON.COM

SCOTT ZIRKEL SCOTTZIRKEL.COM

PATRICK BUSSEY

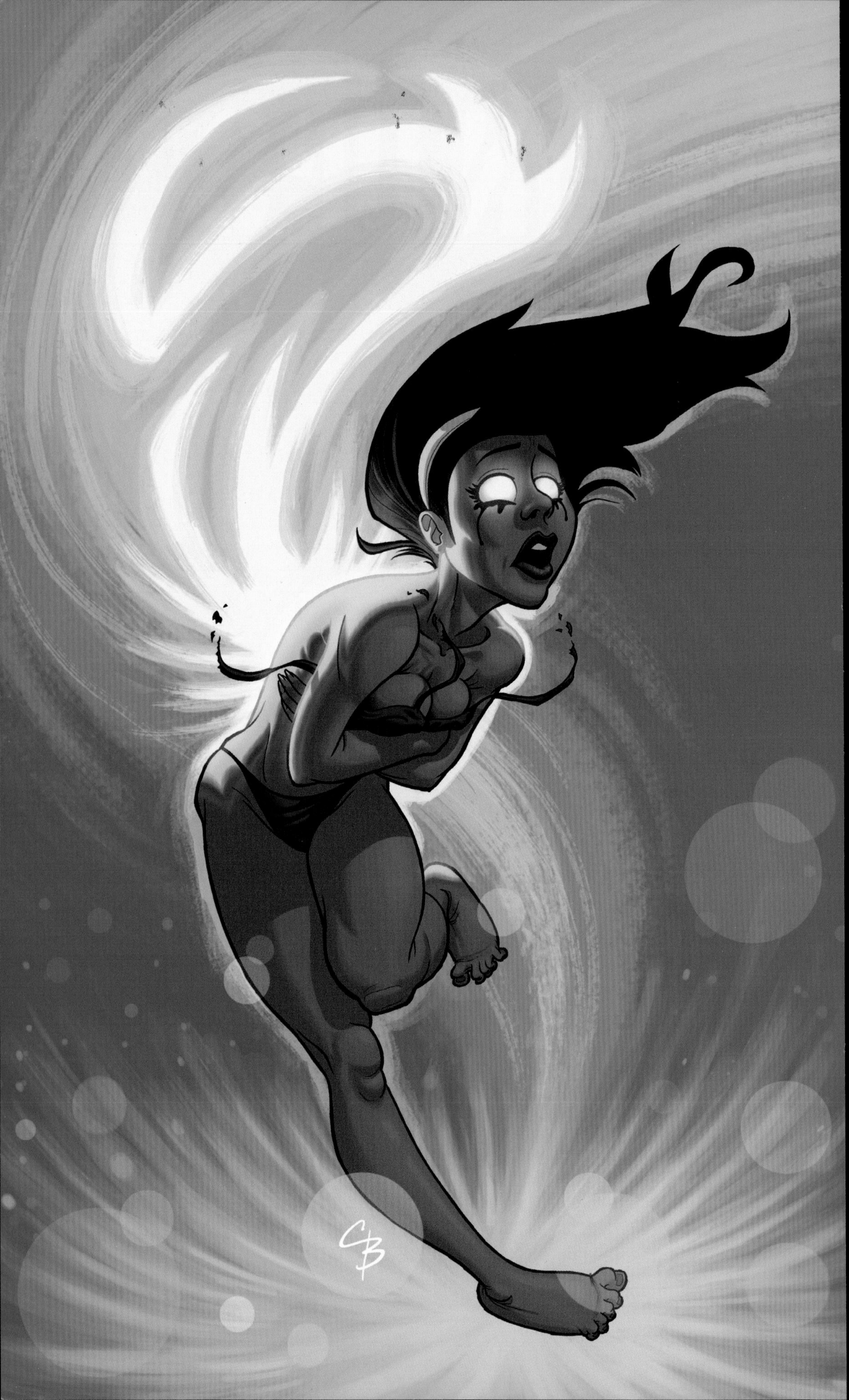

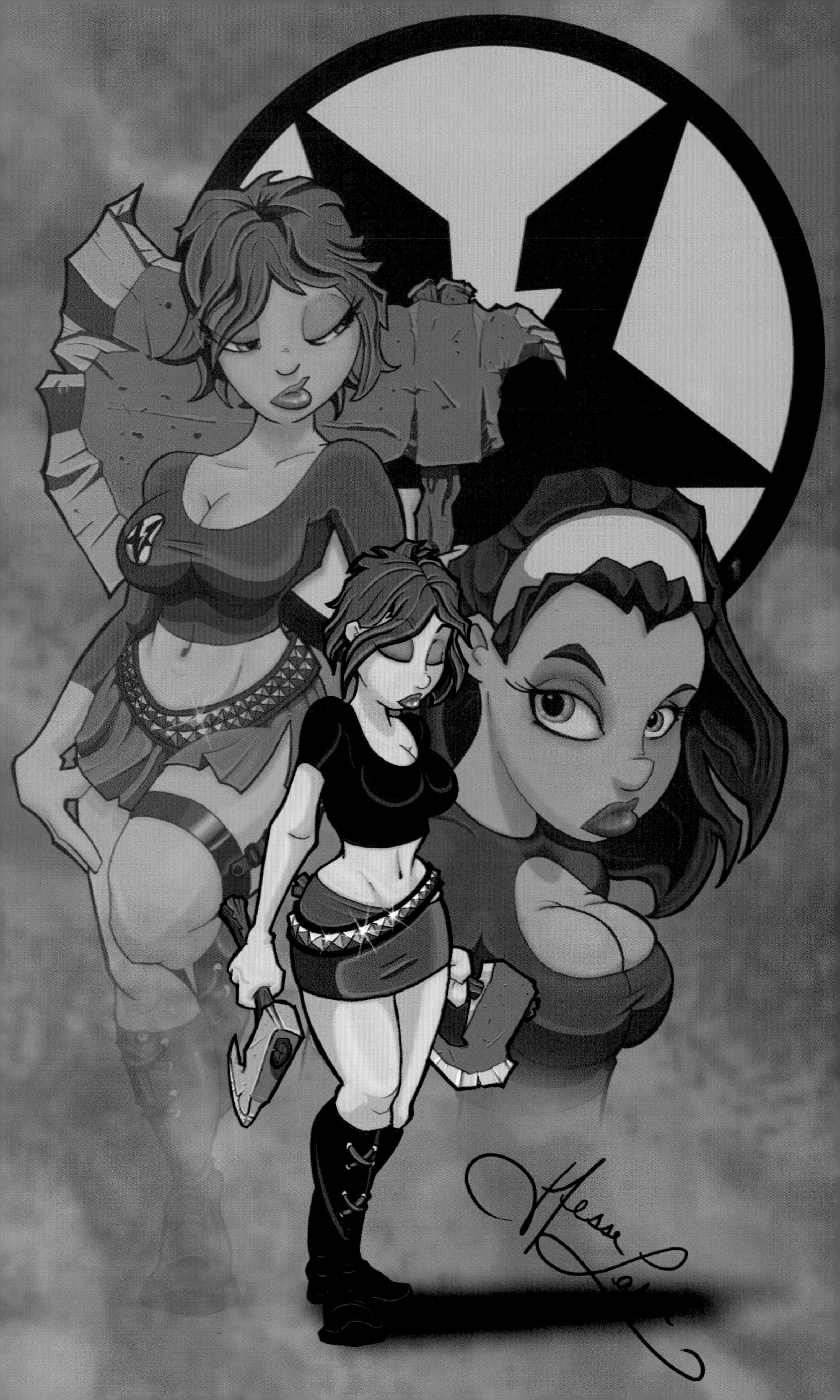

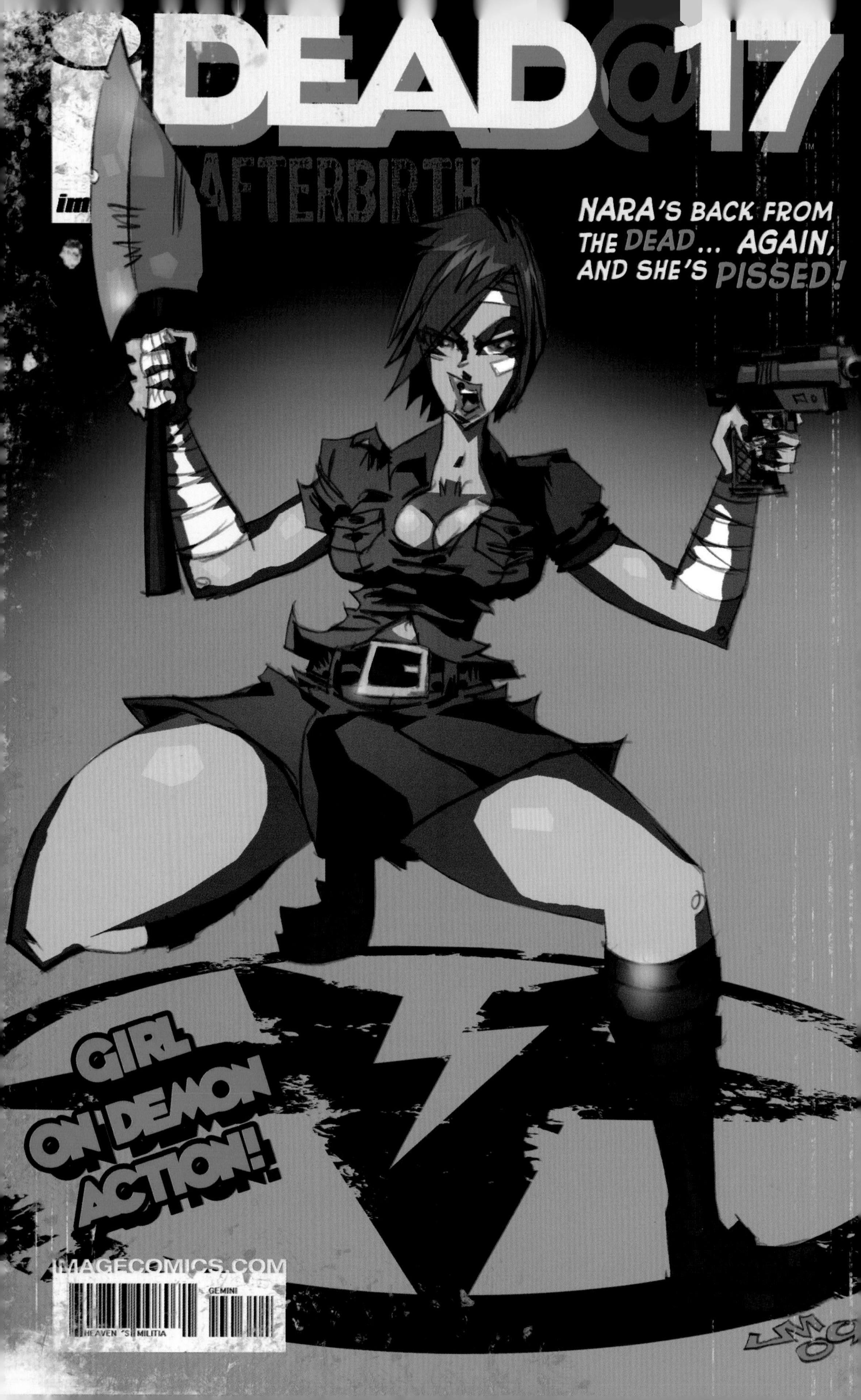

DEAD@17
AFTERBIRTH
NARA'S BACK FROM THE DEAD... AGAIN, AND SHE'S PISSED!
GIRL ON DEMON ACTION!
IMAGECOMICS.COM
GEMINI
HEAVEN'S MILITIA

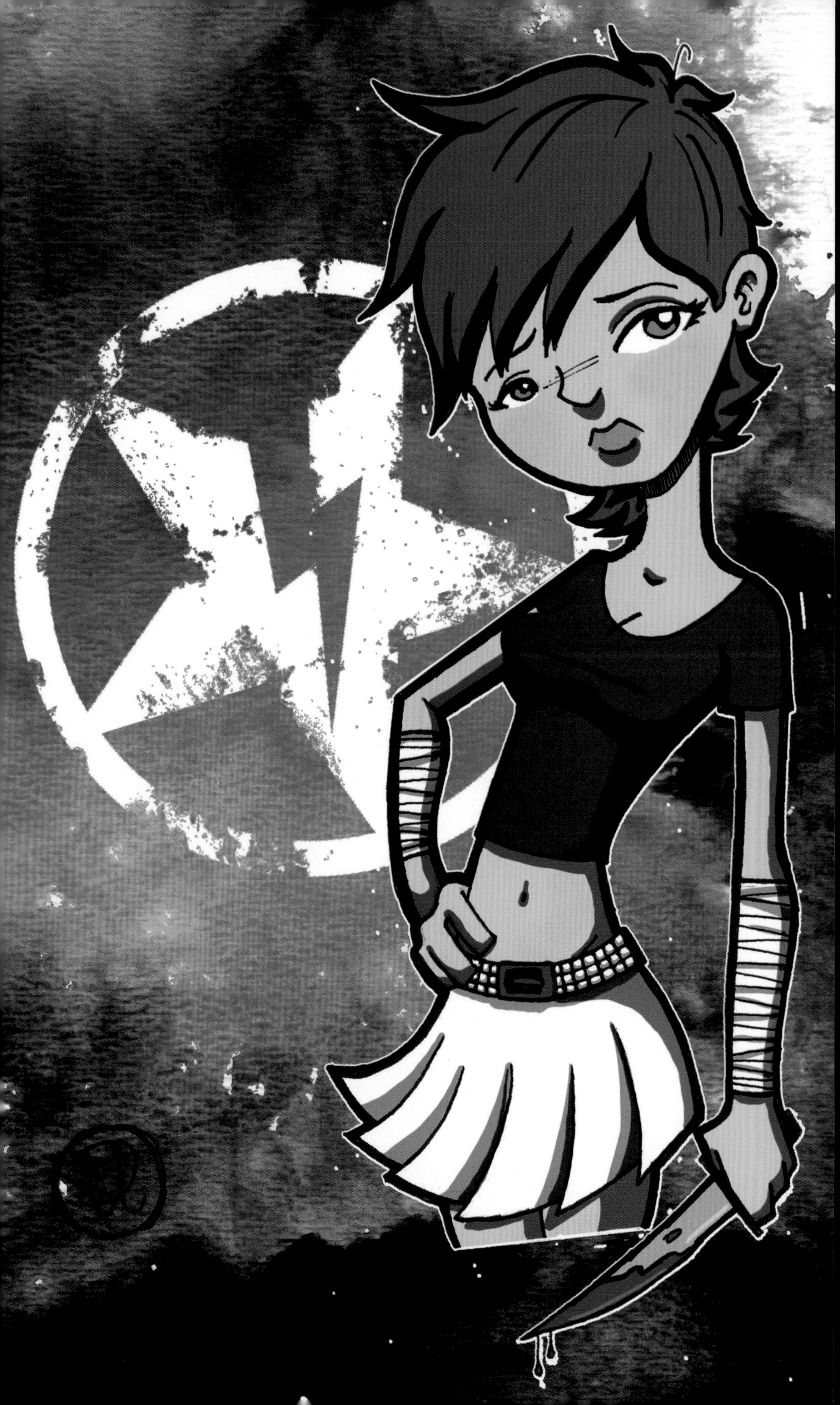

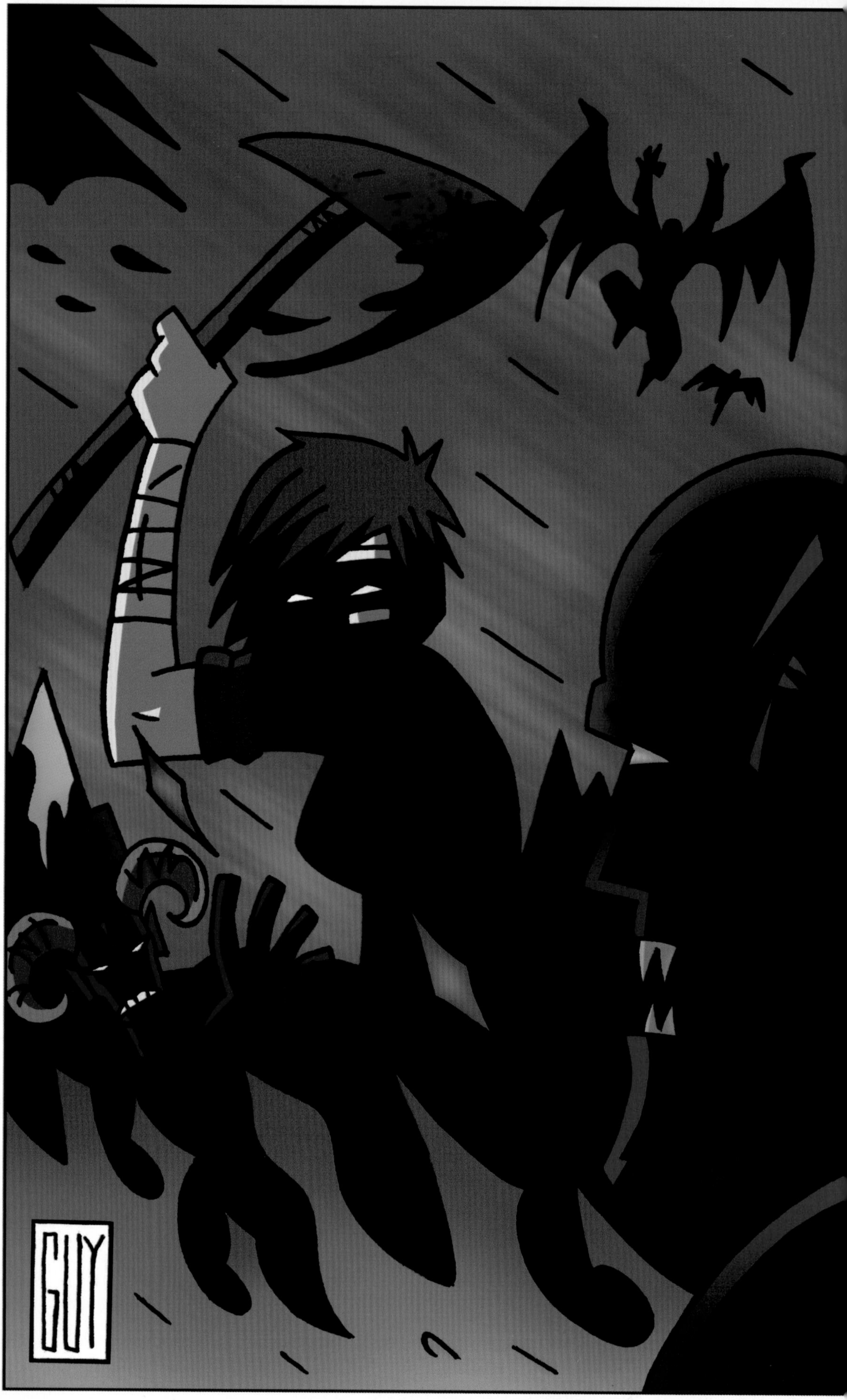
GUY

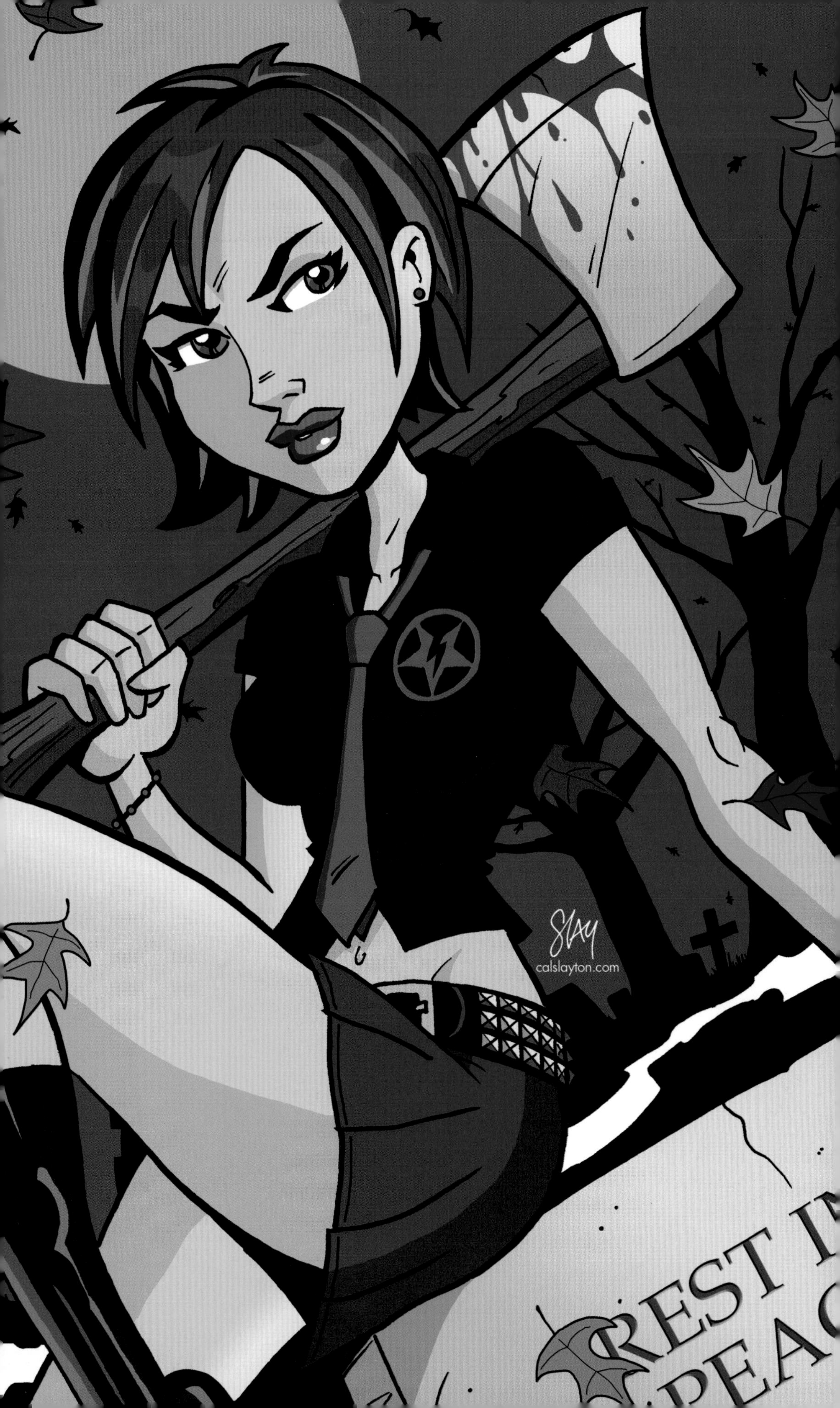
SLAY
calslayton.com

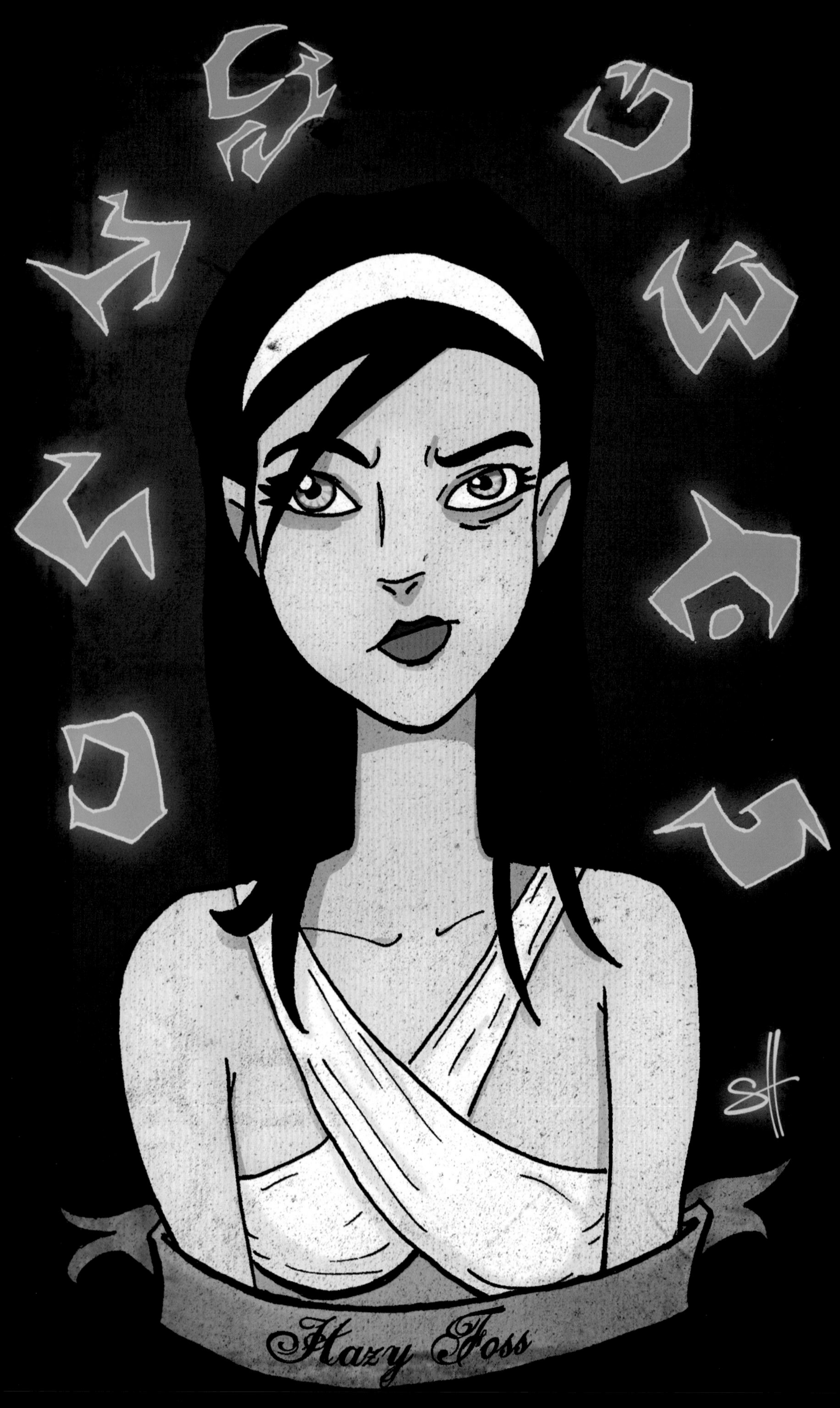
Hazy Foss

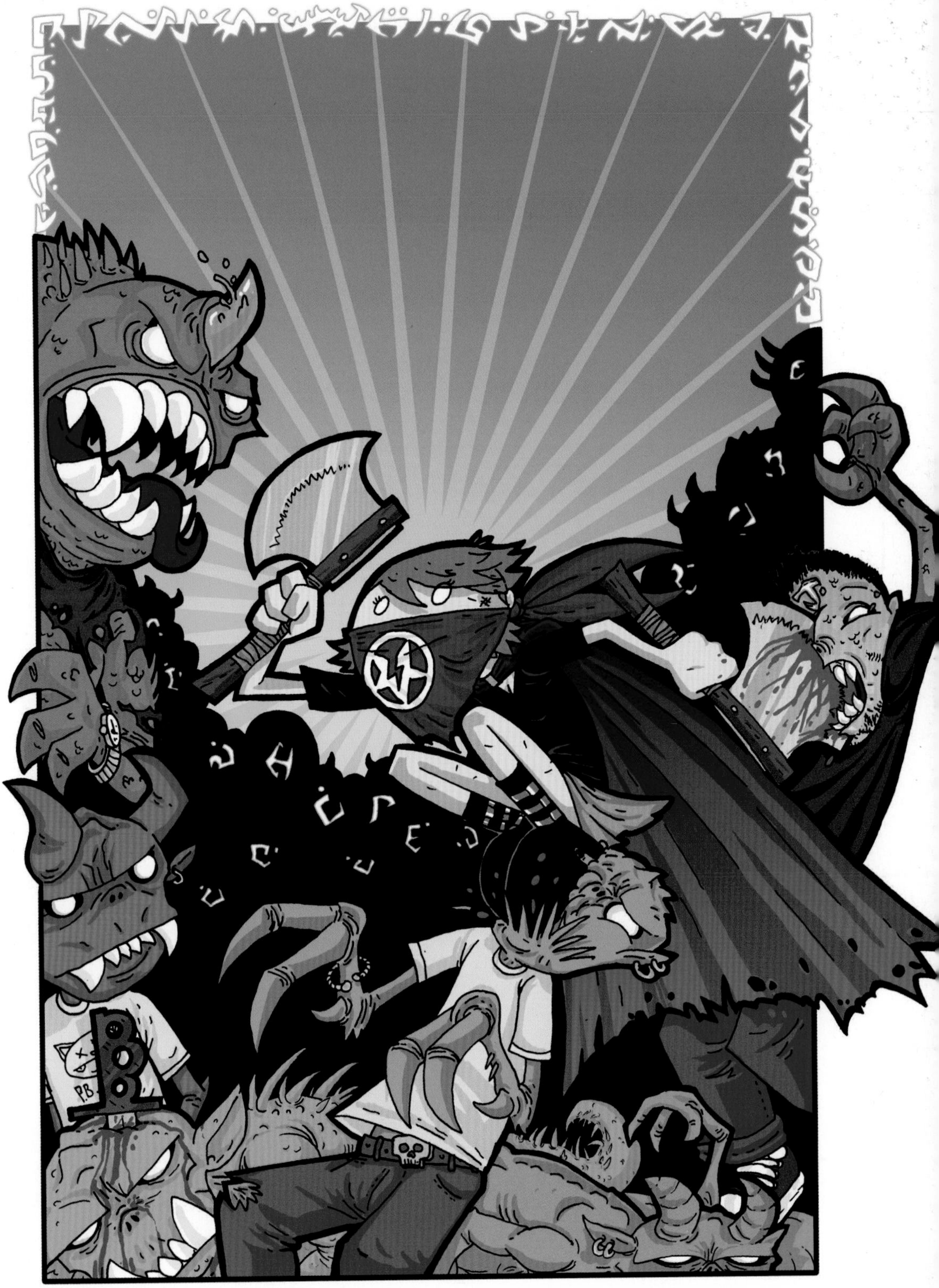
P.B.

MORE GREAT BOOKS FROM IMAGE COMICS!

THE ASTOUNDING WOLF-MAN
VOL. 1 TP
ISBN: 978-1-58240-862-0
$14.99
VOL. 2 TP
ISBN: 978-1-60706-007-9
$14.99

BATTLE POPE
VOL. 1: GENESIS TP
ISBN: 978-1-58240-572-8
$14.99
VOL. 2: MAYHEM TP
ISBN: 978-1-58240-529-2
$12.99
VOL. 3: PILLOW TALK TP
ISBN: 978-1-58240-677-0
$12.99
VOL. 4: WRATH OF GOD TP
ISBN: 978-1-58240-751-7
$9.99

DRAIN
VOL. 1 TP
ISBN: 978-1-58240-752-4
$16.99

LOADED BIBLE
VOL. 1: THE JESUS VS. VAMPIRES GOSPELS TP
ISBN: 978-1-58240-579-7
$16.99

GIRLS
VOL. 1: CONCEPTION TP
ISBN: 978-1-58240-529-2
$14.99
VOL. 1: EMERGENCE TP
ISBN: 978-1-58240-608-4
$14.99
VOL. 3: SURVIVAL TP
ISBN: 978-1-58240-703-6
$14.99
VOL. 4: EXTINCTION
ISBN: 978-1-58240-790-6
$14.99
THE COMPLETE COLLECTION HC
ISBN: 978-1-58240-826-2
$99.99

THE WALKING DEAD
VOL. 1: DAYS GONE BYE TP
ISBN: 978-1-58240-672-5
$9.99
VOL. 2: MILES BEHIND US TP
ISBN: 978-1-58240-413-4
$14.99
VOL. 3: SAFETY BEHIND BARS TP
ISBN: 978-1-58240-487-5
$14.99
VOL. 4: THE HEART'S DESIRE TP
ISBN: 978-1-58240-530-8
$14.99
VOL. 5: THE BEST DEFENSE TP
ISBN: 978-1-58240-612-1
$14.99
VOL. 6: THIS SORROWFUL LIFE TP
ISBN: 978-1-58240-684-8
$14.99
VOL. 7: THE CALM BEFORE TP
ISBN: 978-1-58240-828-6
$14.99
VOL. 8: MADE TO SUFFER TP
ISBN: 978-1-58240-883-5
$14.99
VOL. 9: HERE WE REMAIN TP
ISBN: 978-1-60706-022-2
$14.99
VOL. 10: THE ROAD AHEAD TP
ISBN: 978-1-60706-075-8
$14.99
BOOK ONE HC
ISBN: 978-1-58240-619-0
$29.99
BOOK TWO HC
ISBN: 978-1-58240-698-5
$29.99
BOOK THREE HC
ISBN: 978-1-58240-825-5
$29.99
BOOK FOUR HC
ISBN: 978-1-60706-000-0
$29.99
DELUXE HARDCOVER, VOL. 2
SBN: 978-1-60706-029-7
$100.00

THE SWORD
VOL. 1: FIRE TP
ISBN: 978-1-58240-879-8
$14.99
VOL. 2: WATER TP
ISBN: 978-1-58240-765-4
$14.99

TO FIND YOUR NEAREST COMIC BOOK STORE, CALL: **1-888-COMIC-BOOK**